F
Foster, Alan Dean.
Running from the deity

BY ALAN DEAN FOSTER

Published by Ballantine Books

The Black Hole

Cachalot
Dark Star
The Metrognome and Other Stories
Midworld
Nor Crystal Tears
Sentenced to Prism
Splinter of the Mind's Eye
Star Trek® Logs One–Ten
Voyage to the City of the Dead
. . . Who Needs Enemies?
With Friends Like These . . .
Mad Amos
The Howling Stones
Parallelities

THE ICERIGGER TRILOGY
Icerigger
Mission to Moulokin
The Deluge Drivers

THE ADVENTURES OF FLINX OF THE COMMONWEALTH
For Love of Mother-Not
The Tar-Aiym-Krang
Orphan Star
The End of the Matter
Bloodhype
Flinx in Flux
Mid-Flinx
Flinx's Folly
Sliding Scales
Running from the Deity

THE DAMNED
Book One: A Call to Arms
Book Two: The False Mirror
Book Three: The Spoils of War

THE FOUNDING OF THE COMMONWEALTH
Phylogenesis
Dirge
Diuturnity's Dawn

THE TAKEN TRILOGY
Lost and Found
The Light-years Beneath My Feet

RUNNING
FROM
THE DEITY

RUNNING FROM THE DEITY

A PIP & FLINX ADVENTURE

ALAN DEAN FOSTER

BALLANTINE BOOKS • NEW YORK

Running from the Deity is a work of fiction. Names, characters, places, and incidents are the products of the author's imagination or are used fictitiously. Any resemblance to actual events, locales, or persons, living or dead, is entirely coincidental.

Copyright © 2005 by Thranx, Inc.

Published in the United States by Del Rey Books, an imprint of The Random House Publishing Group, a division of Random House, Inc., New York.

DEL REY is a registered trademark and the Del Rey colophon is a trademark of Random House, Inc.

Library of Congress Cataloging-in-Publication Data
Foster, Alan Dean
Running from the deity / Alan Dean Foster.
p. cm.
"A Pip and Flinx Adventure."
ISBN 0-345-46159-2 (alk. paper)
1. Humanx Commonwealth (Imaginary organization)—Fiction.
2. Flinx (Fictitious character)—Fiction.   I. Title.

PS3556.O756R85 2005
813'.54—dc22   2005041324

Printed in the United States of America on acid-free paper

www.delreybooks.com

2   4   6   8   9   7   5   3   1

First Edition

Text design by Niqui Carter

For my nephew,
Shawn Lee Stumbo

RUNNING FROM THE DEITY

CHAPTER

1

At first thought, you'd think it would be easy to find a missing planet. Even a methane dwarf. Except that the missing tenth world of the outlying Imperial AAnn system of Pyrassis was not a world, but an immense automated weapons platform of the long-extinct race who called themselves the Tar-Aiym.

Actually, Flinx mused as he held out his arms and let the magnetically charged droplets of water swirl around him and scrub his lanky naked form, one would think it would be even simpler to find a planet-sized weapons platform than a small planet itself. The only problem was that in the absence of standing orders to guide its revived behavior, the monstrous ancient device had gone looking for some. Since to the best of current knowledge the last of those beings who might be capable of issuing such directives had died half a million years earlier, more or less, the prospects of said intelligent weapons platform stumbling across relevant instructions on how it ought to proceed were slight indeed. Flinx suspected that it would do no good, should he somehow actually succeed in tracking down his galactically perambulating quarry, to point out that the species it was built to fight, the Hur'rikku, were as dead and gone as the massive machine's original Tar-Aiym builders.

Find it first, he told himself as he did a slow turn beneath the recycled spray from the shower. Semantics follow function.

He did not need to pivot for purposes of cleanliness since the water beads automatically enveloped him in their attentive aqueous embrace. They avoided only the special shower mask that shielded his mouth and nose. Without such a mask, someone making use of such a shower conceivably could drown—though it was an easy enough matter simply to step sideways and clear of the open-sided, freestanding facility.

"Are you finished yet?" The voice of the *Teacher*'s ship-mind reached him through the stimulating vertical bath.

"Almost. Why? Are you going to suggest that after I finish bathing I take another 'vacation'?"

"It is interesting how sardonicism tends to shed efficacy over time," the ship-mind replied tartly. Having suggested that Flinx spend a while resting and recuperating on the out-of-the-way world of Jast, only to see him nearly murdered by one of the expatriate AAnn officials residing on that world, the AI was understandably disinclined to discuss the subject. Knowing this, Flinx lost few opportunities to bring it up.

"I take your point, by which I assume that you're not going to make such a suggestion. Good."

As he stepped out of the shower, the ready and waiting dryer scanned his dripping body. Preprogrammed to his specified level of individual comfort, it set about evaporating from his skin the water and the dirt it had englobed. Standing there, alone in his personal hygienic facilities within the ship, Flinx contemplated his immediate future and regarded it as fraught with uncertainty, danger, and confusion.

Not that it had ever been otherwise.

Some days he chose to dress while at other times he moved about the *Teacher*'s interior quite naked. As the only human on board, there was no need to concern himself with violating nudity taboos. Pip certainly did not mind. Rising from the resting place where she had dozed in utter indifference to her master's peculiar habit of immersing himself in gravity-defying liquid, she landed on his bare right shoulder and settled down. Her slender serpentine shape was warm against his freshly scoured skin.

Pulling on lightweight pants and a feathery comfort shirt, he made his way to the *Teacher*'s bridge. Around him, the product of the Ulru-Ujurrian's creative engineering genius functioned smoothly. It would have been dead silent inside the ship, except that dead silence smacked too much of death itself. So at present, and in response to his latest request, the hush was broken by the soft sounds of a Sektakenabdel cantata. Like many of his kind, Flinx was quite fond of the often atonal yet oddly soothing traditional thranx music, which in this particular composition sounded like nothing less than lullabies sung by angry, but muted, electrified cimbaloms.

As the ship sped at unnatural velocity through the nebulosity of higher mathematics colloquially known as space-plus, Flinx settled into the single command chair to gaze moodily through the sweeping, curved forward port. Though shifted over into the ultraviolet by the ship's KK-drive posigravity field, the view of the distorted universe surrounding him was, as always, still spectacularly beautiful. Pulsars and novae illuminated nebulae while distant galaxies vied for prominence with nearby suns.

Meanwhile, out beyond it all, in the direction of the constellation Boötes, something unimaginably vast and malevolent was coming out of a region known as the Great Emptiness, threatening not merely the Commonwealth and civilization, but everything within his field of view. His mental field of view, he reminded himself. Hence the need, however hopeless the notion of fighting something so immense and alien, to find allies. Such as, just possibly, the primeval weapons platform that had for millennia masqueraded as the tenth planet of the system known as Pyrassis.

Thinking of it made him want to go stand and soak beneath another shower.

A reaction as ineffectual as it was childish, he knew. He could no more wash away the distinct memory of the evil he knew was out there than he could that of his troubled childhood, his subsequent erratic maturation, and the pressure to succeed that had been placed on him by his good friends and mentors Bran Tse-Mallory and the Eint Truzenzuzex. Just as with his unstable, if escalating and potentially fatal Talent, he could not wish such things away.

He stared out at the universe and the universe stared right back, indifferent. Exactly how *was* he supposed to go about finding the wandering planet-sized Tar-Aiym device? The brilliant Truzenzuzex and the insightful Tse-Mallory had been unable to give him much advice. Since he was the only one who had experienced (or suffered, he corrected himself) mental contact with the machine, it was hoped that if he deliberately went looking for it he might make such contact with it again. Strike up a casual conversation with an all-powerful alien artifact, it was supposed.

And, he mused, in the unlikely event that he did? How to convince such a relic to participate in the defense of the galaxy. Nothing of overweening importance—just your average galaxy, in which he, and everyone he knew, happened to live. Reposing in the chair, he shook his head dolefully though there were none present to note the gesture save Pip and ship.

"I don't see how I can do what Bran and Tru asked," he muttered aloud. He did not need to explain himself. Ship-mind knew.

"If you cannot, then no one can," it replied unhelpfully. As befitted its programming, it was doing its best to be supportive.

"A distinct and even likely possibility," he murmured to no one and nothing in particular. He glanced in the direction of the main readout. "We're still on course—if you can call heading in a general direction hundreds of parsecs in extent a 'course.'"

As usual, the *Teacher* sounded more relaxed when responding to specifics of ship operation than it did when trying to understand the often unfathomable complexities of human thought and behavior.

"We have re-entered the Commonwealth on intent to cross vector three-five-four, accelerating in space-plus on course to leave Commonwealth boundaries beyond Almaggee space, subsequent to entering the Sagittarius Arm and the region collectively known as the Blight."

The Blight, Flinx thought. Home to long-vanished species among whom were the ancient Tar-Aiym and Hur'rikku. The Blight: an immense swath of space once flourishing with inhabited worlds much of which had been rendered dead and sterile by the photonic plague unleashed by the Tar-Aiym on their ancient Hur'rikku enemies half a million years ago. Like those who had hastily and unwisely propounded it, the all-destroying plague had long since consumed itself, leaving in its wake only empty skies gazing forlornly down on dead worlds. Here and there, in a few spatial corners miraculously passed over by the plague, life had survived. Life, and memories of the all-consuming horror that had inexplicably skipped over them. No wonder the inhabitants of such isolated yet fortunate systems gazed up at the night sky with fear instead of expectation, and clung tightly to their isolated home systems.

Somewhere within that immense and largely vacant chunk of cosmos, the re-energized Tar-Aiym weapons platform had gone searching for instructions. Hunting for those who had made it. That there were none such to be found anywhere any longer was not sufficient to discourage it from looking. Such was the way of the machine mind. A mind he somehow had to make contact with once again. A mind he had somehow to persuade.

A hard task it was going to be, if he continued to have trouble convincing himself that the enterprise he was engaged in had not even the remotest chance of success.

When applied to most people, the expression *have an open mind* was merely rhetorical. Not so with Flinx. In fact, for much of his life he had prayed for the ability to have one that was closed. Intermittently and uncontrollably exposed to the emotions of any and every sentient around him, he threatened to drown in a sea of sentiment and sensation whenever he visited a developed world. Feelings flooded in on him in endless waves of exhilaration, despair, hope, remorse, anger, love, and everything in between. With each passing year he seemed to become more sensitive, more alert to those inner expressions of thinking beings. Not long ago, he had unexpectedly acquired the ability to project as well as receive emotions. This capability had proven useful in his search for the truth of his origins as well as in escaping those who intended him harm.

Yet for all his escalating skills, he had yet to learn how to master them. Defined by their erraticism, he had long ago decided that they might forever be beyond his control. That did not keep him from trying. Not only because a Talent that was wild was of far less usefulness than one that could be managed, but because the severe headaches he had suffered from since adolescence continued to grow more frequent, and more intense. His ability might be his savior—as well as that of billions of other sentient beings. It might also kill him. He had no choice but to continue wrestling with it, and with what he was, because he was special.

He would have given up everything just to be normal.

Sensing her master's melancholy, Pip rose from her resting place on his shoulder, the deep-throated humming of her wings louder than the ambient music that was being played by the *Teacher*. Circling him twice, she settled down on his other shoulder, wings furled tightly against her slim, brightly colored body. Wrapping herself around the back of his neck, she squeezed gently and affectionately, trying to reassure him. Reaching up with his left hand, he absently stroked the back of her head. Small slitted eyes closed in contentment. Alaspinian minidrags did not purr, but the strength of the empathetic bond between him and his scaly companion managed to convey something like the emotional equivalent.

Leaning back in the command chair, Flinx closed his own eyes and tried to open his unique mind further, to reach outward in all directions. Though he could readily identify the target he sought, he could not have defined with precision the exact nature of what it was that he was searching for. But, like the caressing hand of a beautiful woman, he would know it when he felt it. Out, out, away from the ship, away from himself, he searched. His field of perception was an expanding balloon. But no matter how much he relaxed, even with Pip's aid he sensed nothing. Only emptiness.

Occasionally, as the *Teacher* drove onward through the outer reaches of the Commonwealth, his Talent was tickled by sparks of sentience. A flash of feeling from distant Tipendemos and, later, stronger bursts of emotion out of Almaggee. Then, more nothingness as he left the region of developed systems and sped through space-plus toward the Blight.

There were worlds in that vast section of the Sagittarius Arm that had once been inhabited, and worlds that were habitable still. No doubt someday, as the human and thranx population continued to expand in every direction, those worlds would once again resound to the voices of sentience. But not for a while yet. The Commonwealth itself encompassed an enormous section of space replete with hundreds of worlds yet to be settled or even explored by robotic probes. However enticing, the ancient worlds of the Blight would have to wait.

In its search for those who had built it, the wandering Tar-Aiym weapons platform would have hundreds of square parsecs in which to roam without encountering intelligent life of any kind. Making contact with anything in so vast a place seemed impossible. What swayed Flinx to try was the imploring of those wiser than himself. That, and the fact that on more than one occasion in his short life he had already achieved the impossible.

Having more or less resolved in his own mind to at least attempt the search, the last thing he expected as he entered the Blight was to have his resolution temporarily countermanded by his own ship.

He was taking his ease, as he so often did, in the central lounge. With its malleable waterfalls and pond, its fountain that sent heavy water trickling down and light water floating upward as decorative bubbles, it was far and away the most relaxing part of the unique vessel. Hailing from many worlds, the lush greenery that now packed every corner of the carefully maintained chamber filled it with wondrous scents and extra oxygen. Of course, he could have achieved a similar effect by simply directing the ship-mind to alter the composition of the internal atmosphere. But artificially regenerated oxygen lacked the subtle smells that accompanied air exhaled by growing things. Merely reclining among the running water and miniature forest helped him to unwind, and allowed his mind to roam free of anxiety and headaches. Green, he reflected, was good for the soul.

Nearby, Pip was pursuing something through the underbrush. It was harmless, or it would not be on board the ship. It was also confined to the lounge area. Chasing such harmless bits of decorative ambulatory life gave her something to do.

Unlike me, he thought.

"There is a problem."

Reluctantly, he bestirred himself from daydreaming of warm beaches on a recently visited world, and the passionate company he had kept there. "If you're trying to astonish me with revelation, you need to choose a less recurrent subject."

Ignoring the cynicism, the *Teacher* continued. "You are not the only one who suffers from stress, Philip Lynx."

Frowning, he rolled over on the supportive lounge. "Don't tell me that *you're* having mental problems. That's supposed to be my area of expertise."

"Mechanicals, however sophisticated, are fortunately immune to such intermittent cognitive plagues. My current situation involves stress of a purely physical nature. That does not render it any less serious or in need of attention. Quite the contrary."

Mildly alarmed now, Flinx sat up straight and set his cold drink aside. "You know how I hate understatement. Tell me straight: what's wrong?"

"We have done a great deal of traveling together, Flinx. In all that time I have endeavored to protect and care for you to the best of my abilities, according to the programming installed within myself by my builders."

"And an admirable job you've done of it, too." Flinx waited uncertainly for whatever was coming.

"We have crossed and recrossed vast sections of space. Because of a singular adaptation of KK-drive technology exclusive to my drive system, I have been able to set down on worlds and moons that would otherwise require visitation in the usual manner, via suborbital shuttle. On your behalf, I have run and I have fought.

"Now internal sensors have detected a disquieting deterioration in certain portions of my makeup. These need to be repaired. I am afraid that continuing on our present course and search without attending to these needs could result in structural failure, eventually of a catastrophic nature."

Flinx knew whereof the ship spoke. KK-drive starships did not fall slowly to pieces, did not wear away like ancient ships of the sea. Bits and parts did not flake off the exterior, exposing gaps and cracks, and still remain functional. Boats traveling on liquid oceans could sustain themselves with such damage and continue to function. So could vehicles traveling on land. But a starship had to be maintained whole and intact, or disintegrate entirely. Tortured metaphors notwithstanding, there was no middle ground in space, to which the doomed crew of the famously lost *Curryon* could no doubt attest.

He took a deep breath. "What do you recommend?"

"We can reverse course and return to the Commonwealth, where repair facilities are widely available and where I judge it should be possible to effect them without arousing overmuch unwanted attention."

Return, Flinx reflected. Go back, risk being discovered by Commonwealth authorities, or members of the Order of Null, or who knew what else, while the *Teacher,* his home and refuge, was laid up in an orbital repair facility somewhere, leaving him no means of flight from possible trouble. Not to mention, once repairs were completed, having to begin this probably vainglorious quest all over again.

"I deduce by your silence that this proposed course of action leaves you less than enthused."

Irritated, Flinx spoke without looking up from the green-and-blue ground cover that gave the floor of the lounge the look of a well-manicured meadow. "What did I just say about understatement?"

"Usefully," the ship-mind went on, "there is an alternative possibility."

"Alternative?" Now Flinx did look up, focusing his gaze on one of the unobtrusive visual pickups scattered around the lounge. "How can there be an alternative?"

Sounding pleased with itself—although it was nothing more than a subset of its conditional programming—the ship-mind continued.

"The structural repairs and reinforcements I need to effect are within the capability of my integrated maintenance faculties. I am convinced that I can carry out the requisite maintenance without outside assistance. Provided, of course, that a location is found that will support my weight while simultaneously making available certain essential raw materials. These consist primarily of carbon and titanium, two quite common elements, that need to be worked under terrestrial-type atmosphere and gravity. It should be possible to locate such a world here within the Blight. This would obviate the need for us to return to the Commonwealth, a course of action I infer from your reaction to my previous suggestion that you would clearly prefer to avoid."

"You infer correctly." Flinx was much relieved. With luck, they would not have to subject themselves to Commonwealth scrutiny, nor retrace the parsecs they had already covered. He did not doubt that the *Teacher* could successfully carry out the necessary repair work. If it was in the least bit uncertain, it would never have put forth the proposal.

For just a moment, he considered instructing the ship to press on ahead and ignore the required repairs. What was the worst that could happen? That the ship would fragment and he would die? In space-plus, the convergent disintegration would occur in less than the blink of an eye. It would all be over and done with: the burden of responsibility, the endless worrying, his confused concerns for Clarity Held, the recurrent head-splitting headaches—all forever finished, and him with them.

Then he remembered what the ever-gruff but affectionate Mother Mastiff had always told him, even when he was a pre-adolescent, about dying.

"Just remember one thing about death, boy," she'd growl softly, in between spitting something better left unidentified into a receptacle in the corner of the small kitchen. "Once you decided to be dead, you don't get to change your mind if you don't like the consequences."

And, he reminded himself, there was Clarity to think of.

A new thought caused him to break out in the slight, subtle grin that always teased and bemused those fortunate enough to gaze upon it. Once again he eyed a pickup concealed among the foliage that enveloped him. "I don't suppose you would by any chance already happen to have located a suitable nearby world?"

"As a matter of fact," ship-mind replied unexpectedly, "there are virtually no systems in the general, let alone immediate, spatial vicinity that fit all of the obligatory needs."

Flinx frowned slightly. "You said *virtually*. Go on."

"There is one. That is, it should prove suitable if the single isolated and relatively old record referring to its location, existence, and physical makeup is of sufficient accuracy."

The sole human on board the expansive, softly humming starship nodded knowingly to himself. "Then we ought to head there, don't you think?"

"I do. Unfortunately, I cannot do that unless you specifically grant permission for me to do so."

"And why is that?" Something small and bright yellow darted between a pair of solohonga trees, energetically pursued by the blur of blue-and-pink wings and body that was Pip.

"Because," ship-mind intoned solemnly, "while the extant situation for a system lying within the Blight is unusual, it unfortunately for our purposes is not unprecedented. This is because the world in question is inhabited."

Even as they changed course to head for the system where the *Teacher* would attempt to carry out repairs to itself, Flinx brooded on whether or not he had made the right decision in authorizing access. Arrawd, as the depressingly inadequate old records indicated it was called by its nonhuman inhabitants, was a Commonwealth-equivalent Class IVb world. Knowing that presented him with an ethical dilemma of a kind he had never before been forced to face.

Class IVb sentients existed at a pre-steam or lower level of technology, usually accompanied by similarly primitive political and social structures. The study of such societies was permitted only after applicants, nearly always scientific and educational bodies, submitted and had their intentions rigorously screened and passed by peer review and the appropriate authorities. Even with suitable safeguards in place, orbital observation was permitted only under advanced camouflage and from strictly regulated distances. Surface study was outright forbidden, actual contact with the species under examination punishable by revocation of academic and scientific accreditation and, in extreme cases, selective mindwipe of the offending individuals.

The *Teacher* was unequivocal in stating its needs. In order to obtain the raw materials to effect the necessary repairs to its structure, it had to set down on Arrawd itself. As for any contact, Flinx determined to hold his natural and inveterate curiosity in check. He would stay inside the disguised ship and wait out the delay while essential renovations were completed.

It had been a long time since the single Commonwealth survey vessel that had filed the only report on Arrawd had visited its isolated system. Though not exceptionally far from Commonwealth space, it lay well within the boundaries of the Blight. As was typical of such remote, inhabited worlds, there were no other populated systems nearby. The likelihood of the *Teacher* encountering another Commonwealth vessel in such a region was more than remote. That comforting improbability did not make his intended visit any less illegal.

His alternative was to reverse course and return to the nearest developed Commonwealth world, there to continue concealing his identity and that of his vessel while the obligatory repairs were surreptitiously carried out. Flinx had never been one to backtrack. Perhaps it was because he was more conscious than most of the absolute preciousness of time.

Also, once a thief, always a thief. In this instance, he would filch an illegal stopover. Somehow it struck him as less unlawful than stealing goods or money. Just a brief, if illicit, visit. Then he would depart, he and his swiftly repaired ship stealing away just as though they had never been there, leaving any natives none the wiser or Commonwealth authorities any the angrier.

So it was with the most righteous and honorable intentions that he entered the Arrawd system, flew past a ringed world that generated unexpectedly powerful pangs of homesickness, and allowed his suitably cloaked vessel to settle into orbit high above the fourth world of the local sun. It was there and then that his virtuous intentions unexpectedly began to unravel.

For one thing, Arrawd was astonishingly beautiful.

Even from orbit, the surface was achingly tempting. In the space immediately in front of him, images of the world below materialized and shifted at his beck and call. There were rainstorms but no hurricanes, seas but no oceans, dry land regions but only unassuming deserts. Capillary-like, rivers threaded their way through rolling plains and dense forests. Jungles matched icecaps in moderation. According to the *Teacher*'s sensors, the atmosphere was almost painfully human-normal while the gravity was sufficiently less to make an athlete of all but the most incapacitated visitor. He could not only survive unprotected on Arrawd's surface; he would have to take care not to let himself go.

As for the local dominant species that carefully crafted government regulations were designed to shield from the potentially unsettling effects of superior Commonwealth technology, there was little enough information on the Dwarra. Since the robotic probe that had discovered and studied their world was prohibited from setting down its surface, all measurements, readings, approximations, evaluations, and opinions of that unfamiliar species were necessarily fragmentary and incomplete.

The last time he had been compelled to call upon the *Teacher*'s prodigious archives to provide him with a portrayal of a soon-to-be-visited alien race, he had been forced to wrap his perceptions around the completely alien (and not a little grotesque) Vssey from the distant world of Jast. So it was with some relief that he found himself gazing upon body shapes that were considerably less outlandish as the ship called them forth from its files. Even the recorded analysis of their primary language was simple and straightforward.

The Dwarra were bipedal, bisymmetrical, and bisexual, like himself. No more reproducing via spores or budding, like the Vssey. Aside from a distinctive slenderness that bordered on the anorexic, their most distinguishing physical characteristic consisted of a pair of short, whip-like antennae that protruded from their flat, back-sloping foreheads. Concerning the possible function of these prominent appendages, the relevant archive was disappointingly uninformative. For all Flinx was able to find out, their purpose might be nothing more than decorative—or they might be equally capable of sending and receiving radio signals. Though the vaguely humanoid Dwarra displayed ample evidence of sexual dimorphism, both genders appeared to sport antennae of equal length and diameter. He had to smile. The fleshy gray protrusions lent their owners something of the appearance of emaciated sprites.

Waif-like bodies suited to the lighter gravity boasted two upper arms that divided halfway along their length into two separate forearms. Instead of hands and fingers, each forearm tapered until it split again into a pair of flexible gray flanges that looked oddly clumsy and flipper-like but were doubtless capable of sufficient manipulation with which to raise a civilization. Legs were characterized by a similarly subdivided arrangement. Two legs and two arms giving way to four feet and eight hand-finger equivalents made for a disconcertingly busy physical appearance. Fortunately, hearing organs and eyes were not similarly partitioned. As in humans, the former were small and positioned on the sides of the narrow head, while the eyes were wide, round, and set in deep, muscular sockets in the center of the equally round face. A single small air intake located just above the mouth slit and set flush with the gray skin of the hairless face completed the alien visage.

In place of body hair or scales, flattened fingernail-sized flaps of skin that ranged in hue from light gray to an almost metallic silver covered the visible parts of the slim body. Varying in length from one to three centimeters, they flapped like leaves in the breeze when the projection demonstrated the Dwarra's ungainly but satisfactorily motile gait. Females tended to be slightly smaller than males. According to the sparse records, the Dwarra gave birth to young who remained encased in a nourishing sac of gelatinous material until they were approximately a year old, at which point a second birthing ritual took place to celebrate the emergence of the infant from its mother's insides and manual transfer to its nurturing pouch, where it remained for an additional year before finally being asked to stand erect on its eight wobbly podal flanges.

As he finished perusing the limited information and waved off the floating, three-dimensional imagery, he decided that perhaps the inhabitants of looming, scenic Arrawd were not as much like himself as he had first thought.

Upon arrival, conducting leisurely observations from high orbit, the *Teacher* was able to reconfirm the available historical data on the state of Dwarran civilization. It was impossible to tell what, if any, advances the locals had made since the time the robot probe had carried out its survey, but there was no question that the alien civilization spreading across the world below remained at a low-tech level of scientific accomplishment. There were cities, but they were unexceptional in size and even under high resolution exhibited nothing in the way of explosive technological development. If there were factories, they were fueled by nothing more exotic than the simplest of hydrocarbons. Though roadways were present in abundance, none appeared to be paved with any material more advanced than stone.

Harbors displayed a more sophisticated appearance, boasting among other recognizable components ingenious slipways for the handling and repair of large vessels. Evidence for extensive commerce was present in the form of extensive built-up areas and warehousing complexes. The seas of Arrawd, many in number and unassuming in extent, would be highly conducive to waterborne transportation. The smaller the body of water, the less ferocious were likely to be any prevailing storms, though the lighter gravity would permit higher waves. Mountain ranges further reduced the efficacy of land-based transportation and would tend to cause the locals to focus even more intensively on waterborne shipping. Even so, further observation revealed the presence of nothing more elaborate or advanced than large sailing craft.

Unfortunately for his purposes, while there were no great, sprawling conurbations, all indicators pointed to a sizable and largely dispersed population. When the *Teacher* finally announced that it had located an area appropriate to its needs, Flinx decided that he'd had enough of staring blankly from orbit. The small peninsula the ship had chosen was reasonably far from the nearest community of any size, distant from even a small harbor, and rippling with titanium-rich sand dunes. There was also ample carbon locked up nearby in the form of an extensive and untouched deposit of fossilized plant growth. No indicators of urban population, no signs of commerce, no agriculture. A better spot might be found, but it would take more time to search.

"I concur," he told the ship-mind. "Take us down as fast as practical. At the slightest sign of reaction from the native population, return to orbit and we'll try again on another continent."

"I will be as subtle as possible," the ship-mind replied. A slight lurch indicated that the *Teacher* had already commenced its owner-approved descent.

Of course, what it was doing was not only highly illegal, but almost universally thought to be impossible. By their very nature, KK-drive craft were not supposed to be able to come within a specified number of planetary diameters of any rocky world without causing destruction on the ground and damage to the ship. Only the Ulru-Ujurrians, who had fashioned the *Teacher* as a gift to Flinx, had been able to find a solution to the problem, which continued to bedevil the physicists and engineers of all other space-going species.

Not that the Ulru-Ujurrians could properly be called space-going, Flinx mused as the ship continued to drop surfaceward. More like otherwhere-going.

The touchdown of the *Teacher* would have enormously impressed anyone on the ground—had there been anyone around to witness it. Executed under cover of night, as far as Flinx could tell the massive shape terminating in its coruscant Caplis projector came to rest in near silence among the thirty-meter-high dunes of the bucolic peninsula unnoticed by any living thing save for a pair of nesting amphibians. What little noise the ship generated was masked by a nocturnal onshore breeze, with the result that even the two jet-black, half-meter-long creatures hardly stirred in their burrow.

For several long minutes, an edgy Flinx paced the confines of the command cabin while the ship-mind made note of and absorbed everything about its immediate surroundings, from the chemical composition of the gentle sea nearby (less salty than terrestrial oceans, its tidal shift hardly affected by the three small moons in the sky) to the efforts of a number of surprisingly mobile nearby plants to uproot themselves and move away from the *Teacher*'s imposing bulk. Walking up to the curving foreport, he gazed down the length of the ship's service arm toward the now dark disc of the KK-drive generating fan. His craft was as exposed, obvious, and unnatural a part of the landscape as a thranx clan meeting in the arctic.

"How much longer?" The ship-mind was sufficiently intuitive that he did not have to specify the subject of his query.

"Working," the *Teacher* replied succinctly. "I do not foresee a lengthy study period. The immediate surroundings are simple and straightforward and will be easy to mimic."

"Then how about simply and straightforwardly concealing us?" Responding to her master's uncharacteristic irritability, Pip looked up from her resting place on the forward console.

"Processing." The *Teacher* could be talkative when the environment was relaxed, and equally concise when the situation demanded it. "Observe."

Once again, Flinx turned his attention toward the bow of the ship. It was no longer there. In its place was a narrow, low dune that terminated in a higher barchan of mineral-rich sand. The programming and complex projection mechanics that enabled the *Teacher* to alter the appearance of its exterior to resemble anything from a contract freighter to a small warship also allowed it to impersonate more mundane surroundings. Gazing at the forward part of his vessel, a relieved Flinx had no doubt that the larger habitable section that formed his home now also blended effectively into its immediate surroundings.

Not far off to the left, a placid sea glistened invitingly in Arrawd's dim, tripartite moonlight. After weeks spent cooped up on board, the thought of a nocturnal swim in tepid salt water was tempting. No doubt his presence in such waters, however, would prove equally enticing to whatever predators roamed the perhaps deceptively sluggish shallows. Taking a reckless plunge in an alien sea was a good way to meet one's maker in advance of one's designated time. He would wait until morning, see what developed, have the *Teacher* run a bioscan out to depth, and then decide if his present locale was safe enough for him to take the plunge.

Seduced by the serene, moonlit surroundings of solid ground, he had already set aside his promise not to emerge from the ship.

"How soon before you can begin acquiring necessary raw materials and commence repairs?"

"I already have," the ship informed him. Somewhere deep within its self-maintaining mass, faint mechanical noises sifted upward into the living quarters.

Flinx gestured toward the console. Obediently, Pip rose on thrumming, chromatic wings and glided over to settle on his shoulders. "That's great. If I'm not up, wake me at sunrise."

The ship responded affirmatively, even though it knew the request was unnecessary. The ability of its human's biological clock to reset itself almost immediately to whatever new world Flinx happened to find himself on was one that never ceased to amaze the multifaceted artificial mind. Flinx called it "making myself at home."

Perhaps, ship-mind thought to itself, the human had developed this unusual ability to make himself at home wherever he happened to be because he had never really had such a place of his own.

CHAPTER

2

Ebbanai made sure each thorall bulb was planted firmly in the sand before starting to insert the next one. It was not a difficult task, but did require attention to one's work. Jam it too deeply into the shallow rippling sands in the waist-deep water, and much of the thorall's bulb would be hidden, rendering it useless. Set it too high, and the occasional gentle wavelet might dislodge it and send it floating away. Gathering thoralls required time and effort, and he had no intention of wasting even one tonight.

They squirmed against the pair of strong opposing flanges that gripped them, reluctant to comply. There was little more they could do. The filter feeders at the top of each glowing sphere lay flat against the curved, semi-gelatinous surface, helpless and useless when out of the water. Once implanted where he wanted them, they would hesitantly extend their feathery tendrils and resume feeding on the tiny pisceans and rotoforms that came into the shallow bay to feed at night, safe from the voracious predators that haunted the deeper waters beyond. In turn, larger sinuous marrarra and fat ferraff would come to feast on the smaller creatures.

Implanting the last of the thoralls by jamming its single spike-like foot into an appropriate segment of sand, he stood back on both legs to survey his handiwork. Water lapped against his four forelegs and his unshod feet. His efforts had resulted in the creation beneath the surface of a neat half circle of phosphorescent light. Walking to one end of the semi-circle, he lowered his torso into his pelvis and settled himself down on all fours into a comfortable holding squat as he prepared to wait. Marrarra and ferraff were choosy about when they would enter the shallows. Ebbanai glanced skyward. Arrawd's three moons had last been high in the sky together nearly a forenight ago. Nighttime harvests had been sparse since then. Hopefully, tonight would see him bring in a good haul. He needed to. He was hungry, and Storra would lambaste him unmercifully if he returned yet again with an empty collecting sack.

The sea was warm against his bare foot-flanges and ankles. On this pleasant eve, he wore only a conical kilt and a light vest. Both were cut and shredded appropriately to allow him to raise and lower the epidermal flaps that covered his body. More close-fitting attire would have held these flat against his musculature. Unable to ventilate his body by raising and lowering the hundreds of small skin flaps, he would rapidly have developed all manner of unpleasant diseases.

As he stood there, the small bits of his epidermis rising and falling reflexively and in unison to catch every slight breeze wafting in off the bay, he reflected on his life. It could be worse, he knew. Owning a piece of patrilineal land on the bay brought with it the right to harvest its bounty. While his mate of ten years might use her flexible palate to occasionally mouth-lash him, that same orifice was skilled at obtaining the highest possible price in the town market for his catches as well as for the fine, sturdy cloth she wove from the seashan he gathered during the day. As a mated couple, then, they had access to both food and clothing without having to pay money for it. The ancestral stone home that as a sole offspring he had inherited upon the untimely passing of his parents was both solid and spacious. *Sfaa,* he decided contentedly. While they were not of the nobility, or even the upwardly mobile business class, their lives were certainly better than those of many commoners.

Leaning forward slightly but not moving his legs, he contracted his eyes in their muscular sockets to focus on sudden movement within the semi-circle of light he had made. A pair of marrarra in the catch-cup already, feeding on the rich faunal soup that had been drawn to the thoralls' lights. And wasn't that a ferraff next to them? One big enough for broiling, no less, and not just for the stewpot. He felt relieved. As long as the wind didn't pick up, it was going to be a good night.

One double-jointed, double-limbed arm bent backward to reach around behind him and remove the neatly rolled net from the bag slung across his back. Skin flaps rising and falling with anticipation, he methodically unscrolled the fishing gear. Fashioned from the toughest fibers of the same seashan Storra loomed into cloth, he shook it out preparatory to casting. Properly thrown, it would seal the mouth of the thorallian cup. Forcefully nudging a thorall or two would cause the legless creatures to blink their lights with furious intensity. Designed to startle and frighten off possible predators, the reaction should scare the feeding marrarra and complacent ferraff straight into the waiting depths of his net.

He held the braids of the latter in the four grasping flaps of his left hands and readied himself to cast it with those of his right. A poor throw and his quarry would panic and might slip away. It could happen, even to one as experienced as himself. Antennae stiff and protruding forward from his forehead, he kicked at the thorall nearest him, moved quickly to the next and repeating the action. Taking their cue from these first two, the other thoralls in the semi-circle responded by pulsing violently to scare off the perceived threat. Quickly, he drew back all four forearms simultaneously and heaved. Flying into the darkness and expanding as it caught the night air, the weighted seashan latticework struck the water with a gentle slap, sinking quickly downward to trap and entangle everything trapped beneath its inescapable mesh.

Sucking air through the vent in his face, Ebbanai moved fast to check on his catch. There was one marrarra, there the other, and—not one sizable ferraff, but two! Two ferraff broilers, and on his first throw of the night. Rightly and for once, Storra would be full of praise for his efforts. Perhaps even enough to alter her body chemistry and render it suitable to generate the necessary hormonal flash that would permit copulation. He tugged eagerly at the net, pulling it in, closing the trap on the fine catch. Glancing gratefully upward, he gave thanks to the three moons Hawwn, Terlth, and Vawwd for their bounty this night.

And that was when he dropped the net.

Slipping slowly from his usually strong grasp, the slick strands of tough seashan fell into the water. As the mesh expanded, now floating aimlessly, the panicky marrarra and greatly desired ferraff found the gaps that resulted from inattention and sprinted unhesitatingly for the safety of deeper water. If not for the small weights sewn intermittently along its edge, the net itself would have drifted out to sea.

Ebbanai did not care. He could not pick up the net, did not watch as his fine catch made its escape. His thoughts were no longer on harvesting, or his mate, or on anything else. Every iota of his being, every fraction of his attention, was focused and locked on the impossible thing he was seeing.

A fourth moon had appeared in the sky, and it was falling straight toward him.

He wanted desperately to move, to run, to flee—but he could not. His legs would not work. The slender muscles were as paralyzed as his thoughts. As the incredible, implausible fourth moon came ever closer, he saw that it was flecked here and there with colored lights brighter than those of any thorall; more intense even than those that bedecked the castle of His August Highborn Pyr Pyrrpallinda of Wullsakaa.

Thoughts of the Highborn finally gave him the push he needed to react. Getting all four legs under him, he broke for the nearest beach dune. Knowledge of what Storra would have to say if he returned without the precious net was imprinted on him deeply enough to make him pause just long enough to gather up the precious folds and take them with him. With bits of mesh trailing behind and on both sides and threatening to trip him at every stride, he ran through the shallows as fast as his podal flaps would propel him, not caring how much noise he made or what potential catch he might be frightening away.

Seizing on the first dune whose crest rose higher than his head for a suitable hiding place, he threw the sodden net down to one side and collapsed his legs beneath his body. Trying to squeeze his torso down into his hips, breathing hard, he peered over the crest of the dune and through a clump of thin, trembling chourdl as the swiftly descending moon settled to ground.

His astonishment was only magnified when he saw that it was no moon, but an artificial construction of some kind. While one end was huge and rounded like a flattened bowl, it was the size of the apparition that awed him: the machine, or whatever it might be, exceeded in length the walls of the Highborn Pyrrpallinda's fortress. In height it was taller than even the great waterwheel at Pwygrith. Wishing to hide in the sand but unable to wrench his gaze from the sight, he tried to determine the nature of the material from which the arrival had been fashioned, only to realize that he could not. Surely something so immense had to be made of metal, but in the light of the three moons it did not look like metal. It had a soft, almost pliable appearance, which was of course quite impossible. But then, the notion of something so large and angular managing controlled flight without the aid of gas-filled lifting bags was equally impossible.

If he thought the night's wonders had come to an end with the appearance and touchdown of the machine, he was much mistaken.

Coming to rest among the dunes well inland of the high-tide mark, the massive mechanism settled partway into the sand. The depth to which it sank with no visible effort was indicative of its great weight. A high-pitched squeal, just at the limit of Dwarran hearing, escaped from somewhere within the dark depths of the device. Following this mechanical ululation, the lights that dotted its curving flanks and the great dish shape at one end went dark.

Then the entire great, impossible alien mass began to disappear right before his astonished stare.

Ebbanai's eyes contracted in disbelief, and his skin flaps pressed so tight against his body that he feared he would sprain every one of them. Before his gaze the exterior of the immense intruder seemed to shimmer, as if the very moonlight illuminating it had begun to flex. Under his stare, towering, smoothly curving flanks of maybe-metal were altering their appearance. They became less foreign, less solid, and more—sand-like.

It was all over in less time than it would have taken Storra to spit and braise one of the marrarra. Where the piece of sky had lain, dominating the moonlit eastern horizon, there now rose a new series of interlinked, rippling sand dunes. Only their height hinted at anything out of the ordinary. Only one who had witnessed the actual transformation would recognize that the outline of the new dunes closely paralleled that of the machine that had preceded them. Even in the depths of his terror and bewilderment Ebbanai had to admit that the illusion, if that was what it was, was perfect. Of course, it would be a simple matter to establish if the new manifestation was nothing more than an illusion. All he had to do was walk over to it and touch it.

In fact, he had almost managed to convince himself that he was the victim of nothing more threatening than an elaborate hallucination when a small portal appeared in the side of one soaring dune, and the creature came out. Or creatures, he corrected himself, once more spellbound by the sight of the impossible. There were two of them.

Though of average Dwarran height, the larger of the two alien beings exhibited a build that was heavier and more muscular. It had two lower limbs for locomotion and two upper, the latter presumably intended for manipulation, though neither was subdivided. Gawking at it in fascination, Ebbanai wondered how the creature managed to stand upright on only two forelegs. Furthermore, its hands appeared to split into numerous smaller digits instead of the usual solid, gripping flanges. Its eyes were almost tiny and placed right out front, vulnerable and nearly parallel to the rest of the face. He could not think of a function for the small projection that thrust outward from the center of the face, nor those that protruded from the sides of the head. The cranium itself was covered with what appeared to be hundreds, if not thousands, of tiny red tentacles. Though the visitor was very different in appearance, it was not entirely horrible to look upon.

The second creature was small and winged. As it rose into the air, its pleated wings gave off a steady thrumming sound. It was swift, agile, and curious, darting from one place to another as it examined its surroundings while never straying far from the much larger being.

Then the latter bent its ridiculous knees and jumped high into the air.

Given the visitor's apparent mass, the vertical leap was extremely impressive. Only the most athletic Dwarra could have hoped to have equaled it. What other remarkable abilities the alien might possess Ebbanai did not know. What he did know was that he was not about to wait around, in the middle of the night, to experience them first-hand. When the creature turned away to inspect the massive sand dune where its vehicle, or whatever it was, had been, the terrified net-caster took the opportunity to make a break for the inland path. Glancing back over a shoulder, he had a moment of fright when it seemed as if the colorful winged thing had spotted the movement and was coming after him. But in response to a loud mouth-noise from its companion, it whirled in midair and returned to its larger companion.

Breathing with difficulty, all eight bare foot-pads swishing sand beneath him, Ebbanai ran until he couldn't run anymore. Following that, he walked, until after what seemed like an eternity the lights of his solid, ancestral home welcomed him at the base of the path.

Thankfully, they were not brightly colored, and the house did not transform itself into a dune or anything else as the exhausted gatherer staggered toward the wide, arched entrance.

"Pip!"

Just the name was all it took. He didn't have to whistle, didn't have to yell, did not have to utter a complicated stream of commands. Actually, even the use of the minidrag's name was superfluous. Flinx's heightened anxiety would be enough to draw her back to him as she sensed his shift in mood. But it always felt right to call her by name.

Mildly curious as to what had momentarily drawn her attention away from him, Flinx peered into the Dwarran night. The three small moons cast just enough light for him to make out the rolling edges of the surrounding dunes, like so many ocean waves frozen in time and blasted beige by the sun. Odd flora responded to the occasional breeze off the nearby bay by bending low to hide their sensitive heads in the sand. A few burrowing creatures of as yet undetermined lineage made fitful dashes from hole to hole. Overhead, yet another new set of constellations peered down at him.

So many worlds circling so many distant suns. In his short life he'd already seen too many of them, and yet not enough. Or at least, he corrected himself, not the right ones.

So far this one seemed amenable, if not openly inviting. Unable to see anything that might have drawn Pip's attention, he tried to reach out with his Talent, only to find that, as was too often the case, it had decided to shrink to an unperceiving blur in the back of his mind. Such lapses in his singular ability had become less and less common as he grew older, but they still struck him with alarming unpredictability.

Unable to perceive any emotions in his immediate environs save his own, he decided to carry out physiological experiments instead. Bending his knees, he executed another vertical leap. Due to the lower gravity here, he found that he could jump much higher than the terrestrial norm. Contrary to popular belief, bounding about in light gravity was not all pure exhilaration. He would have to watch his stride lest he put his feet down in awkward places they would automatically avoid on t-gravity-normal worlds. For example, if he did not gauge distance correctly, he might find himself accidentally leaping over a cliff—or into one. On the other hand, he would be able to cover longer distances on foot than was normal, and with less effort.

Not that he intended going for any long walks. He knew little enough of this world, could at present sense nothing of it, and the *Teacher*'s archive had been less than all-inclusive on the subject. He was, after all, embarked on a journey of some importance. Futile as that might seem, he was anxious both to be on his way and to avoid contravening any more of the Commonwealth restrictions that applied to a society like that of the Dwarra.

Glancing back, he studied the curving side of the sham dune. "Good job," he told the ship. "I can't detect any sign of artificiality even up close."

"My work is invariably first-class," the *Teacher* replied softly via a temporarily extruded external speaker disguised to look like a specimen of local vegetation. Its reply was a statement of fact. Artificial intelligences were immune to such weaknesses as false pride.

"How long?" Even as he posed the question, Flinx was aware that his usual impatience would do nothing to accelerate their departure.

"I told you. When it's done. The ore here is of good quality and should be simple to process. While the amount of carbon locked in fossilized vegetation is located deeper, I will manage as necessary. Meanwhile, why don't you try to relax?"

Flinx made a low sound. "Like on Jast?"

The ship sighed. That, it was programmed to do. "Like you are the first human to set foot on this world, a circumstance that is entirely probable. The climate is salubrious, the air devoid of pollutants natural or otherwise, and my sensors perceive nothing potentially dangerous in the immediate vicinity. While I would not advise going for a nude swim in the absence of additional information on the local water-dwelling life-forms, I see no harm in taking a short stroll. You have your minidrag with you, hand weapon, communicator, survival gear, and can walk for a considerable distance without traveling beyond range of my instrumentation. Why should you not enjoy your immediate surroundings? Are you not glad to be outside of myself?"

Pursing his lips, Flinx once more studied the dunes and shallow bay. "It's been my unfortunate experience that during my many travels my immediate surroundings have a way of jumping up and biting me on the ass. But you're right, as usual. A walk would be nice." He inhaled again of the fresh, pleasantly scented alien atmosphere. Above him, Pip whirled in effortless circles, scanning their surroundings.

From beneath the *Teacher* rose the heavy, muffled sounds of machinery starting in motion. The ship would carry out the necessary mining of the sands on which it rested and was currently mimicking with a minimum of noise and disturbance. Long, tentacle-like manipulators would extend outward, away from the camouflaged vessel and beneath the surface, to collect the large volume of fossil carbon from which it would extract the other raw material it needed. Other devices would suck titanium sand into refining processors. Meanwhile, as there was nothing for him to do, and since he was already outside anyway, he decided he might as well follow the ship's advice.

He had no compunction about starting off into the dunes. This close to the *Teacher*, it would warn him if it detected anything sizable in his immediate vicinity. Of course, it was often the case that the smaller an alien life-form, the more threatening it would turn out to be. He was not especially concerned. He had spent time on far more overtly dangerous worlds, among life-forms that made no attempt to disguise their lethality. As he climbed a low dune for a better view of his surroundings, he felt comparatively safe. No doubt this planet was home to dangerous creatures of one kind or another—but it was readily apparent from the little time he had already spent on its surface that this was, for example, no Pyrassis or Midworld.

As he strolled, with Pip circling overhead, he tried to get a better look at the small, scurrying things that were darting about among the dunes. There was not enough light, and he had not brought one from the ship. That lack would force him to turn around soon enough, he knew. Most importantly, as he felt his talent beginning to return to strength, he could not perceive any of the kind of complex emotional resonance that would indicate he might be in the physical presence of a higher intelligence such as the dominant local species. For just an instant on first emerging from the *Teacher,* he thought he might have picked up something emotive as well as alien. It had disappeared almost as soon as he had sensed it. Some mental illusion; a misperception on his part. He shook his head and smiled. No matter how increasingly proficient he grew in its use, his Talent could prove as erratic as ever.

On a Class IVb world, he knew, it was as incumbent on him to stay out of view and not reveal himself to the locals as it was for the *Teacher*. The mere sight of an obviously otherworldly being like himself could be dangerously disruptive to the local culture.

It was an effect, in fact, that he had had on others before.

CHAPTER

3

Ebbanai did not stop running until he reached home. The sight of the sturdy, domed structure standing foursquare and isolated in the first patch of tillable soil to shoulder its way between the dunes was a grateful reminder that he was not mad, and that he had not fallen into some loathsome, spirit-inspired nightmare. Beyond, barely discernible in the moonlight, other houses were just visible, spotted along the winding road that led to Metrel City.

As he raced down the last gentle slope, a wandering perermp crossing from cover to cover got snarled in Ebbanai's two right front legs. Long, lean, half the net-caster's body length, and built low to the ground, the slow-moving perermp found itself tangled up like some animate length of ship cable in the frantic Dwarra's lower limbs. Four-legged Dwarra and multi-limbed herbivore found themselves tumbling over and over downhill as each sought frantically to extricate its entwined limbs from the other. As they rolled, Ebbanai strained his antennae toward those of the perermp, trying to indicate that he meant it no harm, but the twin protrusions of the lesser creature remained maddeningly out of reach.

Coming to rest at the base of the slope, more irritated than angry, Ebbanai relaxed the skin flaps that had been reflexively held close to his body so as not to become abraded or, worse, ripped away. Rising, he methodically unwrapped the clumsy creature from where it remained tangled around his legs. Its wide-spreading mouthparts were flat and fleshy, suitable only for munching on the soft, low-growing, moisture-laden vegetation that covered the dunes. Even so, it did its best to bite him, antennae flailing and meeping feebly as the net-caster flung it over the nearest hillock. Landing with a heavy thud, it promptly righted itself and scrambled off in search of the nearest hole large enough to admit its bruised, attenuated body.

Breathing hard, Ebbanai plunged down the entry path paved with flat, irregular stones he had laid with his own hands. He even forgot to extinguish the greeting light, leaving it to flicker away atop its post, wasting oil. This far from major arteries of commerce and the sins of town, it was not necessary to lock the front door. Everyone along the inland peninsular road knew one other.

Storra was waiting for him. On the nights when he went out with the net, she would stay up working at the loom located in the forepart of the house, utilizing her weaving to keep awake until he returned. The pungent aroma wafting from the kitchen smelled of jent leaf and koroil: she always prepared a late-night snack for him, knowing how hungry he would be after long, hard hours spent casting and pulling in the weighted net.

As he drew up sharply, his thin torso expanding and contracting with the exertion of the single, pleated lung within, she turned from her loom and eyed him up and down. While the piquant food simmering in the kitchen hinted of her concern for him, her tone did not. That was Storra: an unpredictable ongoing collision of the caring and the caustic.

"You're home early," she observed succinctly.

"I saw—I saw . . . !" His upper body sank down into its more flexible lower half. The nature and evolutionary design of the Dwarran spine prevented them from bending over very far. He fought to catch his breath.

Rising from her comfortable squatting position before the loom, she set aside the length of indigo-stained seashan she had been working into the half-finished carpet and glanced behind her mate.

"Not anything edible, it seems. I see net, but no feyln, no mararra, not even a handful of soft-shelled tibordi."

He started, looked suddenly embarrassed. He had forgotten to leave the still-damp net outside, on its drying rack.

Hurriedly, he retraced his steps and dumped it outside the front door, not even bothering to ensure it was properly folded. Her eyes contracted suspiciously when he, for the first time she could remember, threw the bolt that secured the door against the outside.

"You have not been working," she accused him deliberately. "You have been off stargazing and sipping brew with those two no-goods Brrevemor and Drapp!"

"No, no," he hastily corrected her. "I swear on my father's heritage, I haven't seen anyone else all night long!" Starting at the crest of his smooth skull, a perceptible shiver started southward, traveling the length of his body until his podal flaps were visibly quivering.

Her annoyance changed quickly to concern. "Are you ill, Ebbanai?"

"No, I'm not." Coming closer, he extended all eight gripping flanges. "At least, I don't think I am."

Inclining his head forward, he extended the two fleshy antennae that protruded from its forepart. They made contact with those of his mate. The emotional charge that coursed through him and into her was strong enough to shock. Startled, she untwined her antennae from his as fast as if they had been greased, and drew back. This time her eyes were wide, having expanded considerably within their flexible sockets.

"*Mersance!*" she exclaimed, her attitude toward him completely altered by the emotions he had conveyed. "What happened, mate-mine? What *did* you see out there?" Her characteristic sarcasm had now given way entirely to concern.

"I'm not sure. A miracle, or a bad dream, or maybe something else. Something impossible, that's for certain." Moving past her, he slumped into a collapsed crouch beside the entrance to the kitchen. When she acknowledged the gesture with one of her own, he entered. But though the night-stew she had boiled for him beckoned, he found he was too nervous to sup. Instead, he edged cautiously toward the single window to stare out into the night. Coming up behind him, she placed both sets of right flanges on his shoulder.

"I had set the thoralls and was casting the first net of the evening," he told her without tearing his gaze away from the view, "when something came down out of the sky."

Her expression was pinched. "Down out of the sky?"

His antennae wove patterns in the air. "I thought a fourth moon had appeared and was falling toward me. When it drew nearer I saw that it was not a moon, but a machine of some kind." Seeing the look on her face, he hurried his explanation. "It touched down not far from the place where I ran and hid. Even as I was staring at it, it changed and became a line of large dunes. Then a hole appeared in the side of one of these new dunes. It was filled with light, from which a strange being emerged." Though she was now looking at him with something less than concerned compassion, he resolutely soldiered on.

"This creature was unlike us, but not unrecognizably so. It stood upright, but had upper and lower limbs that did not properly divide. Though no taller than I, it was much broader. It had two absurdly small eyes, and skin as smooth as a sheet of fabric, and a thick cluster of red tendrils atop its head, though because of the distance and the darkness I could not tell if they were for feeding or had some other purpose." His antennae bobbed significantly. "Certainly they were too numerous, too small, and too thin to serve for touching.

"The being was not alone. It was companioned by a small, brightly colored winged creature that seemed to respond to its mouth-noises. Or maybe to the gestures the larger creature made." He shuddered again at the remembrance of that unnatural, monolithic arm and its multiple digits gesturing into the night sky.

"When it turned to look back at its dune-machine, I took the opportunity to run away. I didn't stop running until I came through our portal."

She stared at him for a long time, the stew simmering on the cookbin behind her. "Well, *something* certainly scared you." Her antennae twitched expressively in his direction. "I felt the truth of that. The question is, what?"

He was breathing without effort now, if not necessarily more confidently. "I told you, Storra. It is just as I've told you."

"Is it?" Two sets of gripping flaps were clasped together in front of her torso. "Who ever heard of such a thing? Falling machines that turn into dunes. Lumbering beings who have lost arms and legs and don't even have Sensitives." The pair protruding from her head rubbed against each other. "Would not any creature capable of mastering such marvels have to be of a high order of intelligence?"

"*Vyst,* certainly," he agreed, wondering what she was getting at.

Her antennae thrust out straight toward him. "But without Sensitives, how could any being communicate its true feelings to another?"

In his fright, he had not thought of that. "I don't know."

"Of course you don't," she snapped as she turned toward the cookbin and picked up a ladle to fill a bowl for him. "Because it's impossible."

"I know what I saw." In the face of her sarcasm, not to mention her logic, he remained adamant. Assuming a squat feeding position, he began to dine, sipping the steaming contents of the feeding bowl she handed him from one of its two supping spouts. "This is delicious. I've always said that you are expert at weaving more than just fabric."

"Thank you, mate-mine. It is interesting to live with someone who is at once complimentary and crazy."

He looked up from his energetic slurping. "This thing *happened*. The consequences remain."

Her antennae flattened back against her smooth skull in a clear sign of disapproval. "*Something* happened. I suppose I should grant you that much." Eyes flexed. "It's true that things that happen require an explanation. Perhaps what you 'saw' and experienced has differed from what you believe." When he did not reply, she squatted down opposite him. Her right pair of forearms brushed against his upper left arm.

"Ebbanai, one who goes out with the net, alone and at night, is subject to sights unfamiliar to those who farm the land, or work in town. Is it not possible that you fell and hit your head, and had a wild dream from which you awoke confused, hurt, and believing it to have been real?"

He paused with the spout touching the lower portion of his round mouth. "What could I have hit my head on except sand? The bay where I was casting is empty of rocks."

She persisted. "Then if there was a rock buried in the sand, and you fell and struck it, and coming back to consciousness you believed there to be no rock, would that not only enhance the illusion of the experience?"

His antennae twisted and coiled like worms. "You are a good mate, Storra, and a good provider, but too often your words make a sickness in my head."

"If not that," she continued, "then could there not be some other explanation?" She stared at him out of wide, round eyes that were purple on silver. "Which is more reasonable? That you fell and hit your head and had a bad dream, or that you saw a giant machine descend from the sky, turn to sand, and spit out alien beings?"

Setting the now empty bowl aside, he looked up at her cautiously. When she wanted to, and given enough time, Storra could reduce a normally suave and articulate school instructor to a babbling idiot. "I'm tired, mate, and my head hurts."

She erected triumphantly. "Just as I was suggesting!"

"Not from hitting any rocks!" he hastened to correct her. "Soon you'll have me believing I'm a flying coretret that's spent too long in embryo." His expression brightened. "Come with me tomorrow and you can see for yourself. In daylight, it will be impossible to deny the reality of the thing!"

"It will certainly be impossible to deny some things." She spoke irritably, gesturing toward the front half of the house. "I have work to do. And so, in case you've forgotten it, do you."

"If you're going to doubt me," he pressed her, "you owe me the chance to prove you wrong."

Her Sensitives twitched in annoyance. "What a waste of time! Searching for the source of a bad dream." A pair of opposing flanges gestured. "If you're not going to do proper work tomorrow, it would be better if you traveled into Metrel to see the physician Tesenveh. Perhaps he can help you better than I. Myself, I have only words with which to try and cure you."

"Physicians are expensive." He placed the empty bowl in the cleaning basin. Sensing the proximity of food scraps, the horde of minuscule pekcks that lived beneath emerged from their burrows and began to hungrily scour the ceramic bowl. When they had finished, they would retire swiftly to their nest to quietly await the next bounty from the sky.

Straightening, Ebbanai moved toward his mate until they were touching Sensitives as well as all four upper limbs. "You can feel my self like none other," he told her softly but intently. "All I ask is that you spend a little of one morning with me. If I am wrong, if I imagined what I saw, I will perform a whole quarter's worth of abasements."

"You will, too," she told him—but tenderly. Then she sighed and pulled away, her Sensitives unwinding from his. "The lunacy one has to endure for the sake of maintaining a relationship."

"It is not lunacy," he assured her. "It is a giant machine and an alien that dwells inside. Two aliens," he corrected himself.

She made a spitting noise. "You came in here swollen with fear. Are you no longer afraid of what you think you saw?"

"Of course I am still afraid. But I will go back nonetheless."

He did not add that he would do so because he was more afraid of her continuing disdain than anything he might encounter. Besides, nothing could be as menacing in the bright light of day as it was at night. And this time he would not be alone.

His matchless, strong-willed mate, he was certain, was spirited enough to stand up even to oddly jointed, thick-bodied aliens.

Flinx estimated each leap covered half a dozen meters. One such jump might not be considered exceptional by a good athlete. Making such leaps in rapid succession, one after another, was another matter entirely. The low gravity allowed him to cover considerable distances with far less effort than usual. Though he was firmly rooted to the ground, the exuberant bounds conveyed something of the feeling of flying. By combing a short run-up with a strong jump, he discovered he was also able to soar over obstacles that on a t-normal world would have forced him to scramble over them or find a way around.

For her part, Pip dipped and plunged through a succession of aerial acrobatics that would elsewhere have seen her dangerously close to crashing. Anyone watching them would have been hard-pressed to tell who was having the better time: man or minidrag.

Then something stepped out from among the plant-laced dunes to confront him directly.

The size of a small bear, it had a low-slung jaw that made up fully a third of its length. Four squat, stumpy legs separated at the midjoint into pairs that terminated in a total of eight blocky feet. Hairless, earless, and colored a splotchy blue-black, it sported a smooth pair of fleshy appendages that protruded from the top of its head. Though the teeth in the extraordinary mouth were flat and designed for masticating vegetation, the two short horns that tipped both the upper and lower jaw looked sharp enough to do real damage.

As startled by the sight of the taller but lighter human as Flinx was by the sudden appearance of the bulky herbivore, the creature's large eyes contracted in their bony sockets. Uttering a cross between a snort and a whistle, it started toward him: slowly at first, but rapidly gathering momentum.

Flinx knew it was startled because he could sense that particular emotion emanating from the oncoming animal. Could sense it without even having to try. It was among the clearest emotional projections he had ever received at any time in all his many travels. He did not have to extend his perception at all, as he often did at such moments of stress. Proper perceiving was even more difficult when the subject was nonsentient. But this charging creature was laying its emotions out in his mind as clearly as if they had been printed to hard copy and handed to him for his leisurely perusal.

Above, Pip sensed her master's sudden stress, folded her wings, and dove. Her intervention was not necessary. Exerting only a minimal effort, and without even trying to focus his attention, Flinx simply thought at the beast that he meant it no harm. Normally, he would have had to concentrate forcefully and hope that the creature possessed sufficient neurological complexity to be affected by the projection. If not, Flinx was fully prepared to dive aside and pull his handgun while his flying snake engaged and diverted the onrushing animal.

It stopped dead in its tracks, its dark blue pupils squeezing together even more tightly than they had thus far. The two appendages that protruded from its head were pointed straight at Flinx, and quivering. Simultaneously relieved and bemused, the tall young human stared back. He had only concentrated once on the suggestion, and that almost indifferently, that the advancing creature should halt its charge. Yet it had done so with such alacrity that it was almost as if it had received and reacted to a recognizable spoken command. What was going on here?

Flinx allowed himself to feel at ease, relaxed, nonthreatening. The jaw-bear's cranial appendages relaxed. Letting out a soft snort, it turned and ambled off into the brush, not even looking back to see if the strange, angular being that had surprised it in the midst of dense vegetation was making an effort to follow.

That was odd, Flinx reflected. Usually, his singular ability allowed him to empathize only erratically with nonsentients. He was better at it now than he had been years ago, but it was a talent that was still far from perfected. Yet convincing this startled alien planteater that he represented no threat to it had required hardly any effort at all.

He shrugged it off as a fortuitous coincidence. That rationalization lasted until he encountered a small herd of long-eared, long-tailed browsers.

There might be trees elsewhere on this world, but at least on the sandy peninsula where he had landed, the tallest vegetation was comprised of numerous variants of single-bladed pseudo-grasses. Some species were striped, some blotched, while others flaunted extraordinary and sometimes bizarre variations in color. And size. A few individual blades soared to heights high overhead. Providing a strong contrast was a pinkish stubble that in places grew together tightly enough to form a pale carpet under his feet. Everywhere he looked, diminutive and fast-moving creatures scurried through the diverse, angular grassland.

Striding along, trying to gain a sense of the place while having to remind himself not to take giant leaps, he topped another dune, pushed through a closely packed stand of yellow-striped, single-leafed vegetation, and found himself confronting a pack of creatures busily cropping fat blue blades that grew in dense, solitary clumps. Unlike the bear-thing, these browsers were built low to the ground, though they featured the same arrangement of subdividing limbs as the larger animal. There the resemblance ended.

Each individual was about the size of a small pig. Their front ends were narrow, the opposite terminus broad and flattened. Once again, each sported four legs that separated further into eight forelegs. A single small eye stared up at him from a globular housing near the tip of the pointed end, while a much larger one was located directly behind it and higher up. Speculating on the unusual in-line ocular arrangement, Flinx hypothesized that one eye was permanently focused for close-up work while the other searched for movement at a distance. Like the jaw-bear, their bodies were smooth and, except for a few gray and black patches here and there, a startling creamy white. And just like the bear-being, each of them had a pair of cranial appendages protruding from the front of its skull. At present, every one of them was pointing directly at Flinx.

Half closing his eyes to relax himself, he felt that he was projecting a sense of complete well-being, of calm and contentment, that bordered on lethargy.

In seconds they were clustering around him, rubbing up against his legs like so many arrowhead-shaped alien house cats. At the same time, they began vocalizing sharp clicking sounds that reminded him of recordings he had heard of terrestrial crickets. In this case, exceedingly large terrestrial crickets.

The feelings, in the best sense of the term, were mutual. The more he relaxed, the more the arrowhead cats did, and the more he felt himself at ease. So much so that despite some nervousness on Pip's part, he felt safe in taking a seat in the midst of the pack. They swarmed him immediately, chattering away like a dozen attenuated snare drums come to life, the emotions they were registering anything but hostile.

Attracted by the noise, another couple of representatives of the local fauna appeared, pushing their way forcefully through the high, solo-stalked flora. The newcomers were considerably larger than the arrowhead-shaped creatures, each massing about as much as a heavy dog. Their appearance being notably less benign than that of the browsers clustered around him, Flinx started to scramble to his feet. As soon as he sensed what both of the new arrivals were feeling, however, he allowed himself to relax once again.

The new arrivals had eight main limbs apiece, four to a side, each further dividing according to the apparently dominant local pattern into a pair of separate forelegs. That gave them sixteen legs apiece to go along with the four bright eyes: two facing forward to provide binocular vision, one each aimed to either side to supply tracking in parallel. Coupled with a narrow mouth full of slim but sharp centimeter-long teeth, it was clear that these most recent visitors had evolved to eat something more substantial than grass.

Yet as they approached the wary but still-seated Flinx, not only did they ignore the potential arrowhead-shaped prey crowding around him; they positively purred. While their scaly flanks were not nearly as velvety to the touch as those of the clicking, chattering arrow-cats, they made up in displays of affection what they lacked in suppleness.

Landing on her master's shoulder, Pip surveyed the alien lovefest, flicked out her tongue several times in a reptiloid gesture whose meaning was beyond Flinx's purview, coiled her hind half snugly around his neck, and settled down for a nap, oblivious to the activity around him. Meanwhile, the arrowhead cats and the two predators had been joined by a dozen or so much smaller creatures, each no bigger than a wingless pigeon and considerably more wiry. They boasted the same pair of peculiar cranial appendages possessed by every example of the local fauna he had encountered so far. While built close to the ground, these latest locals to push up against him were not devoid of limbs. Each had two, appropriately separated into two more.

Eyeing the mass of alien affection swarming over his lower body and nuzzling his back, Flinx decided that instead of Arrawd, this world might more appropriately have been called Legs, if only by the Commonwealth probe that had surveyed it.

Cuddly as was the creature conclave, before the sun reached its midpoint in the sky he wanted to see as much as possible of the region that lay within easy walking distance of the *Teacher*. Of course, the light gravity considerably aided the number of kilometers he could cover. Careful not to kick or step on any of his captivated local admirers, he rose, having to gently dislodge or brush several of them away from the legs of his jumpsuit. Primitive though were the simple emotions engulfing him on all sides, he found he was able to perceive their collective disappointment without straining.

A single leap, a giant stride, and he was off and running. Jolted from her brief nap, Pip rose complainingly into the air as she was forced from her perch on his shoulder. Leave it to a minidrag to throw a hissy fit that was literal as well as metaphorical, he thought as he joyfully extended his bounding stride.

What he forgot to keep in mind, because he was not used to taking such long steps, was that the sudden ability to span additional space also exposed one to additional dangers. One such, as treacherous as it was innocuous, took the form of an unexpectedly deep hole that had been inadvertently camouflaged by its excavators. As Flinx's right foot descended, the occupants of the hole took scampering flight. When his boot entered the burrow, the owners were no longer present.

A surprised look on his face, he threw out his hands and arms to break his fall as he went down. Lesser gravity or no, he hit hard. An electric pain shot up his right leg, and he was grimacing as he hit the ground.

Angry at himself, he gently disengaged his right foot from the gap that had momentarily swallowed it and began to feel gingerly of the limb from toe to knee. Nothing appeared to be broken, but when he tried to stand and put pressure on it, the injured area protested vehemently. It took only another minute to trace the problem to a sprained ankle.

He was in no particular danger. A quick call via the communicator that was part of his service belt would cause the *Teacher* to send out the small skimmer it carried in its cargo hold. The danger was not to him, but to Commonwealth protocol regulating Class IVb worlds. Unless the initial planetary survey had been very wrong, or severely limited in scope, or the local dominant species had made unexpectedly giant strides in scientific achievement that he had somehow overlooked during his own admittedly brief survey from orbit, the skimmer represented technology far in advance of anything yet developed on Arrawd. It was incumbent on him to make every effort to ensure such a device was not observed by the locals.

He considered how to proceed. The craft could fly low, just above the tips of the tallest growths, and at slow speeds made very little noise. Furthermore, he had chosen an area of sparse population in which to set down. Even if the skimmer was seen by a couple of locals, it was unlikely any report they might decide to make would be believed. Circling low, Pip regretted the absence of any vegetation with branches, and had to settle for landing on the sandy soil. Head up, wings half furled, she watched Flinx carefully as she monitored his pain.

A second try at standing proved as futile as the first. While there was plenty of fallen and dried plant matter scattered about, none of it proved strong enough to serve as a temporary crutch. Lips tight, he reluctantly reached for his communicator, and was about to request that the skimmer be dispatched when a thought stopped him.

No, not a thought. A feeling. Paired.

Each was among the clearest emotional projections he had ever received, even from others of his own kind. Though not human, they were startling and uncompromising in their clarity. The first was a rapidly and continuously shifting blend of anticipation, determination, and fear. The second was unchanging and relentless in its light-weight fury: anger underlain with resentment. For all his practice in reading the emotions of others, in all his years of trying to gain control of his erratic, sometimes pain-inducing Talent, this was the first time perceived feelings had leaped out at him with such crystalline transparency.

What sort of beings could project their emotions as sharply as if they were shouted words? His fingers hesitated above the communicator. He knew he should not have any contact with the local sentients. By doing so, he would be flouting a long list of elemental Commonwealth laws. On the other hand, he told himself as the emotional clarity of the two individuals approaching the clearing where he was sitting continued to intensify, he had been raised a thief. In his time, he had been compelled to steal many things. He had already stolen time on this world. Taken in that context, the theft of a little information, without anyone continuing any the wiser, to satisfy his own private curiosity and without any intent to disseminate, seemed but a minor infraction.

His hand drew away from the communicator and moved to position itself near the needler attached to his belt. While their emotions were presently nonthreatening, he had no way of knowing how those coming this way would react at the sight of him. Nor did he know if they were armed, and if so, with what. Death brought about by primitive devices was no less final than that begat by advanced weaponry. He needed to be prepared for anything. As he had been all his life.

Calling Pip to him, he bade the flying snake curl up in his lap, leaned back with his palms pressing into the cool, slightly moist soil, and waited to see what was about to step through the surrounding vegetation.

CHAPTER

4

"Are you sure you know where you're going?"

Storra was tired, bored, and frustrated at the waste of time. She should be home, finishing the fringe work on the magaarje runner. It was a particularly fine piece of work, incorporating both suru and sjal patterns, and it ought to bring a high price in Metrel's southern marketplace. If she was ever allowed to finish it, that is. She resented every timeclick that took her away from the work. It was beginning to look like this wild wandering of her beloved mate, she reflected dourly, would end up costing her an entire morning.

Ebbanai's confidence was starting to ebb even though they were still some distance from where the arrival had taken place. Storra's uncompromising resort to logic and reason was beginning to have an effect on him, wearing down his conviction like gherowd bone beneath a file. Had he truly seen what he claimed to have seen? Or, as she had suggested, had he taken a fall after all, and hit his head, and dreamed everything but the falling and the head-hitting?

No. He rose a little higher, lifting his upper torso another fold out of the pelvic buttress. He had not been dazed, or dreaming. It had all been real, as real as the sand and dirt presently passing beneath his four sandal-shod foot-pads. What he *did* fear was that the machine he had seen had swallowed up its creatures and left during the night. If that was the case, and no proof of its ever having been on the beach had been left behind, he would never hear the end of it. For the rest of his life, Storra would drag it out in the middle of every argument and use it against him.

The machine-dune had to still be there. It *had* to be. He pushed through a denser clump of tall cherkka—and then it no longer mattered whether the gigantic apparition remained on the beach or not.

Because its occupant was not with it. It was here, right in front of them.

Alongside him, he heard Storra react, her startled inhalation a fusion of whistle and gasp. Every one of her skin flaps lifted and extended to its maximum, giving her the temporary appearance of a threatened horwath raising its defensive spines. Her eyes widened such an extent that they threatened to sprain the encircling muscles. All her anger, annoyance, and uncertainty evaporated in the space of a second.

As for the creature, neither it nor the smaller, winged being coiled about its upper arms made any effort to stand in response to their arrival. Nor did either of the alien beings react sharply. Their calm in the face of the confrontation almost suggested that the arrival of Ebbanai and his mate had been anticipated.

Nearly as shocking to Storra as their appearance, and certainly as much to Ebbanai, were the mouth-noises the alien spoke. These were directed not at them, but toward a small device the creature took from a belt and held up to its enormously wide, flattened mouth. Alien noises went in, but comprehensible Dwarrani came out.

"My name is Flinx. I am an intelligent being like yourselves." A single hand at the end of a single forearm pointed skyward, and a stunned Storra could not keep from looking for its missing counterpart. "I come from far away, from a world that circles a star not unlike your own." The alien arm lowered to indicate a leg that terminated in a similarly solitary forelimb. "I was running, and I've injured myself. I mean you no harm."

He did not have to say so. Both Ebbanai and his mate already knew it.

They knew it because they could sense it. How, neither of them could understand. They had made no contact with the alien's Sensitives. They could not do this, because it *had* no Sensitives. Except for the peculiar short, red tendrils that sprouted somewhat gruesomely from its skull, it was evident that the alien had nothing of that vital nature to conceal. Yet despite the creature being Sensitive-deprived, they could perceive its feelings as clearly as if that myriad of tiny red tendrils possessed the same function and were presently coiled tightly around their own antennae.

Somehow it was communicating its emotions to them without physical contact. Ebbanai would have declared this to be impossible, if not for the indisputable fact that it happened to be taking place. He turned to Storra.

"Are you feeling these—these projections, as I am?"

Openmouthed, she indicated assent. "How can this be happening?" She looked back down at the alien. "I've never heard of such a thing."

"Of course not." Her mate spoke with quiet but unmistakable satisfaction. "It's impossible, remember?" With both of his right hands, he indicated the incongruous creature seated before them. "Just as is the undeniable existence of this being."

She found herself grateful to her mate twice over. First, for having had the strength of character to persist in his beliefs and insist she come see the truth of them for herself. And second, for not shaming her with his triumph. Other females might seek mates with money or reputation: once again she found herself content to have chosen one whose most outstanding asset was a goodness of spirit and soul. Moving impulsively close to him, she flicked her Sensitives against his.

The depth of feeling that passed between them was not lost on Flinx. He understood immediately the nature of their relationship without having to inquire.

Despite the additional forelimbs, their movements were somewhat awkward, as if their lean and willowy bodies did not quite know what to do with the extra forelegs and arms. No doubt that was just his own alien perception. In all probability they considered themselves quite graceful. He marveled at how the quartet of forelegs worked in concert, when it seemed certain every second step would see them getting entangled and tripping all over themselves.

"You two are related, and very fond of one another." He spoke gently into the translator he held.

Contact between them broke as both regarded him with fresh astonishment. "How—how can you know that?"

Seeing no reason to withhold information about himself that would never leave this isolated world, and feeling that revelation of his ability to communicate on the emotional level could only enhance his stature among natives who did likewise, he told them.

"I can perceive what others are feeling." He gestured with the translator as Pip stirred in his lap. "Just now, you two were expressing the warmest sentiments toward one another."

While making no effort to hide her astonishment, Storra was also suddenly wary of this creature. She brushed two hands across her head, pressing her antennae gently back against her smooth skull. "If you can comprehend what we are feeling, and without Sensitives, then how can we be sure without any kind of physical contact between us that the emotions we are receiving from you are a genuine expression of your own feelings?"

Flinx started to rise, grimaced, and sat back down. "I'd be happy to make physical contact, but I can't stand up." Once again, he indicated his right leg. "I told you; I've injured my ankle."

"And with only two instead of four to call on for support." Despite the exhibition of unimaginably advanced technology he had observed the night before, Ebbanai was moved to sympathy for the creature.

When it came to a proper number of limbs, its ancestry was decidedly shorted.

"Storra, I'm sure there's no deception here." His Sensitives flicked toward her but did not reach for contact. "Touch or no touch, I'm confident the emotions we are receiving from this—visitor—are authentic. It's no threat to us, and it's hurt." All four fingerless, flange-tipped hands gestured toward the seated figure of Flinx. "It makes no threats, though I suspect that if it wished to do so, it could. It shows no fear. In fact, the only concern I feel from it is for *us* and for our state of mind—not for itself."

Ebbanai had voiced exactly what Storra was feeling, though she was reluctant to admit it. As the one who did all the trading and bargaining in the marketplace, it was natural that she should be the more suspicious of the pair. Staring down at the Sensitive-less being, she found her eyes drawn to the device it held that allowed them to communicate, then down to the belt it wore. All manner of interesting devices were visible there. If half of what her mate had told her was true about gargantuan machines dropping from the sky and turning themselves into sand dunes, what other possibly useful wonders might this visitor command? What miraculous devices did it possess? And how could she, and Ebbanai, possibly profit from them, and from the presence of their visitor?

It was a tried and trusted tenet that an injured traveler should be given succor. If they helped this creature, would it not be grateful? It certainly struck her as completely civilized. Though they knew nothing of its ethics or those of its kind, its comments were not those of a hostile barbarian. What did they have to lose by showing a little compassion? If it wanted to harm them, surely it would have done so by now, out of fear of what they might do to it. She still could not get over her amazement at its ability to project and receive emotions in the absence of Sensitives or, for that matter, any kind of physical contact. Thus far it had projected nothing but calmness and concern for their reaction.

She came to a decision.

Flinx knew about it before either of the Dwarra could say anything. He felt the subtle shift in their feelings toward him; from initial fear, to amazement, and now to concern.

"Up, Pip." As the minidrag, on command, took to the sky, Flinx extended an arm toward the two natives.

After a quick glance at one another, they cautiously approached. Ebbanai slipped all four forearms underneath the alien's right arm while Storra did the same on the other side. "Together now," he urged the creature. Bracing himself against the support of the two natives, Flinx clenched his teeth and pushed himself upward.

All three of them nearly went down. Though no taller than the locals, Flinx was considerably heavier. Furthermore, the disparity in weight reflected more than just a difference in bodily proportions. Evolved to cope with heavier gravity, his muscles and bones were significantly denser than those of the Dwarra.

"Freint!" Storra exclaimed as she struggled to keep all four feet under her and the hundreds of skin flaps that lined her body untensed. "Are your people made of stone?"

"I'm sorry." Flinx tried to place more of his weight on his good leg as he hopped along between them. "My world is different from yours. Higher gravity there means living things have to develop dense muscles and heavier, thicker bones just to support themselves."

"What's gravity?" a curious Ebbanai asked, when no equivalent was forthcoming from the translator device hanging around the alien's neck.

For the first time, the initial Commonwealth survey's designation of this world as one supporting no more than Class IVb technology was confirmed in person. Flinx did his best to explain.

"It's a force that one object exerts on another," he told the male Dwarra. "It's what keeps everything fixed to the surface of the world and prevents it from flying off into space."

Bent under her share of the burden that was their guest, the female made a gargling noise in her throat. "I won't argue with alien notions of how things work because I'm not familiar with them, but everyone knows that weight is what keeps things fixed to the ground. When you drop something, weight is what makes it fall."

While the two explanations were not irreconcilable, Flinx decided that now was not the time to begin lecturing his amiable hosts on the finer points of elementary physics. He needed to concern himself with more prosaic matters: such as where they were taking him.

"To our home, of course," Ebbanai informed him when he voiced the question. "To a place where you can heal."

Flinx did not counter that better facilities for speeding his recovery were available on board his ship. He thought it unlikely these remarkable folk would willingly board his craft. They might be bold, but if confronted by something as intimidating and alien to them as the *Teacher,* their resolve was likely to shrivel. Better to engage them on ground and terms they found familiar.

As the trio made their way northward through the dunes, with Pip patrolling lazily overhead, it became clear to him that these creatures were not true empaths like himself. Whereas he could perceive their emotions effortlessly, they could not tell what he was feeling unless he worked to project his emotions directly onto them. Moreover, they could only recognize each other's feelings when physical contact was made through the cerebral transmitter/receivers they called Sensitives.

That aside, with the exception of Pip, with whom he shared a unique mental connection, they were more like him in their emotionally perceptive abilities than any species he had ever encountered. The feelings he received from them were as clear and pure and easy to interpret as words on a screen. He felt an instant rapport with these simple sentients of a kind he had never experienced before, not even with another human being. Well, with the exception of perhaps one or two human beings, he corrected himself. And a certain thranx.

It was as if, after searching for uncomplicated, straightforward empathetic connections all his life, he had finally stumbled on a situation where they were not only not special, but a natural component of everyday person-to-person existence. The realization left him more than a little overwhelmed.

Careful, he admonished himself. Thus far, he had only met two of the natives. Their mental condition might be as unique as it was isolated. He knew nothing of the rest of the population. He needed to reserve judgment concerning the abilities of the species as a whole until he had experienced a substantially greater number of encounters. Appearances, even mental ones, could be deceiving.

He nodded toward the native on his right. Though the representatives of the two sexes were approximately the same height, the limbs of the male were larger in diameter than those of the female, while the lower torso of the latter was wider. He recalled the unique birthing process described by the *Teacher,* but saw no sign that the female was carrying pouched young.

A slight misstep sent an electric sting up his right leg, and he winced. "Is it much farther?" he asked via the translator swaying on the retractable cord around his neck.

"Not so far." He found himself looking into the large, inquisitive round eyes of the female. "Why didn't you just fly there? Ebbanai said that you arrived here in a great flying machine."

"That's just it," he told her, sidestepping mention of the shuttlecraft and skimmer snugged in the *Teacher*'s support bay. "It's not feasible to have a large vessel engage its engines to travel such a short distance."

Ebbanai freed one double-flanged forehand long enough to make a crisp gesture. "What powers your craft, Flinx? I would say that maybe it is like one of the wondrous new steam devices one hears about, though I saw no evidence of such."

More indications of the level of local technology. "Not steam," he replied as they followed a well-trodden path through a pair of dunes thickly clad in tall, single-stemmed vegetation. "A kind of energy that would be hard for me to explain to you."

The Dwarra accepted the demurral—for now. Time enough later

to seek more detailed explanations. As the initial shock of the creature's reality continued to fade, other ideas, other notions, began to fill the empty space in his head. Especially the portion that was devoted to contemplation of future possibilities. Looking past the struggling, limping alien, he could see that his mate's thoughts were running along similar lines.

Not every successful voiceless communication required the entwining of Sensitives.

The home of Flinx's new friends was not properly a farm. There were only two buildings, both dome-shaped. The smaller featured tall, narrow windows, a single door, and a slender clay pipe chimney. The other was somewhat larger with no chimney or windows, but it boasted a much larger set of double doors.

"That's where we keep our wagon and overnight the baryeln," Ebbanai explained in response to his query.

"What's a baryeln?" Flinx asked via the translator. The sounds of Dwarrani were not complex. Already he found himself beginning to recognize simple words. Always good at languages, he had no doubt that with a little effort and practice, he would soon be able to manage basic phrases. The translator would always be available to back him up.

Ebbanai looked again at his mate. It was clear that this creature, for all its impressive technology and physical stature, was ignorant of a great many basic things.

"We'll show you," Storra told him. Her right hands indicated his bad leg. "Unless you are too tired and wish to rest first."

Flinx tested his ankle. There was no way he could walk on it, but the worst of the pain seemed to be ebbing somewhat. After the assisted hike across the dunes, rest was certainly in order. But he knew that once he sat down he would not feel like getting up again for a while. Better to view the enigmatic baryeln first, then relax.

Interestingly, there was no fence around the buildings, or anywhere that he could see. "How do you define your property limits?" he asked.

"There are stone markers," Ebbanai told him.

"And the baryeln don't wander off if you let them out of their enclosure?" Overhead, Pip soared effortlessly on a mix of sea breezes and lighter gravity.

"You will see," Storra told him. This alien was going to need much education, she thought, if she and her mate were going to pursue some of the ideas that were just beginning to coalesce in her mind.

Hinged at the sides—the Dwarra had advanced far enough to smelt metal, Flinx noted—one of the double doors was pulled aside by Ebbanai while Storra fought to assist Flinx in remaining upright. As the two of them helped him hobble inside, he saw that individual pens held what at first appeared to be decapitated creatures. They were not headless, however, and he eventually found the fore end of each animal by seeking out the now familiar pair of Sensitives that protruded from the skull of every higher-order land-dweller on Dwarra.

The baryeln were so rectangular in shape that except for their four legs—which underwent the standard Dwarran subdividing to form a total of eight forelegs—they might be shipped by being stacked one atop another as neatly as crates of comparable size. Tailless and virtually featureless except for their Sensitives, they stood motionless in their stalls, the only sound in the stable or barn the sound of hundreds of flat mouthparts masticating kilo after kilo of harvested verdure.

Walking over to the nearest enclosure, Ebbanai opened the simple but sturdy gate and beckoned Flinx come closer. He did so, hopping on his one good leg and using the solidly built fencing for support. Up close, the baryeln were as dull in appearance as they were from a distance. Their bulky, squarish bodies were adorned with dozens of small, pyramidal nodules. In color they ranged from a pale blue to a deep violet. Some featured horizontal streaks of white or beige. As they ate, their Sensitives bobbed up and down like paired metronomes. Placid and bovine, it seemed they would be easy to care for.

"The baryeln are our life," Storra explained. "They provide us with meat, gryln, and transportation."

One word had failed to translate. "What's *gryln*?" Flinx asked innocently.

"Watch." Moving to one fence, Ebbanai removed what appeared to be a long, narrow funnel and a feather-tipped stick from among a cluster of identical utensils. Approaching a baryeln, he selected one of the many nodules on its back and began to stroke the area around it with the feather-stick. In less than a minute, a glistening, pink-tinged fluid began to ooze from the tip of the nodule. It flowed slowly, gleaming with a consistency like glycerine. After a few tea-spoons had issued from the spot, the flow stopped.

Bringing the funnel-like collection device over to where Flinx stood propped up against the fence, Ebbanai held it up to the visitor. "Gryln is refined in many ways, and used in many different forms, but those of us who are fortunate enough to own our own baryeln enjoy it fresh." He held it out to the human. "Please, try some."

They were both watching him carefully. Fortunately, they did not possess sufficient cultural referents with which to allow them to interpret the expression on his face. He swallowed hard. Removing the analyzer from his belt, he carefully pushed the sampling probe into the viscous fluid. Unfortunately, the device promptly pronounced the amalgam of alien proteins and sugars perfectly harmless to his system. It did not, of course, reference something as subjective as taste. His principal excuse for not accepting the offering now demolished, he smiled wanly and took the funnel from the eager Ebbanai's gripping flanges.

The thick liquid was warm, which did not surprise him. The taste, however, did. His face rapidly unwrinkled. The viscous fluid was simultaneously sweet and sharp, like honey doused with pepper. Though perplexing to his palate, it was anything but unpleasant, despite the immediate and unsettling proximity of its ambulatory alien origins. He handed the funnel back to his host. Moments passed and his stomach did not rebel.

Storra's mouth was flexing in a series of expanding ripples. The local equivalent of a smile, perhaps. "Welcome," she declared heartily. "Wherever you have fallen from, Flinx, you are welcome in this house."

"Where our tired and sore guest should be resting," Ebbanai chided them both. He had to admit that it had been interesting to see the alien drink gryln fresh from the baryeln. Perhaps they were more alike than not.

Their visitor chose that moment to remind them that the gap between them was also defined by things that could not be observed.

"That baryeln there." Halting on the way out of the building, Flinx halted and pointed at one of the creatures in a stall opposite.

Storra looked at the animal and wondered why the alien was singling it out. "That is orv-six. Something about it draws your attention?"

Flinx did not bother to nod, knowing that the gesture would pass unrecognized. "Something's wrong with her. She's in pain."

Eyes contracting slightly, Ebbanai walked over to the stall in question. Entering, he studied the nearly motionless animal, walking all around it, collapsing his upper body into the lower in order to peer beneath the stolid creature. All the while it ignored him, making no sound beyond a soft humming noise.

"I see no injury, or sign of difficulty." He peered at his alien guest. "What leads you to suspect such a thing?"

"I perceive it," Flinx told him. "That's all I can tell you." On his shoulder, Pip stirred slightly.

Now both Dwarra were staring at him. "It is not possible." Like individual flower petals caught in a stiff breeze, Storra's skin flaps slowly rose and fell against her body. "People are advanced enough to transmit their feelings to the lower animals, but they cannot read the emotions of the lower orders, no matter how tightly they might try to entwine their Sensitives with them."

Lest unflattering conclusions be drawn, Flinx held back from pointing out that even in the complete absence of the sensitive cranial protrusions, he could easily read her emotions. "Check again," he urged his hosts. The pain from the creature was sharp and clear, the mental equivalent of pouring lime juice into an open cut.

Once more Ebbanai moved to examine the animal called orv-six. This time, he used the eight gripping flanges at the ends of his fore-arms to prod and press against different parts of the animal. Nothing happened—until one firm inward thrust caused the creature to bark crisply, lean forward, and strike out sharply with all four of its rear legs. Only by scuttling swiftly to one side did Ebbanai avoid a nasty kick.

Keeping a wary eye on the now visibly disturbed baryeln, Ebbanai rejoined the alien and his mate. "Some kind of severe upset of the third digestive tract. A purgative may be in order, or a change in diet. Unquestionably, something is wrong." Turning, he regarded his singular guest with something approaching awe. "Devoid of Sen-sitives," he commented aloud, as if the alien were not present, "yet it can identify emotions not only in Dwarra, but in simple animals. Re-markable!"

"And useful," the ever-practical Storra observed. With both left hands, she indicated the other stalls. "What of the rest of our pack? Can you probe their feelings as well?"

Flinx could, and did. "Everyone else seems to be fine," he as-sured her. "Content."

She made a clicking sound in her throat signifying approval. "It's clear our new friend is the master of many surprising talents—even if fixing its own leg is not one of them."

"Actually," he told her, "I can do that, too. But in order to do so properly I need a place to rest."

"Of course, of course!" Ebbanai hastened toward the propped-open double doors. "In our amazement we forget ourselves, Storra. Come into our home, Flinx, and partake of my family's hospitality."

The dome house was surprisingly well decorated, full of carv-ings and attractive weavings that made good use of local colors and materials. It was also notably, almost shockingly, devoid of furnishings.

A mite bewildered, Flinx noted the paucity of furniture. "I don't see any chairs or benches. Where do you sit?"

"Sit?" Mate and mate looked at each other before returning their attention to their guest. "What is *sit*?"

This was an aspect of Dwarran culture the *Teacher* had neglected to expound upon, Flinx observed. Come to think of it, from the moment he had set eyes on them, he had not seen either of the natives sit down. Instead, their upper torsos sank down into the lower portions of their bodies, which were appropriately wide enough to receive them. Supported by a quartet of forelegs, it was evident that they did not *need* to sit down. At least, not in the human sense. He wondered if they were physiologically capable of it. Instructively, the house was destitute of furniture for the purpose. There were no chairs, no couches, not even a lounge. He began to wonder what position they used for sleeping.

"Well, in order to work on my leg, I need to sit down." He proceeded to explain what was required.

Did the alien's legs tire so easily that they could no longer support it? Ebbanai mused. The absence of furniture specifically designed for the human's need was not a problem. A family wooden chest carved with rough bas-reliefs served the purpose admirably. Open-mouthed, he and Storra looked on in fascination as the visitor actually *bent its body in the middle* and rested it on the chest. Such remarkable flexibility in one so bulky, she marveled, had to be seen to be believed.

Opening a pouch on his service belt, Flinx removed a small tube, unsealed it, and squeezed a little of the ointment it contained onto his open palm. Pip's tongue immediately darted in its direction, and he had to use his other hand to push her head back toward his shoulder. Peeling down the top of the boot on his right foot, he applied the ointment to the swollen, slightly reddened flesh. Immediately, his injured ankle was suffused with a soothing warmth. A couple of applications should restore the stressed spot to normal, he felt.

Meanwhile, he would try to relax and learn as much as he could about his hosts before it was time to take his leave of them. Thankfully, except for their understandably roiled emotions, all was quiet within him as well as without.

"You're quite isolated here, I see," he murmured into the translator's pickup.

"Oh no." Storra hastened to correct him. "We have many near neighbors. This is a productive fishing and growing area, well-populated." Her Sensitives dipped toward him but did not make contact. "Because Ebbanai's ancestors were among the last to settle this peninsula, our home is the farthest out. But between here and Metrel City there are many hundreds of homesteads and several small villages."

That was not possible, Flinx reflected. No matter the world, if it was inhabited by sentients capable of a minimum of cognitive thought, their projected feelings invariably found him smothered beneath an unending torrent of emotion. Struggling to ignore that constant emotional pressure was one of the hardest things he had to do in life. It was why he did not mind spending so much time traveling between worlds. Only in the vastness of interstellar space could his mind be fully at ease, free from the interminable storms of love, hatred, desire, lust, fear, uncertainty, and all the other emotions intelligence was heir to. Once down on an inhabited world it was a constant battle to keep that emotive babble pushed sufficiently far into the background just so he could retain his sanity. Less complex animalistic emotions he was able to ignore.

Sensing the uncertainty and concern and emotions of only his two hosts, he had naturally assumed he had set down in a sparsely inhabited area. Now they insisted the reality was otherwise. Could there be more to the local mental state of affairs than first appeared? Carefully, he reached out with his Talent; seeking, searching.

There—another set of emotions. And there another. And another. Storra was being truthful. Yet when he closed down his perceptive ability, the other individual emotive projections disappeared. And not only them. He found he could shut out the feelings he was receiving from his hosts as well.

As far back as he could remember, he had been able to read the emotions of others—whether he wanted to or not. In cities, he sometimes had to resort to music or other forms of continuous noise just to gain some relief from the emotional cacophony by overriding it with something else capable of holding his attention. Over the last few years, he had discovered that he had within him the ability to project emotions onto others.

But this was the first time, and the first place, ever, where he had been able to completely shut them out.

He sat there dazed, like a man who has just found he can turn his sense of hearing on and off at will. As his Dwarran hosts eyed him uncertainly, he practiced alternately perceiving with and then shutting his Talent down. One moment their emotions were there, clear and sharp in his mind as if he were studying words carved in stone. The next, with minimal effort on his part, all was silent. Silent, and quiet. A type of quiet he had never experienced before in his life.

He wanted to cry out with delight.

On his shoulder, an Alaspinian minidrag wondered at the rush of buoyant emotion that was surging through her master. She began a curious and ultimately futile search for its cause.

"Are you all right?" The radical shift of expression on the alien's face alarmed Storra.

"I—I'm fine. Remarkably well, I think. It seems that this world, and your—kind—are full of surprises."

Ebbanai felt pleased without knowing quite why. "We're happy you find your surroundings agreeable. Hospitality is a hallmark of my family."

Rubbing another daub of ointment into his ankle, Flinx looked up at the angular, big-eyed Dwarra. "You have no idea how hospitable I'm finding it. Maybe before I leave I'll find a way to explain why."

Ebbanai glanced at his mate, then back to the alien. "Surely you need not rush away. You have questions for us, but we also have some for you."

Flinx was immediately on guard. While he had already violated the strictures governing contact with inhabitants of Class IVb worlds, he fully intended to minimize the damage by telling them as little as possible about himself, the Commonwealth, and its technology. He supposed he owed this particular couple a few answers in return for their help, even if he would have been quite capable of surviving his injury without their intercession.

But he would keep any replies to their queries as simple and harmless as possible.

It was hard to restrain his elation. If Storra was being truthful, there were within reception range of his Talent dozens, perhaps hundreds, of fully aware minds constantly generating all manner of emotions. And he was, almost without conscious effort, shutting them out. He was among emotives, but his consciousness was at peace. He luxuriated in the remarkableness of it.

Different neural pathways, he thought. The Dwarra were wired differently from any sentient species he had yet encountered. Just enough to allow him to have some peace. Barring any sudden and unexpected changes, here was an intelligent folk among whom he could spend time without having to constantly guard against the uninvited intrusion of distressing emotions. Yet whenever he wished to do so, he could apparently access them with the same ease as he did those of other sentients. And there was something else. It had been nagging at him ever since he had first stepped out of the *Teacher* to inspect its external camouflaging and his new surroundings.

He had not experienced even a suggestion of a headache.

His constant companion since childhood, they were always worse on civilized worlds, festering inside him until they exploded in pain that nowadays was sometimes severe enough to incapacitate him. During his recent visit to Goldin IV, one such attack had put him in a dangerous coma. Since arriving on Arrawd, even the familiar faint throbbing he normally experienced in the company of other sentients had vanished.

His mind was not cured—but it was at peace.

Among the gear that filled out the belt around his waist was a medipak crammed with all manner of medications designed to alleviate his recurring cerebral pains. Glancing in its direction, he eyed it as if he had a sleeping taipan snaked around his waist. Not his waist, he corrected himself, adjusting the metaphor. His head. But his mind was easy, the genetically altered neurological processes that alternately thrilled and tormented him presently tranquil. Had he finally, accidentally, stumbled upon that which he thought he would never find? An inhabited world full of expressive, thinking beings whose emotions he could perceive or ignore at will, without existing in continual fear of being overwhelmed by them? And if the corollary was a cessation of his tormenting headaches . . .

He dared not think about it too much lest a sardonic Fate suddenly decide to prove him wrong. He smiled inwardly. Thinking too hard on the subject might—give him a headache.

"You're sure you are well? You squat so still and silent." Storra was eyeing him evenly—but the emotion she was feeling was one of honest compassion. He knew that for a fact, and smiled.

"I'm fine," he told her via the translator. "In fact, I haven't felt this good in years."

Ebbanai puckered his round mouth and exuded satisfaction. "This is a healthy place," he affirmed, innocent of the reasons behind his guest's declaration. "Much better for the body than the town or the city."

"My mate is all country at soul," Storra confirmed. "If you are then feeling good, could you answer some questions for *us*?" She glanced over at her mate. "Both Ebbanai and I have queries that burn within us."

Flinx nodded. "I'll answer what I can," he told her guardedly, "as best I can. And in turn, you can answer some additional questions for me. I'm going to try to learn something of your language, so be patient with me."

Despite all the evidence of its technological prowess, Ebbanai saw, the alien was not domineering, nor did it choose to act toward them in a superior manner. That was promising. If only they could find ways to keep it from leaving as soon as its leg was healed. Language instruction might be one way.

It certainly put a new twist on the old adage that he who speaks slowly is the one who stands to learn the most.

CHAPTER

5

When it came to learning languages, Flinx had two advantages. His travels had exposed him to a great many varieties of communication, including some that were only borderline verbal, and the ability to read the emotional outpourings of others allowed him to understand the substance of a phrase even as he struggled to reproduce it aloud. Under Ebbanai and Storra's kindly tutelage, he made impressive progress.

His hosts, of course, were astonished at his facility—as they were by other abilities of their guest that were only gradually revealed. For example, so rapidly did his injured ankle recover that one could practically see it healing. As his leg became stronger, their guest began to demonstrate physical abilities that were commensurate with his mental talents.

On the day before he had indicated he was going to return to his machine, which was truly a vessel for traveling between worlds, he tested his leg by taking a short run around the homestead. With his flying pet accompanying him all the way, the alien covered ground with bounding strides of such length that his hosts were left staring in stunned disbelief. Fences that would have stymied even Ebbanai's athletic neighbor Tebenrd were cleared with ease. Breathing effortlessly, the alien even tried to jump over the house. He did not make it, sliding down its curving flanks while laughing loudly to himself, but he came nearer accomplishing the seemingly impossible feat than could any Dwarra.

"It's because the gravity is stronger on the world where I matured than it is on Arrawd," he explained yet one more time to his awestruck hosts.

"That expression again." For a second time Storra struggled with the untranslatable term, which clearly had as much to do with the matter of weight as it did with the weight of matter, but which she did not understand. If this "gravity" forced the alien to become heavier, then how was it he could move about more easily on Arrawd? Shouldn't the opposite be the case? Though she prided herself on her intelligence, clearly there was some alien concept here that would require much mental struggling to properly comprehend. She was determined to manage it, however, as was Ebbanai.

Understanding would require a greater effort on the part of her mate. Ebbanai was a fine, upstanding, devoted male, but in matters involving mental as opposed to physical resolution, he tended to leave the decision making to her. That only showed how smart he really was. There is no greater sign of high intelligence than realizing that another person is cleverer than you, and having the strength of character to rely and act on their opinion.

So she was reasonably confident of convincing him of the course of action they needed to take when she confronted him in the baryeln barn later that afternoon. The alien was out studying vermin in the verdure, an activity she found revolting as well as pointless. Still, she made an effort to understand the why of it. Comprehending the alien's motivations was vital to her intentions.

"Flinx says its leg is almost fully healed and that it intends to leave us tomorrow morning."

Her mate looked up from where he was tapping imv-nine, their second-best producer. The mature baryeln stood quietly as the sweet, high-protein, glucose-rich fluid it secreted upon external stimulation flowed glutinously into several dozen waiting catchments.

"I know. A shame, really."

"It need not be." She did not lower her voice. The alien had many abilities, but it had already demonstrated that its hearing was not exceptional. Whether it could detect at such a distance what she was feeling at the moment, she did not know. She could only try to control her emotions and hope that her true feelings were passing unnoticed. Moving closer, she entwined Sensitives with Ebbanai's so that he would know exactly what was going through her as she spoke.

"I don't understand." This close together, Sensitives locked, he had nowhere to look but into her eyes.

"If we are to gain anything from our acquaintance with this visitor, we must find a way to make it remain among us." Behind them the indifferent, placid baryeln continued its consumption of silage and secreting of gryln, its complex internal organs turning the harvested one into the profitable other.

Ebbanai's eyes contracted slightly, indicative of skepticism. "And how are we to do that?" He looked suddenly alarmed. "You cannot be thinking of restraining the alien by force! Surely it possesses advanced means of harming as well as of healing."

She gestured with all eight gripping flanges. "Of what use would it be to us even if we could somehow take it and hold it prisoner? To make use of the alien, we need its willing cooperation. An attempt to forcibly detain it would only have the opposite affect."

Ebbanai's eyes contracted until they were reduced in their sockets to the size of marbles. "Then how can we possibly manage to obtain both its continued presence and its cooperation?"

Storra's mouth expanded in the Dwarran equivalent of a smile. "By throwing our humble selves on its mercy and appealing to its instincts as a greatly superior being."

Her mate remained unconvinced. "I don't see how that will be sufficient to convince it to stay with us."

"It will, when we beg it to help with your injury."

"My injury?" Ebbanai's uncertainty increased. "But I am not . . . oh. I see. I will fake an injury, and we will appeal to the alien to help us as we helped it."

"Not exactly." She spoke slowly, methodically, so he would be sure to understand and so that she would not have to pause to correct any misconceptions. Keeping their Sensitives entwined helped. "Remember that the alien can read our emotions as if they were an open book. It would instantly detect any attempt at propounding such a thorough falsehood. Any pain of injury cannot be faked. It must be real. Your suffering must be genuine, the damage perceptible, or this subterfuge will not work."

He twitched one pair of arms. "Yes, you're right, Storra. As always. I see that it has to be that way. One question." His eyes met those of his mate. "Why me?"

Anticipating the query—she would have thought less of her mate had he failed to ask it—she had readied an answer. "While one of us is laid up, the other will be busy working to make use of the accident. We both know which of us would be the better at that." When Ebbanai did not disagree, she continued. "Also, since you were the first to encounter the alien, I believe it may feel more responsible for anything you may suffer as a consequence of its presence among us than it would if I was the unfortunate one."

Her mate pondered the prospect for another moment before reluctantly conceding his concurrence. "Very well, Storra. I will suffer the injury." He hesitated. "Looking always ahead, I assume you have something already in mind. Something that will be convincing but hopefully not too painful?"

"Not if it is executed properly," she told him.

He did not sound entirely assured. "I wish you would have chosen another way of putting it."

They were in the barn examining the baryeln. Their visitor had expressed an interest in learning more about the animals that supplied so much nutrition in such a peculiar manner, and Ebbanai had agreed to further enlighten him. Storra remained behind, in the house, while her mate gave the alien a thorough explanation of baryeln anatomy and history.

"You see how many gryln collectors can be placed on a single animal." Ebbanai indicated ijv-three, their best producer.

As he took mental notes on the relevant biology and process, a curious Flinx could not keep from mentally substituting the term *lactation* for *secretion*, even though nothing about the practice had anything to do with milk. "If manual stimulation is required to start the animal producing, how to you persuade them to keep it up? Do you have to continuously work the herd, going from one to another?"

"Exactly." Ebbanai proceeded to demonstrate, moving from one animal to the next. As he did so, a curious Pip hummed along overhead, alternating her attention between the activity taking place below and the interesting alien vermin that infested the upper reaches of the building.

Flinx studied the Dwarra's hectic movements. "There ought to be a way to automate the process," he murmured, more to himself than to his host.

"*Automate?*" Working a fourth animal, Ebbanai wondered at the alien's thought processes. In order to induce them to produce lavishly, baryeln required constant attention and care. How did one automate attention and care?

Its focus elsewhere, the alien's pet dropped in his direction. Flinx seemed momentarily distracted, closely examining the most recent animal Ebbanai had stimulated. Time to act, Ebbanai realized. Tilting back his head, he glanced upward more sharply than was necessary. As he did so, his eyes expanded and he began waving his forearms over his head and shouting wildly.

A surprised Flinx turned toward the native. "It's all right, Ebbanai! You know she won't hurt . . ."

Stumbling around in a panicky semi-circle as the "frightened" Ebbanai sought to avoid the minidrag's "attack," both of the native's right forelegs slammed up against the back legs of the baryeln he was working with. Knowing he might not get a second chance, he made sure to throw his legs solidly against the animal's much sturdier hind limbs. The startled baryeln uttered a sharp grunting noise and hopped a couple of steps forward. One hind limb came down on Ebbanai's outer right foreleg. This unforeseen reaction had a consequence that was undeniably beneficial, though Ebbanai would have preferred to have avoided it. At least he was spared the need to try to force the appearance of discomfort.

The slender foreleg snapped as it was stepped on.

He screamed; a high-pitched whistling sound that had nothing of the forced or fake about it. Flinx was at his side immediately. As the heavy-bodied alien biped hauled his softly caterwauling host out of the stall, the wounded Ebbanai was yet again made conscious of the alien's physical strength. Whether due to lower "gravity" or something else, those otherworldly muscles handled his broken body effortlessly.

Storra joined them quickly—almost too quickly. She had been waiting for the yell, though its volume and intensity had surprised her. Rushing from the house toward the barn, she mentally complimented her mate on the veracity of his screams—until she saw his leg. Before she could even think to prevent it, or modify it, a mix of sympathy and admiration flowed out to him. Since their Sensitives were not in contact, Ebbanai didn't receive it.

Flinx did. It puzzled him. What, exactly, was the native female feeling? Compassion for her injured mate, certainly. But he was picking up indications of something else. Something almost contradictory. It made no sense.

He had no time to analyze it. There was no ambivalence about his own emotions. He felt terrible. His friendly, obliging host had been seriously injured while taking time to accommodate the wishes of his guest. Flinx eyed Pip disapprovingly. The flying snake was not intelligent enough to understand what, if anything, had gone awry. She had no sense of having done anything wrong. She perceived only that her master was unhappy with her. Fluttering above all the sudden activity, she did not know what to do except stay out of the way.

A detailed examination of her mate's second right foreleg was not required to tell Storra what had happened. "It's broken," she announced immediately. Given the unexpected extent of the injury, she did not have to fake surprise. "How did this happen, Ebbanai?"

Through pain considerably greater than that which he had expected to have to experience, Ebbanai grimaced at her. His prepared speech fell by the wayside as he found himself speaking the actual truth, as opposed to the one he and his mate had so carefully rehearsed.

"I was working with three when our friend's pet dove down and startled me. It caused me to kick ijv-three's back legs, which upset it, and in trying to get away it stepped on me."

Flinx looked on anxiously. "Is there anything I can do?"

This was going to be easier than they had planned, Storra thought—except for the fact that Ebbanai's leg actually was broken, instead of merely strained as they had intended.

"Our business requires my presence in the city tomorrow." All four forearms indicated her collapsed, injured mate. "But I can't leave Ebbanai alone like this." She turned what she hoped were soulful, pleading eyes on their alien guest. "I know you intended to leave us very soon, but if you could see your way to remaining for just another few days, to watch over Ebbanai, I could successfully conclude our business in town and return to take up his care."

It was not the kind of request Flinx had expected. "By offering to help, I meant with his actual injury. I have a device called a beam-healer that promotes a body's ability to repair itself, by encouraging the increased production of calcium, and . . ."

Seeing that they were staring at him uncomprehendingly, he trailed off. Anyway, while the beam-healer could to a certain extent be adjusted, he would first have to analyze the composition of Dwarran bone before it could be recalibrated to the appropriate setting. Dwarran skeletal structure might incorporate more silicon and less calcium than human bone, for example, in which case stimulating the injured area to produce more calcium might do more harm than good.

Just hanging around for another couple of days would not require the serious recalibration of anything but his travel plans, which were themselves in a state of flux. While he did not warm to the idea, there were still things here to be learned, and acquiescing to the request would be comparatively painless. After all they had done for him, openly and without complaint, he could hardly refuse such a simple request.

If only the feelings he was perceiving were less ambiguous. There was no mistaking the authenticity of poor Ebbanai's injury and the emotions that flowed from him. But the more the three of them talked, especially Storra, the more Flinx sensed an underlying current of eagerness that seemed at odds with his host's undeniable pain and discomfort.

Still, a request was a request, and a simple one at that. If all they wanted from him was a little of his time, that he could certainly spare.

"I don't know how I can be of much help around here, but if that's what you want me to do . . ."

A demonstrably excited Storra came toward him, started to dip her Sensitives toward his forehead, remembered that he did not possess the pertinent appendages, and stood back. "It will allow us to continue business with our waiting contacts in Metrel. I will be back in less than three days' time, I promise. Meanwhile, Ebbanai can tell you what to do to keep things functioning here." Four forearms reached out to him expectantly. Choosing a pair of gripping flanges at random, he grasped them politely.

"I can't tell you how much this will help us, friend Flinx." Ebbanai spoke through the throbbing pain in his leg. "With your assistance, nothing need go undone here while Storra is in the city."

Flinx nodded absently. It was clear he was going to learn more about collecting the liquid bounty produced by baryeln and the process and procedures required to support it than he had ever anticipated.

Overhead, Pip remained puzzled and confused. But if her master was now at ease, there was no reason why she should be otherwise. Settling herself across his left arm and shoulder, she warily eyed the barn's two other sentients. She could perceive they meant neither her nor her master any harm.

But that did not mean she had to like them.

Time spent at the homestead in Ebbanai's company passed swiftly, thanks to Flinx's insatiable curiosity and his host's willingness, even eagerness, to satisfy it. In return, Flinx used the medical instrumentation he always carried with him to perform the necessary analysis of Ebbanai's bone structure and consequent injury. As it developed, the beam-healer did not require much adjustment to speed the healing of Dwarran bone. Watching an injury that would normally take eight-days to heal rapidly repair itself, Ebbanai's astonishment knew no bounds.

"How is this possible?" The native was standing in resting pose just inside the barn, his upper torso sunk partway into the lower and supported by his three undamaged forelegs. In the cool shade, with a light, crisp breeze blowing intermittently outside, he had leaned back against the wall to examine the bandage-wrapped injured member. "It must be some kind of magic!"

"Not magic." Standing nearby watching a pair of baryeln lap up the moist plant mash Ebbanai had just dumped in their stalls, Flinx idly stroked the back of Pip's head with one hand as he spoke. "Science."

Gingerly, Ebbanai set his second right foreleg down and put a little weight on it. Normally, it would have been another couple of eight-days before he could have done so. Thanks to the ministrations of the alien and his mysterious devices and mendicants, after only a

couple of days of treatment the limb could now provide the first un-
derpinnings of support.

"I've heard of science. There are many who believe in it, especially the builders of the new factories and the sailoring merchants
who are always looking for safer and faster ways to cross the seas.
Equally, there are others who prefer to rely on the old ways and beseech the assistance of spirits and gods. And there are some, not
wishing to take chances, who implore the help of both."

Flinx nodded understandingly. His host's description of Dwarran
society placed it well within its exploratory Commonwealth classifi-
cation. "My people have come to rely on science to explain the natural cosmos. In time, so will yours." He did not add, *If they survive the
necessary difficult social adjustments that affect all such sentient
species at such critical times.*

Ebbanai took an experimental step with his treated foreleg, marveling at its unnaturally restored strength. "If such 'science' can do
things like fix a broken leg in less than an eight-day, I certainly will
be among the first to salute its primacy." Wide round eyes regarded
the pouch and instrument-laden belt that encircled the alien's waist.
"What other wonders do you carry around so casually with you?" he
asked eagerly. A bit too eagerly, Flinx thought.

Well, such envy was only natural. "Just enough to look after myself. Emergency rations, both for myself and for Pip. A device for
purifying water. The means with which to communicate with my
ship. Medical supplies and equipment, as you already know."

An entranced Ebbanai forgot himself completely. Had his mate
been present, she would have kicked him for his candor. "Weapons?"
he asked enthusiastically, and was immediately sorry for his zeal.

His guest did not seem upset by the query, much less alarmed. "I
always have with me the means for defending myself. When you find
yourself in a strange place, that's always the prudent thing to do." He
smiled reassuringly. "Of course, if I'd been able to foresee what a
kind reception I was in for, I could have left that on my ship."

Could have, the alien said, Ebbanai noted carefully. Not *would have*. It was not a warning, or a sign of displeasure. If their situations were reversed, Ebbanai would have done no less. For example, he never went into Metrel unarmed. The city could be dangerous, especially for a nonresident, and it was only a fool who entered such places unprepared.

Abruptly, and unexpectedly, the alien turned away from him. Its posture stiffened, and the flying creature that never strayed far from its side took to the air, rising toward the domed roof of the barn. Both beings' attention was focused on the main doorway.

"What is it?" Approaching as close as he dared without being invited, Ebbanai directed his own gaze toward the entry. "Is there something wrong, friend Flinx?"

His guest did not reply. Flinx's eyes were on the barn entrance, but his perception was roving beyond. Luxuriating in the mental peace and quiet, he had only intermittently allowed his Talent to break through the silence and reach outward, especially when he was in the perceived comfort of Ebbanai's presence. He had just sampled the emotional aether in the immediate vicinity, only to be rewarded not with the expected continued stillness but with a number of highly energetic emotional projections. Many, in fact.

Frowning, he turned back to Ebbanai, who did his best not to look blameworthy. Flinx wouldn't have recognized the equivalent Dwarran expression in any case, but he didn't have to. His host's guilt flowed out of him like smoke off a coal fire.

"Ebbanai, what is this? What's going on?"

"What is what?" The shamefaced Dwarra tried to stall, ineffectually.

Flinx nodded in the direction of the doorway. Now that he had once again opened himself to external Dwarran emotions, they were flooding in on him simultaneously from several directions. "You told me Storra was expected back today. Nothing was said about her bringing others with her."

Ebbanai tried hard not to look up at the hovering Pip, whom his guest had informed him was capable of dealing out a particularly lethal toxin. Where was Storra and why didn't she hurry up? Where were his tongues when he needed both of them so badly? He stammered, found his tongues tied up in his chewing plates, and managed to utter only a few feeble inconsequentialities.

I've been deceived, Flinx thought to himself as the pack of approaching emotional outpourings grew louder and stronger in his mind. The question was, to what purpose?

Then the barn doors were dragged aside and a veritable flock of Dwarra were visible bunched up tightly together in the entrance. One set of wide round eyes after another gaped at the alien standing before them. In the center, looking tired but triumphant, was Ebbanai's mate Storra.

"There it is," she declared into the verbal but not emotional silence. "Just as I described it. *Now* who calls me a liar?"

There was a pause. The cluster of awestruck Dwarra stared at Flinx. Flinx gazed back at the Dwarra. Then, assured by Storra of his friendliness—that she could not guarantee it did not stop her from offering the assurance—they surged forward and into the barn.

A multifaceted flood of emotion washed over Flinx as he left himself open to them. Anxiety, hope, intense interest, desperate need, and not a little fear were the most common feelings he perceived. Effortlessly he shut them out, then let them flood in on him again. Nowhere else in all his travels had he found himself with the ability to so painlessly turn the rush of surrounding, sentient emotion on and off as easily as he might control the flow of water from a tap.

At the first sign of the incoming crowd Pip had lifted herself from his shoulder. Now she hovered high overhead, near the apex of the barn's dome, watching. She was not alarmed. None of the new arrivals projected hostility toward her master. Wariness, yes. Suspicion, yes. But no enmity.

They didn't want to hurt him, Flinx sensed equally well. The depth of feeling he was picking up was indicative of something else. Via the limited knowledge of Dwarrani he had acquired and with the aid of the translator still in place around his neck, it soon became clear what they wanted from him.

Dwarran parents with suffering offspring jostled for his attention with aged partners in need of miraculous and biologically implausible rejuvenation. Gatherers and farmers wanted an assortment of missing limbs and digits replaced. The mentally disturbed wished to be restored to sanity. Victims of marauding warlords desired that their wounds be made whole again. Veterans of pillaging armies wanted shattered bones rebuilt. All of them pushed and shoved and crowded close to beseech the alien whom Storra had declared could work these miracles. Dozens of pairs of Sensitives fluttered in his direction, as if by merely making contact with him the needs of their owners could somehow be met. Their collective desperation was overwhelming. Off to one side, Storra had rejoined her mate. She looked pleased. He looked guilty.

Hemmed in on all sides by imploring Dwarra, a perturbed Flinx bent his knees and sprang. In Arrawd's lesser gravity, his leap carried him over the heads of the tightly packed throng and onto a rending platform none could reach without one of the triple-wide ladders designed to accommodate their rangy frames. A loud exhalation somewhere between a mass hiss and stunned whistling greeted his astounding physical feat. Catching his balance, he turned to look back down at them. If anything, his new position high above made him appear even more transcendent, though the appearance of the Alaspinian minidrag that settled itself on his shoulder and neck was anything but angelic.

There was no point in pretending that he was ignorant of their reason for coming. No doubt Storra had already regaled them with tales of his empathetic abilities—suitably enhanced. Relying on his translator to correct and adjust his speech patterns, he addressed the crowd. The instant he started talking, they went silent, astonished in spite of what Storra had told them to hear their own language coming from the vicinity, if not always the mouth, of the alien. His words also had the effect, he noted, of calming the storm of competing emotions.

"It's true—I am a visitor from another place, another world." Perfectly round oculars eyed him raptly. "And it's also true that I can do certain things you cannot. But I can't help any of you with your problems, or with your questions, because it's against the laws of the government where I come from."

There was the briefest of silences, followed by a concerted rush toward the high platform on which he was standing. No matter where he went, he thought grudgingly, no matter how hard he tried, he always seemed to end up the center of attention.

"Didn't you hear what I said?" he barked at them wearily. "I can't do what you want!"

"Why not?" While he had been addressing the crowd, Storra had climbed a set of wide stairs located at the rear of the platform and now stood to his left, confronting him. "Perhaps to do such things *is* against the laws of your government. But your government is not here. I'm sure it is a long, long way away, or we would have seen your kind before now, and would know about you." She gestured with all four sets of gripping flanges. "We helped you. You've helped my mate." She indicated the still guilty-looking Ebbanai, who had remained down on the floor with the rest of the crowd.

"Help these others." Both left hands indicated the milling supplicants. "These are poor people, like Ebbanai and myself. Our friends and acquaintances. They have little money. Their afflictions are many. You are great and powerful. How can you withhold your help from them and still call yourself a civilized, compassionate being?"

Her words were straightforward, but her emotions were more complex, Flinx noted. There was honest entreating, yes, but it was mixed with hints of other feelings. Expectation, and eagerness. Eagerness for what? To see him perform more "miracles"? Or thoughts of turning a situation to personal advantage? Clever female . . .

"Please, help my offspring!" An elderly Dwarra, upper legs

trembling with age, pushed forward with a blank-faced young adult in tow. The emotions streaming from the senior overflowed with anguish and despair. In contrast, those of the offspring were—sluggish. The native was brain-damaged. Flinx could do nothing for it even if he tried.

But there were others—others with broken bones and torn muscles, with horrific scars and missing digits—whom he *could* help. Already adjusted to Dwarran biology, his simple beam-healer could speed curing in many of the cases he saw. Similarly recalibrated, the synthesizer on board the *Teacher* could turn out basic medicines that could likely cure at least some of the ills that afflicted this crowd of several dozen desperate supplicants.

The nonmedical questions they continued to bawl loudly and often frantically at him were another matter.

"Where do the stars go in the day?"

"The priests say different things," bellowed another, "but where do we really go when we die?"

"Why must I mature?" asked a youth whose undeveloped lower limbs seemed hardly sturdy enough to support the angular adolescent alien body.

"Are there others up there besides your kind?" wondered another elderly petitioner as two pairs of gripping flanges gestured at the roof of the barn.

"Please, please," Flinx implored them. "I can't answer your questions."

"Because it's against your 'laws,'" Ebbanai suddenly called out from below, sounding resentful, "or because you are so superior to us that you think we won't understand your answers? My mate and I helped you, and you reward us with your contempt."

Flinx's gaze narrowed. In response to his darkening emotions, Pip began to circle more anxiously overhead. "What about your broken leg, Ebbanai? Did I treat *that* with contempt?"

"No. No, you did not," the net-caster admitted as others in the crowd turned to stare in his direction. "You treated it well, as you would have your own. For that, Storra and I are grateful." He spread all four forearms. "Will you not share such goodness with a few others? Just those who are here now, and then you can go. To wherever it is in the sky that calls so strongly to you. I ask, we ask, only for the help of one who is greater than ourselves. Is that so much?"

Once again, Flinx opened himself to the outpouring of emotion before him. These simple folk did not wish him dead, like the Order of Null. They did not seek to use him for their own ends, as had the Meliorare Society. They did not want to arrest him for violating assorted laws, as did the Commonwealth government. Nor were they after the secrets of his Ulru-Ujurrian-built ship. All they wanted was a little care, a little compassion. Help to make a disfiguring scar go away, or for broken bones to knit. Answers to questions that, if they were passed on, none of their brethren were likely to believe anyway.

He'd already broken the laws against contact with peoples inhabiting a Class IVb world. What did that transgression amount to, anyway? Who promulgated such restrictions, and who decided when and where they should be enforced? These people were unbelievably isolated on one of the few inhabited worlds within the boundaries of the Blight. When he took his leave, they might remain so for another century, or for millennia. For the life of him, he could not see what harm it would do for him to use his skills and resources to help a small handful of forlorn locals. He inhaled deeply.

"All right," he told the waiting Storra. "I'll do it. I'll try to help those who are here." The outpouring of gratefulness that rose from the assembled as his translator conveyed his decision threatened to overwhelm him. "But only these. Once I've finished with the last of those you've brought, I'm leaving."

It was only a half-lie. Regardless of how he chose to spend his remaining time on Arrawd, he couldn't truly leave until the *Teacher* had finished its repairs. But he could certainly disappear within her bulk, as he had planned to do, isolating himself from these despondent natives as completely as if he were looking down at them from the surface of one of their world's three moons.

"Of course." Storra's Sensitives were waggling like semaphores. "That is all we ask."

Her emotions said otherwise, but it didn't matter what plans she might be concocting, Flinx knew. He would insist that she and Ebbanai remain at his side, to "help" him with his work. Regardless of how events developed, there was clearly nothing on this backward but developing world that was capable of restraining him any longer than he wished to remain. That much he was sure of.

Of course, in the course of his complicated and singular life he had frequently been sure of many things, only on more than one occasion to find himself proven quite significantly wrong.

CHAPTER

6

"Visitors from the sky?"

As far as he was concerned, His August Highborn Pyrrpallinda of Wullsakaa never had any time to rest. There were judgments to be handed down, regulations to be reviewed, proclamations to be promulgated, evildoers to be sentenced, sentences to be commuted, petitions to be heard. Add to that the constant jostling for position and influence at his court, the endless intrigues, the complications posed by developing technologies that could not simply be stayed or supported by simple decree, the physical responsibilities placed on him to produce several potential heirs, and constant worries about the weather. Throw in the always present threat of war with any one of several confrontational neighboring states and the occasional assassination attempt, and circumstances made for anything but a relaxed lifestyle. A ruler who did not pay attention to all these things was liable to find his reign, along with his neck, cut short.

Other than immortality and invulnerability, neither of which was available to him, the next-best thing someone in his position could have was trusted and true counselors. A judicious and experienced appraiser of others, Pyrrpallinda had over the years managed to gather around him several such invaluable advisors. Most were specialists. Treappyn was not. Knowledgeable in many facets of daily as well as government life, from foreign affairs to the price of chetke fruit in the main marketplace, he was the Highborn's most trusted associate. That they were nearly the same comparatively young age made Pyrrpallinda even more comfortable with Treappyn. While one was the ruler of Wullsakaa's government and the other only a glorified employee, their relationship was that of close friends, if not equals. Pyrrpallinda often found himself differing with Treappyn on numerous matters of administration, but even when they argued, he never failed to respect the other Dwarra's opinion.

Even when the counselor chose to speak of something as absurd as visitors from the sky.

"Only one, actually, Highborn. Or two, if one counts the domesticated flying creature that accompanies it."

Treappyn, who was unusually stout for one of his kind, approached the work desk behind which his liege was presently squatting. Holding a stylus in one right gripping flange and another in a left, the Highborn was writing in florid qeslen style, simultaneously from right to left and left to right, with both lines eventually meeting in the middle of the page. It was a skill not everyone could master. Now he paused and set both writing instruments aside, placing them on opposite sides of the desk according to tradition.

"Very well, then. One or two, it makes no actual difference. Either this is a real thing, or else it is nothing more than a creative rumor spawned by country folk." The ruler of Wullsakaa placed all eight gripping flanges on the table. "I find myself very much inclined to believe the latter. Visitors from the sky!" To emphasize his disdain, he tilted back his head and peered ceilingward. "The stars are points of light. Nothing more. So say those who sacrifice to assorted gods. Among the scientists with an interest in astronomy, I believe there are some who think the stars may be suns not unlike our own. Suns are clearly too hot to support life. Any fool can see that."

Unintimidated as always, Treappyn begged to differ. "Your pardon, Highborn, but many of our younger and brightest academics believe there may be other worlds circling them, much as Arrawd circles a sun of its own. The possibility of life like ours existing there is one that they have often speculated upon."

"Proof of which is now alleged to have arrived here. On the largely empty, windblown Pavjadd Peninsula, no less." The Highborn emitted a discordant whistling grunt. "Such a journey, from one star to another, must demand a ship with a considerable span of sail."

Treappyn smiled inwardly. "The mechanism by which the alien arrived has apparently been seen by only one citizen, Highborn, and nothing was said of sails. This vessel is supposedly still there, but has changed its appearance so that none can recognize it."

"Sounds like the work of a merchant trying to hide from creditors, not that of an explorer. Am I supposed to mobilize a response based on the outrageous claims of one witness?" Pyrrpallinda glanced at a note on his desk. "A childless net-caster, no less. What more proof is needed? Let us call out the army and sound the nereyodes!"

Treappyn grunted sympathetically. "While it is true there appears to be only one witness to the alien's arrival and means of transport, it seems that many others have been the recipients of its largesse." Raising a pair of forearms, the counselor ticked off the alien's reported, rumored abilities one by one. "It is said that he—it is self-declared to be male—can heal the sick in both body and mind, cause crops to mature ten times faster than in nature, answer any question on any subject by communicating with some kind of library on his vessel, and change his own appearance as well as that of his craft. He can also leap higher than any Dwarra and is stronger than our most accomplished athletes."

The litany of accomplishments left Pyrrpallinda more thoughtful, but no less dubious. "No doubt he can also transmute metals and turn night into day, part the sea and raise the dead. A god has come down to us from the stars. With his pet, of course, and a bagful of tricks. A god should always have a pet, and a bagful of tricks." Gripping flanges clenched and relaxed. "Pardon me if I remain skeptical."

"Sensibly so, Highborn," Treappyn readily agreed. Knowing the Highborn for the cautious conservative that he was, the counselor had expected nothing less. "However, bearing in mind that a rumor has a will of its own and a tendency to spread like spit, I think it would behoove the all-embracing, wise government of Wullsakaa to swiftly investigate and ascertain the truth or falsity of this one. Before, say, any of our more quarrelsome neighbors have the opportunity to do so." He leaned over the desk. "On the off chance that there may be some small smidgen of truth to this."

Pyrrpallinda had loaded a suitable response and was preparing to fire when they were loudly interrupted.

"Highborn, Highborn—I have just heard!"

Srinballa came stumbling into the room as fast as his four forelegs would carry him, his conical skirt and matching shirt swirling around his ribbed, aged form like a red whirlwind. The crimson and gold outerwear was trimmed with the finest lacework and fringe obtainable in the main marketplace, imported all the way from distant Berekkuu. For a sober government counselor, Srinballa always had been something of a dandy. Even as a child, Pyrrpallinda remembered the jokes that had been made at the expense of the senior advisor's overdeveloped fashion sense. As ruler, the personal affectations of others meant little to him. He was interested only in a counselor's mind, and what could be wrung from it like a sponge.

Disregarding the hard-breathing arrival's evident anxiety, he responded quietly as a tight-mouthed Treappyn stood aside, "And what, good Srinballa, have you just heard?"

No fool he, the senior counselor swiftly surmised that the Highborn and his youthful friend Treappyn might have possibly been discoursing on just the same subject. Yet having announced himself with such a flurry, he had no choice but to proceed.

"It concerns the increasing number of these folk stories about some all-powerful being who has fallen from the sky." Though he was considerably older than either his liege or Treappyn, Srinballa's words as they emerged from his round mouth were clear and resolute.

"Highborn, if I may . . . ," Treappyn began.

Pyrrpallinda raised a pair of flanges. "You may indeed—in time. Let our elder say what he has come in such a rush to say—as soon as he catches his breath."

"I do not have to catch it, Highborn, as it rarely strays from my side." Srinballa gathered his too-elegant garb about his person and glared at Treappyn. "Surely you do not intend to extend the credibility of the government of Wullsakaa to this preposterous fiction?"

Pyrrpallinda clicked one tongue against his upper, tightly curved palate and his second against the lower. The sound this generated was heard by his counselors though the appendages that produced it were not seen, being of insufficient length to emerge from his mouth.

"As always, wise Srinballa, I grant the government's credibility only where it has already been safely established. I take it by both your words and your tone that you believe there is no substance to these stories?"

"Substance?" As he came forward, the senior counselor was gesturing animatedly with all eight gripping flanges. "A being who comes from the sky? Who is no taller than the average Dwarra but whose strength is several times that of the most powerful soldier? Who can clear the roof of a small building or a high fence in a single leap? Not to mention heal the incurable, dispense knowledge on any subject, and—most wonderfully of all—perceive the true feelings of another *without Sensitives*?" His own pair dipped forward sharply to emphasize the impossibility of it all.

Treappyn was growing mildly agitated. "Why should a previously unknown being not possess such powers, and more? While we know a great deal about ourselves, we know nothing of other worlds and their inhabitants."

"What other worlds?" Srinballa challenged his younger colleague. "The night sky shows us only stars. It is not possible that . . ."

Pyrrpallinda raised a left and a right flange for silence. "I have no time for an extended argument concerning the extent and limits of our current astronomical knowledge. Awkward situations often find a home in the fertile soil that is rumor, and need to be nipped in the bud. I neither accept nor deny the existence of other worlds and those who might dwell upon them."

"*Fithwashk,*" Srinballa grumbled. "This whole business is nothing more than a story concocted by bored coastal folk to garner some attention. If it gets out that we grant any truth to this nonsense, we will be a laughingstock to our neighbors."

"I am already all too aware of the opinion many of our neighbors hold of Wullsakaa." Pyrrpallinda spread all eight flanges out on the table in front of him. "Since it cannot go much lower, I see no reason why we should not investigate these rumors further."

Treappyn's Dwarran equivalent of a smirk would not have been identifiable as such to a human, but Srinballa seized on it readily enough. Their respective expressions, however, were immediately reversed by the Highborn's next remark.

Pyrrpallinda let out a long, gradual grunt that was more like an extended wheeze. "The things a sovereign has to deal with. Treappyn, I accede to your opinion in this matter. We will authorize a look into it. And since you have been the one to convince me of the necessity of doing so, you are obviously the one to follow through on it."

It was the senior Srinballa's turn to smirk. The Highborn was passing the responsibility on to his youthful counterpart, with the expectation that any derision would subsequently fall upon him and not the government. As for Treappyn, he was visibly taken aback.

"Highborn, I'm not sure that I . . ."

Once again, Pyrrpallinda raised open gripping flanges in a call for silence. "No, no, Treappyn, don't thank me. Your willingness— indeed, your eagerness—to pursue this matter to a verifiable conclusion is commendable. I bid you gather a small retinue and start as soon as possible for this—what was the name of that nearest village again? No matter. I'm sure you'll get there and put paid to these absurd rumors before they can spread any farther. As always, the realm owes yet another debt of gratitude to your unbounded initiative."

"Surely, it does," added Srinballa, struggling to conceal his glee.

Swallowing his unhappiness, Treappyn requested and received permission to remove himself from the presence of the August. "I will commence preparations for departure immediately, Highborn."

As soon as he was out of the room, Pyrrpallinda turned to Srinballa. "It will be a lesson for him. Along with his other travel baggage, he will have to carry with him the burden of the credulous."

"Young fool." Srinballa was careful not to gloat overmuch. "The things people will believe. 'Creatures falling from the sky.' As if the government did not have enough real problems to deal with."

"Quite surely so," Pyrrpallinda agreed. "Let us hope this is not another one."

The senior counselor looked momentarily startled. "Surely you don't lend any credence to this rustic nonsense, Highborn? I wouldn't be surprised if this turns out to be an invention of one of our neighbors, designed to disquiet a portion of the population. It's exactly the sort of troublemaking subterfuge I would expect from, for example, the Warden of Nyheurr."

"No, I don't believe it." Pyrrpallinda gazed down at the pile of official documents spread out and piled all too high on the table before him. "But by the same token, Treappyn is right: I can't afford to just ignore it." He glanced toward the doorway that led to the main hallway. "He has been too intense, lately. His mating time is upon him, and he is distracted. This short journey will allow him time to reflect, and to relax. He will return chastened, I suspect, and moderated in manner."

Having made his points, Srinballa was willing to be generous. "The overexuberance of youth."

"Yes," Pyrrpallinda agreed, ignoring the fact that he was little older than the unhappy counselor he had just sent on his way. The matter settled, his thoughts had already moved on to matters of more pressing import—and reality. A pair of gripping flanges grasped a scroll, opened it, and beckoned Srinballa come around behind the desk so that he could also see it clearly. "Now, as to this request to construct a toll bridge in North Province, I would ask your opinion on certain specifics of the proposal . . ."

Despite his hosts' assurances that they had limited those seeking help to the initial group of friends and relatives who had confronted Ebbanai and Flinx in the baryeln barn, more and more Dwarra in need seemed to be finding their way to the isolated homestead. Flinx raised the issue more than once, only to be told that "This group is the last" or "Can't you take pity on them? This family has nowhere else to turn."

What could he do? In the face of desperation, he was reminded of his own difficult childhood. These poor Dwarra were intelligent like himself, capable of the same depth of feeling as he was. Maybe he couldn't track down an ancient wandering sentient weapon, and maybe he could or could not in some as yet unknown, unfathomable way influence a looming galactic cataclysm. But he *could* speed the knitting of a broken bone or the healing of damaged neural connections, or answer a young male's query as to the true nature of what lay beyond his world. He could, and did, do all of these things because he had always, at heart, had more compassion than common sense.

When informed (politely) that he valued his solitude at night, his hosts had not been affronted. Instead, they had rapidly fashioned a separate sleeping place for him in one of the upper barn lofts, where the cooling breezes off the nearby sea made for the most pleasant sleeping conditions. This despite the fact that they believed his preference in climate dangerously chilling, something Storra was at pains to mention whenever the opportunity arose. In this the Dwarran female was more diplomatic than Mother Mastiff would have been. His adoptive mother would simply have told him to shut up and throw on another blanket.

The slimmer bodies of his Dwarran hosts were more comfortable inside their well-insulated home. They slept vertically, in squatting position, their upper bodies sunk as far as possible into the lower, swathed in multiple layers of cloth. In contrast to them, he found the peninsula's sometimes bracing climate downright salubrious.

On this particular evening only Storra was present, having just brought him the nighttime meal she had expertly prepared, when the *Teacher* chose to make contact with its owner. She looked on in fascination as he plucked the com unit off his belt and acknowledged the call. He could have ignored it, waiting until she left, but he had already broken so many laws regarding contact with a species of her level of accomplishment that he barely thought twice about responding.

"Repairs are proceeding smoothly and on schedule," the ship informed him courteously.

"How much longer?" Flinx ignored the captivated, wide-eyed stare of the female Dwarra standing at the top of the rough-hewn wooden stairs that led to his sleeping area.

"As I said, on schedule. With proper facilities, I would be done by now. But I have only on-board tools to work with. Do you wish me to repeat the schedule of work that needs to be done?"

This time, the ship was not being sarcastic. "I remember it, better than I care to. If there is any change, let me know."

"Always."

The transmission ended, Storra could not restrain herself from asking, "Ebbanai and I thought you came alone among us."

"I did. I mean, I am." A pile of furled wings and bright colors, Pip dozed nearby on a pile of raw, unstripped seashan. He carefully snapped the compact communications unit back in place on his utility belt. "That was my ship I was talking to."

Storra was understandably confused. "Your vessel talks to you? But it sounds so much like a person. As if it had a mind of its own."

"It does," he told her. "Sometimes too much of a mind of its own."

Her Sensitives strained toward him, as if by making contact she would be able to grasp what he was saying. "How can a machine have a mind of its own? My loom has no mind. The new steamcraft some of the watermasters are said to be building do not have minds of their own."

"There are machines more complex than you can imagine, Storra." He dug into the food she had prepared. As always, it was plain-tasting and filling, much like the countryside from which the ingredients that had gone into it had been harvested. So far he had encountered nothing in the way of local produce that threatened to upset his digestive system.

"As you are more complex than I can imagine, Flinx." She backed toward the stairs. The Dwarra possessed an excellent sense of balance and considerable confidence in their footing. Not surprising, he mused, when gravity was light and one was equipped with two pairs of forelegs.

"I'm not all that complex," he countered as she retreated. "Confused sometimes, but not complex." It was a comforting lie he did not even believe himself.

She paused at the top of the stairway that led down to the floor of the barn. "I would like to see your ship sometime, Flinx."

"I'll consider it," he told her. In fact, he had already considered it.

Helping injured natives was one thing. Allowing them to explore the interior of a Commonwealth starship, and a uniquely advanced one at that, was simply not in the offing. Not that someone like Storra was likely to take anything but astonishment away from such a visit. She did not possess sufficient references to allow her to understand what she was seeing. What would a tenth-century human, for example, make of a modern timepiece? Or something like the needler holstered at his side? But he saw no reason to disappoint her by turning her down cold.

No one but Ebbanai had seen the *Teacher*. With a little effort, the net-caster could probably find its camouflaged location again, but as far as Flinx knew his host had given no indication he intended to try to do so. Showing disbelieving visitors a large pile of sand and claiming it was a vessel that had come from the sky was not likely to enhance the net-caster's reputation among his neighbors.

Storra was talking to him again. "Whatever you are, you have been a blessing to the afflicted."

"Speaking of the afflicted, while I'm happy to help people as long as I'm here, I expect to be leaving before long. I wouldn't want anyone to have to go away disappointed on my account. As, for example, by having someone else, say an unnamed third party, encourage them to come here seeking my help only to find me gone."

When he spoke the last, he wanted to meet her eyes. But she had already started down the stairs. So he settled for probing her feelings. As was often the case, much more so than when he probed her mate, her emotions were a complex, hard-to-penetrate jumble. There was concern for him, excitement that probably stemmed from his apparent agreement to consider her request to see his vessel, plus overtones of contentment and concern. What he could not do was isolate and identify their root causes. Was she concerned because he had spoken of leaving, or for some other reason? And if the first, why?

At the moment, he was too tired to care. *Blessing to the afflicted* she had called him. Nonsense. Doing good deeds was a way to simultaneously underpin his humanity and alleviate boredom while providing an unmatched opportunity to study the dominant local life-form of the Arrawd system. The way she had phrased it made what he was doing sound almost like a religious experience. Weary as he was, he didn't bother to explore the possible ramifications of his own observation.

He should have.

By the following week it was difficult to say which was being put to more use: his limited store of knowledge, or the medicinal supplies and devices he always carried with him whenever he was out and about on an alien world. Finding itself in daily use, the beam-healer needed constant recharging from the storpak he carried. Eventually, even the pak ran down. This required a trip to the *Teacher* to recharge them both, as well as to replenish his other supplies.

Clearly fearful he might not return, Ebbanai and Storra did everything they could to prevent him from going. He reassured them that as long as honest individuals in need of his aid remained at the homestead, he would return to help them to the best of his limited abilities. He did not add that he might as well do so because he couldn't leave anyway until his ship had completed its necessary self-repairs.

Through the storm of emotions that boiled inside his hosts he could perceive how hard it was for them not to follow. He was gratified when they did not do so. Pip served as his eye in the sky, circling high above as he followed a deliberately circuitous path back to the camouflaged *Teacher*. She could not talk to him, of course, but by reading her emotions he could tell if anything out of the ordinary was active in his immediate vicinity yet outside the range of his own perception. Thankfully, his hike back was as uneventful as the weather: clear skies mottled with gray-white clouds, and a shifting, cooling breeze flowing from east to west off the nearby sea.

The *Teacher* was as he had left it: a high ridge of rippling beach "dunes" whose concealment was all the more effective since real, blowing sand had by now covered parts of the ship's expertly camouflaged exterior. Always seeking to improve on its own efforts, the vessel had responded by adding imitation shoots and sprigs of local vegetation to its outward appearance. One had to admire the result. Without the tracker attached to his belt, he would have been hard put himself to find it again. That it was well hidden from any wandering locals he had no doubt.

He luxuriated in its familiar interior. Even some of the plants in his relaxation lounge seemed affected by his visit. Small vines and creepers twisted toward his feet and legs when he took his ease among them that afternoon. He felt equally at home in their presence.

Something about the imported greenery that decorated the lounge always seemed to relax him.

Of course, he had been relaxed ever since he had first set foot on this world. His ability to simply shut out the babble of sentient emotion surrounding him whenever he felt like it was not only unique to Arrawd, but bordered on the addictive. If only he could do the same on places like Earth, or New Riviera, or Moth, or any of the other inhabited worlds he had visited, his life would be far less stressed and very different.

And still, after the many days he had spent here, not a single headache. Not one. For the first time in his adult life, he was free of such pain. Nor did it seem to matter whether he was utilizing his Talent to scrutinize the feelings of the Dwarra around him or not. In the absence of such pain, and the constant worry attendant on when it might strike, it was as if he had been given a new outlook on life.

He could not keep himself from thinking about the possible ramifications. Could he possibly live here? It was the only world he had found where he could dwell among other sentients free of the intermittent cerebral assaults that threatened not just to inconvenience, but to kill him. He could still assist Bran Tse-Mallory and Truzenzuzex in their quest to understand and hopefully find a way to counter the oncoming evil that threatened galactic stability. Perhaps he might even persuade Clarity Held to join him. The climate was accommodating, the local food tolerable if bland, the natives he had met thus far sociable and welcoming.

There was a whole new planet to explore, and if boredom set in, the *Teacher* would always be available to carry him to other worlds. It was also conceivable that the Commonwealth authorities who sought to question him would ignore him even if they could find him. Not only was Arrawd technically outside Commonwealth jurisdiction, but any forces sent to detain him would themselves be in violation of the regulations governing contact with Class IVb worlds.

He had come to Arrawd to find raw materials for fixing his ship. He had not expected to find himself in a situation that might help him to fix himself. Albeit more than a little far-fetched, the prospect was definitely something to consider.

As a puzzled Pip mused on the current curious state of her master's mind, the endless wanderer seriously considered the possibilities attendant on turning himself into a real immigrant.

CHAPTER

7

Ebbanai and Storra's joy at his return was unbounded. Their skin flaps fluttered uncontrollably as they caught sight of him coming down the path toward the house. The surge of gratefulness he felt from them was submerged by the flood of thankful expectation from the crowd of hopefuls camped out all around their home. Flinx had to smile to himself as Pip adjusted herself on his shoulder. To look at the throng of stumbling, imploring, forlorn natives while simultaneously perceiving their emotions, he thought absently, one would almost think some weird kind of alien messiah had returned to them.

Re-installed in his basic but comfortable upper-level quarters in his hosts' barn, he resumed dispensing his ministrations, his efforts bolstered by the fresh supplies he had brought with him from the *Teacher*. He was more than content—a condition with which he was generally unfamiliar. According to the *Teacher*'s AI, necessary repairs were progressing smoothly and on schedule. Meanwhile, his endless curiosity was being sated by the constant flow of information about the new world on which he presently found himself, and by its eager, grateful inhabitants. Couple that with the longest continuous period of mental peace he had experienced on a civilized world since his childhood, and it struck him that for a change he was not merely tolerating his surroundings, but actually enjoying them.

Though the Dwarra were entirely alien, the reaction to successful treatment of a sick or badly wounded sentient was generally the same irrespective of species. Gratitude and hosannas were heaped upon him in a steady stream. That the majority of supplicants were poor only made their thankfulness that much more heartfelt (the analogy assuming some sort of relevant circulatory pumping mechanism). One especially common injury involved young Dwarra whose quartet of forelegs had not yet fully matured. Apparently, the pace of development of the two upper legs exceeded that of the four lower into which they branched, resulting in a plague of breakage among the lowermost youthful limbs. If not set properly while the individual was young, such injuries resulted in serious consequences as the individual matured. Judicious application with his recalibrated beam-healer caused damaged bones to knit properly and with unprecedented speed.

Eye repair was another area where the simple tools he carried for personal first aid turned out to be capable of working small miracles among the locals. The joy he was able to generate by restoring full sight to the near-blind was unbridled.

It was a wonderful way to spend time while waiting for the *Teacher* to conclude its repairs. He had never been able to seek help for his own singular condition out of fear of alerting the authorities to it or, worse, to his location. He had been forced to flee the one hospital he had recently been compelled to spend time in when a couple of its practitioners had become suspicious of, and interested in, his unique mind. He could not allow that kind of probing. And by not being able to allow it, he had closed himself off from any kind of advanced medical help either for his devastating headaches or for the modified neurological condition that gave rise to them.

Ministering to others served to alleviate the depression that was always close at hand. He had at his disposal the means to do for the natives of Arrawd what no one could do for him. It was very likely he couldn't do anything to rid the future of the vast incoming evil he encountered in periodic dreams—or whatever such episodes actually were—but here he could at least help needy individuals. That they were not human made no difference to him. Sentience was everything; appearance meant nothing. That was a lesson humankind, spreading outward into space, had learned once and for all as a consequence of the Pitar-humanx war.

He knew himself well enough to know that his activities were not purely altruistic. He derived pleasure from helping the Dwarra who came to see him. If that was an indication of selfishness, however slight, so be it. The genuine pleasures to be had from his nomadic, confused existence were few enough. The good feelings rubbed off on—or rather were perceived by—Pip. So relaxed had she become enveloped in the constant air of benign emotion that she spent most of her time sleeping, only occasionally rousing herself to check out a newcomer or hunt for the small, furtive creatures that infested the barn.

As for the Dwarra he aided, they proffered an endless stream of gratitude, and nothing more. It would never have occurred to him to ask for some kind of remuneration for the services he continued to freely dispense. It was in that regard that certain other individuals displayed considerably less restraint, and more foresight.

Ebbanai was relaxing at the small, unprepossessing gate he had constructed midway along the turnoff to his ancestral homestead. Squatting there, alone, with only the sky and fields of seashan that flanked the main road for company, one could grow bored very quickly. On the other hand, it was much easier work than net-casting at night for elusive marrarra. And with each passing day, the unpaved road between Sierlen and Barazoft saw more and more traffic taking the unmarked, previously unheralded turnoff.

Just now a large wagon was easing its way down onto the sandy track that led to his home. It was a solid, well-built vehicle, with raised, gilded carvings on its flanks that bespoke the attention of skilled woodworkers and much money. Drawn by a trio of hulking tethets yoked in single file, the wagon was clearly the conveyance of choice for a prosperous merchant or family. Wealth could be inferred not only from the fine manufacture of the conveyance itself, but from the worked and polished golden metal that capped the trimmed horns of the protesting tethets, as well as from the beautiful designs that had been shaved into their brown, black, and white fur. His suspicions, and hopes, were confirmed when the driver brought the elegant transport to a halt in front of the crude but unavoidable gate. An attendant hopped down to open the wagon's side door.

It required only a single step for the two adult occupants to descend to the road from the vehicle, which was built low to the ground. Circular upper and conical lower attire billowing around them in the sea breeze, they approached the waiting Ebbanai with anxious expressions on the faces of both the male and his mate. The richness of their raiment matched that of their transportation. Ebbanai would have to work most of a year to afford one such flattering outfit. Perhaps Storra had laboriously woven some of the cloth from which these very garments had been fashioned, he mused. On closer inspection he decided not. The fabric was of too fine a thread, and woven from a much more expensive material than seashan.

The female's attire, he speculated thoughtfully, would look even better on his own estimable mate.

Ordinarily, the pair who now confronted him would affect a superior air, especially if they by chance happened to encounter him in town. Here, and under very different circumstances, the situation was reversed. It was they who deferred, almost submissively, to the humble net-caster. While the female spoke, her mate kept casting glances beyond the gate, as if some vast wonderment or apparition might at any moment appear on the horizon.

"You are the one called Ebbanai?" she inquired respectfully.

"I am." It was to Ebbanai's credit that while circumstances

would have allowed him to assume an air of arrogance, such a condition was so foreign to his self-effacing nature that he did not know how to go about doing so.

"You are the one who determines access to the Visitant?"

Ebbanai responded with the sweeping gesture of magnanimity he had developed and refined over the preceding days. "The Visitant is very busy, and has an agenda of its own."

She looked at her mate, apprehension and concern writ large in her lean, rangy face. "Will it see us?"

Ebbanai affected an air of indifference, his skin flaps lying loose against his body. "Perhaps. Which of you is the supplicant?"

"It is neither of us. Our offspring." Turning, she called softly toward the wagon.

A Nurset appeared. Stunted and broad of shoulder and hip, with an extra gripping flange growing from the tip of each forearm, the raisers of Dwarra young comprised a distinct subspecies of the dominant sentients. More than anything, they resembled squashed-down versions of those they served. The relationship was more symbiotic than master–servant. Without the Nursets, the Dwarra could not raise their young properly. Similarly, without the intelligence and abilities of the Dwarra, the Nursets could not long survive on their own.

This particular well- but severely dressed Nurset was, unsurprisingly, carrying a young Dwarra on its broad back. Uncharacteristically, however, the youngster was not gripping the Nurset in the traditional manner. Instead, it was held in place by an elaborate brace. The instant Ebbanai caught a glimpse of the offspring's face, the reason for the adults' visit, as well as their grave concern, became immediately clear.

Their offspring was brain-damaged.

As to the severity of the problem Ebbanai could not speak. This might be one of those cases where even the talented alien biped could do nothing. But Ebbanai did not voice his reservations. He had long ago overcome any compunction against doing so. Besides, in all honesty, he had already seen his honored guest Flinx work miracles, had watched it accomplish feats of medicine beyond the skills of Metrel's most revered physicians. Who was he, a simple caster of nets and collector of baryeln gryln, to say what the alien could and could not do?

The look on the female's face was heartbreaking, her grief profound. Out here, on the outlying Pavjadd Peninsula and far from her fine home, she was not a member of some rich and powerful family; only a mother seeking relief for her broken offspring. Ebbanai looked away, feigning indifference. Under Storra's prodding he had become business-like, but he could not render himself unfeeling. He was relieved the female did not try to twine Sensitives with him. He was not sure how he would have handled the ensuing torrent of emotion.

"Can the Visitant do anything for such a—a problem?"

"I don't know. It's not for me to say. It can only try, I suppose."

"*Will* it try?" reiterated the edgy male from nearby.

Ebbanai's Sensitives thrust out to the sides of his head, an indication of ambiguity. "One can but ask. Such efforts are tiring for it. And it is a complicated creature, one who requires much attention and care."

The net-caster did not have to hold out a hand. The packet that the anxious male placed in the gripping flanges of Ebbanai's second left hand was more than adequately weighty. "A good beginning for you, I am certain," he assured the fretful couple by way of response. Stepping back, he pushed on the counterweight and swung the gate aside. Rejoining the wordless Nurset and its drooling, head-lolling burden, the female re-entered the extravagant wagon. Her hesitant mate lingered a moment longer.

"I know that we have to approach the vestibule on foot. That much was explained to us."

"Yes," Ebbanai acceded. "It is necessary to demonstrate your humbleness, your need." He gestured past the male. "You must also leave your transportation in a designated place, a proper distance from the bar—from the vestibule, so as to further indicate your status as mere hopefuls." He hesitated briefly. "That will not be a problem for you?"

"No, no," the male assured him hurriedly. "Nothing is a problem, so long as the Visitant agrees to see our offspring."

Ebbanai gently hefted the heavy packet. "I think there will be no problem for you. Once you reach the place, my own mate will direct you further. I wish—I hope that the Visitant can help your offspring. There are no guarantees. Its knowledge is vast, but not infinite."

"We know. We have heard," the male murmured. "For our offspring, there is no other hope. Everything else has been tried." Once again, his anxious gaze roved past the gate. "Now this being has come among us, and we have been given another chance where for so long there seemed to be none. That is all we ask for."

That is all you are likely to get, Ebbanai thought—but he did not say it as he stood aside to let the stylish travel wagon rumble past. With both the turnoff and the main road empty once again, he entered the little covered shelter he had built to keep off the sun. Removing a single panel from the simple wooden floor exposed a four-handled portable metal cistern of the kind used to carry gryln syrup to market. Into this he carefully deposited the heavy money packet the male had handed him in hopes of securing access to the Visitant.

Have to move this tonight, Ebbanai thought to himself. The cistern was nearly full, and soon would be too heavy to lift.

Noble Essmyn Hurrahyrad eyed his fellow members of the consecrated tripartite Kewwyd that ruled the expansive territory of Pakktrine Unified, and brooded. Flood conditions had prevailed throughout the western part of the country for several eight-days now, there had been a mutiny in the law enforcement forces of the province of Meydd that had been costly to deal with in both time and money—and now, this.

"There are no gods." Noble Kechralnan looked up from where

she was squatting at the end of the third point of the gemstone-inlaid, three-pointed star table. "There are only the Dwarra, the Nursets, and the lesser creatures." Tilting her head back, she spread both arms and all four forearms wide, grasping flanges open to the high ceiling of the fortress meeting room and by implication all that lay beyond its intricately frescoed ceiling.

Noble Peryoladam begged to differ, albeit not vociferously. Much more excitable than her counterparts, she was bright and efficient—both qualities that had contributed to her stellar ascension to the ruling triumvirate that was the Kewwyd. But she was still unsure of herself in many things, and tended to defer to the more experienced Kechralnan in areas where she had less expertise.

No reason for her to do so now, Hurrahyrad felt, since no one *had* any expertise on the topic presently under discussion.

"I do not feel we should dismiss these rumors out of hand," he insisted, waving his gleaming metal prosthesis. He had lost the first right forearm as a youth. In a battle with the scions of Jebilisk, his war tethet had been slain under him, and in falling had crushed the missing limb beyond repair. As a result he had lost in addition to the forelimb itself two of his eight gripping flanges. But the prosthesis that had replaced the missing limb was excellent for jabbing with, either for stabbing an opponent or to emphasize a point. He used it thusly now.

"Why not?" Kechralnan stared at him, the colorful yet tasteful circular rings painted around her eyes reflecting the ambient light of the well-lit chamber. "If we choose to investigate such obvious idiocies, we only give credence to our own credulity. We are already under fire for our handling of the floods. Why allow our political enemies to add accusations of stupidity to those of incompetence?"

Hurrahyrad was about to snap off a suitable rejoinder when Peryoladam spoke up. Though low in volume, her voice was oddly compelling. "Perhaps Noble Kechralnan is right and there are no gods. But might the greater cosmos not be home to other creatures? Perhaps some even cleverer than the Dwarra?" She gestured upward, though not as expansively or dramatically as had her colleague. "After all, while we know much about Arrawd, we know nothing of other worlds."

"That is because there *are* no other worlds," declared Kechralnan in exasperation. "At least, none boasting the intelligence of the Dwarra. The other planets that circle our sun are empty and dead. The lights in the sky may be other suns, as some astronomers insist, but there is not an iota of evidence to indicate that other worlds circle them, and even less to suggest that another intelligence dwells somewhere way out in the depths of the sky."

Hurrahyrad was surprised to detect a touch of anger in the other administrator's reply. "It must be a great comfort to be so certain of that which we know nothing about."

Forestalling argument that would get them nowhere, and least of all advance the afternoon's already demanding agenda, he did his best to get between them: rhetorically if not physically.

"Both viewpoints are valid, surely. Myself, I tend to think this whole business a clever ploy of the Wullsakaans to distract us, and others, from matters of genuine import. While I refuse to be so easily dissuaded from reality, I see no harm in sending a spy or two to investigate further. It will be done quietly and with as few as possible knowing the true nature of the visit. That way," he added, eyeing Kechralnan, "if this is all nothing but mischief-making on the part of Wullsakaa, our interest will pass unremarked upon."

Despite her counterpart's assurances, the other senior administrator could not resist one more objection. "Everything costs money these days. Even spies require taxes to support their activities."

Hurrahyrad dipped his Sensitives in her direction. "Then we will only send a little spy. One who does not eat very much, and files reports but sparingly."

Shrinking down into her lower torso and deliberately holding her Sensitives back, she responded with a disparaging wheeze. Kechralnan's unmatched experience and vast knowledge, Hurrahyrad knew, allowed one to overlook her utter absence of humor. But only just.

Thinking the matter done and dealt with, he was prepared to move on. But Peryoladam was not quite finished. "I believe there is one more thing to consider in regard to this matter before we can consider it as closed. Or, more properly, tabled."

Hurrahyrad felt like shoving the second point of the table through the middle of her body. He was tired, and it was growing late. "What might that be?" he inquired wearily of his persistent younger colleague.

She was not intimidated. She rarely was. There was a difference between showing deference and being intimidated. "What if the rumors are essentially true?"

Kechralnan could hardly hide her contempt. "You think a god has come down to Arrawd?"

"Not a god, I suppose, no. I don't know that anything has come down to Arrawd. But if something has—a being from another world such as ours, and a superior one at that—then we have no choice but to consider how to deal with the development, which is complicated by one significant factor."

Hurrahyrad tried not to stare at the bejeweled, freestanding chronometer in the far corner of the room. "Which is?" he asked impatiently.

Her gaze did not waver as it shifted between the two other members of the Kewwyd. "The creature, if it truly exists, is dwelling and working in the land of Wullsakaa, and not glorious Pakktrine Unified. No matter what its nature either as an individual or as a representative of another intelligent species, I submit that this geographical reality cannot be to our advantage."

It was true. The junior administrator had raised a conundrum that could not be ignored—much as Hurrahyrad might wish to do so.

As if this day had not started out with problems enough.

What am I doing here? Treappyn found himself wondering as he guided his tethet off the main road and onto the sandy dirt track. This was no place to advance oneself. The farther he got from Metrel, the deeper he sank into gloom. Worst of all, he could not get the image of that decrepit oldster Srinballa smirking snidely as his younger counterpart was hoisted by his own hubris.

Treappyn knew it was his own fault. When he had argued that the rumors of a miracle-working alien needed to be checked out, he had never dreamed that the Highborn would order him, personally, to perform such a task. That was footwork best left to the lower ranks. Now he found himself nearly at the tip of the Pavjadd Peninsula, far from the nearest decent eating establishment, forced personally to seek verification or refutation of a rumor.

The country simpleton half asleep at the gate that barred the counselor's progress had to be roughly jostled awake by one of Treappyn's two accompanying bodyguards. At least the bumpkin was properly deferential. But there was about him also an air of confidence that did not fit with his apparent station in life.

"Your pardon, Noble Treappyn. I did not recognize you."

Was this cloddish individual having a joke at his expense? Treappyn wondered. The counselor's unusually expansive frame was well-known throughout the length and breadth of Wullsakaa. Still, in a backwater like this, he supposed such ignorance was possible.

"I must make a note to ensure that you are not one of those assigned to man a critical border entry in time of war," the counselor harrumphed. While two sets of gripping flanges clutched the side prods that guided his tethet, he gestured forcefully with the other pair. "Please move the barrier so that we may continue onward."

"You have come to seek the blessings of the Visitant?" Ebbanai asked tentatively.

So that was what they were calling it. The rumor had a name. "I come in search of a degree of reality, not some quack remedies for imaginary ills."

"That will be easily acquired, Noble." Ebbanai stood waiting patiently.

Waiting for what, an increasingly irritated Treappyn could not imagine. "Well—move the gate so that we may proceed."

Ebbanai remained deferential, but insistent. "There is the matter of access, Noble. Caring for the Visitant's needs is an endless and often difficult task. It requires constant supervision. The cost . . ." He let his words trail away, to be carried off by the sea breeze.

Sudden realization of what the speaker was hinting at struck Treappyn, leaving him with a modicum of astonishment. If nothing else, one had to admire the bumpkin's boldness. "Ah. Now I understand completely." The gripping flanges of his second right hand reached toward his side. Ebbanai looked on expectantly.

His expression changed sharply when the Noble withdrew not a money packet, but a longknife. Flanking him, his bodyguards proceeded to unsheathe their swords. Their expressions were not benign.

"Noble, what is this?" Moving a pair of forelegs, Ebbanai took a nervous step backward. "I don't understand."

"It's very simple. You say that this individual requires constant care. Clearly, he would be better off in the absence of parasites. Such as yourself."

Ebbanai began backing away, all four forelegs working nervously beneath him. "Noble Treappyn, I assure you that—I am certain an exception can be made for the good of the Highborn's representative. I did not mean to suggest—"

"Yes you did," declared Treappyn, interrupting briskly as he resheathed his weapon. "No matter. As counselor to the Highborn, it is incumbent on me to encourage the enterprise of Wullsakaa's people. Just not when it happens to be directed personally in my direction."

Ebbanai relaxed—but not completely. The counselor's bodyguards still had their swords out. "I will bring you to the place myself, Noble Treappyn."

He had to run hard to keep up with the three mounted visitors from Metrel. Only the short limbs of the tethets allowed him to do so.

Built low to the ground, they could trot along all day on their power-ful eight legs, but their short stride did not allow for great speed.

"So this 'Visitant' has come to us from the sky?" Treappyn ad-dressed his wheezing guide without looking down from his saddle. All four feet were firmly ensconced in the forward stirrups, his legs parallel to the ground as he rode. "It must be very strong indeed, to have survived such a great fall."

"It did not fall, Noble." Ebbanai was panting hard as he ran alongside the government representative's steed, his lung slamming against the inside of his chest wall. "It—he—arrived in an enormous vessel, a kind of flying machine."

"I see." Treappyn's unhappiness over having to undertake the journey from Metrel began, just barely, to give way to curiosity. "This machine—was it drawn by tethets? How big was it? As big as a good-sized wagon, no doubt, to survive such a fall."

Ebbanai looked up at Treappyn. "It was bigger than the fortress at Metrel, Noble."

That put the poised counselor off stride. "Really? And how, pray tell, did such an enormous vessel touch down without crashing to the ground? Its wings must have been many hundreds of times larger than those of the piercing verohjard that lives in the high mountains."

Ebbanai leaped, one foreleg after another, over a rock in his path. "It had no wings, Treappyn. It was very long, with a bulge at one end, a great glowing disc at the other, and many lights set along its length."

If nothing else, Treappyn mused, the locals hereabouts could boast of vivid imaginations. "I would certainly like to see such a wonder." He looked to his left, scanning the seashan-thick terrain. "Is it nearby?"

"I could take you to it, Noble, but you would not see it. Its ap-pearance has changed since it touched down among us. Somehow, the Visitant caused it to become just like the dunes among which it rests."

"Ah," murmured Treappyn. "How convenient." His escalating curiosity immediately began to recede. The local's reply was clever—and exactly what might be expected of an adroit liar.

Cynicism gave way to astonishment when he and his bodyguards pushed through a last high clump of green-brown seashan and saw the scene spread out before them. All manner of conveyances were drawn up in two traditional circles to the left of a simple domed building. Stretching from the circles around to in front of the building and nearly to where he sat on his patient tethet were the scattered encampments of dozens of families and individuals. Unable to take it all in at one glance, Treappyn nevertheless decided that there were more than a hundred people present, from the elderly creaking along on four bad leg joints to scattered playgroups of energetic youngsters. In contrast to what one would expect from such a scene on, say, the outskirts of Metrel itself, it all looked very orderly and serene.

Noting the look of uncertainty on the Noble's face and back on his home ground, Ebbanai's confidence rebounded. "The Visitant will not stand for chaos where he is working. My mate and I have organized all this." And then, in a not-so-subtle dig at his overlord's parsimony, "All this takes time that we would otherwise be able to use in supporting ourselves."

Treappyn was not so easily ambushed. "Then why bother with it?"

Ebbanai's expression was deliberately enigmatic. "There are compensations."

Ordinarily, the unexpected appearance of senior counselor to the Highborn Treappyn in the company of well-groomed and heavily armed bodyguards would have attracted shouts of recognition, appeals for charity, or at the least a running, trailing escort of shrieking, laughing youngsters. He was both appalled and intrigued to find himself ignored. *Something* was certainly afoot here on this meager homestead, though he was not quite ready to attribute it to the presence of alien visitants from the sky. He had not expected to find much of anything. Yet here he was, surrounded by hundreds of fellow Wullsakaans, all drawn to this humble out-of-the-way place by—what?

He needed to find out, and the Highborn certainly needed to know. Whatever was going on here was clearly of considerably more import than the government realized.

As his bodyguards helped him to dismount—a process rendered difficult by his unusual bulk—the net-caster who had greeted him was in turn met by a female whom Treappyn assumed to be his mate. For the first time this day, one of his assumptions proved accurate. He deigned to touch Sensitives with her, voicelessly conveying his feelings of superiority and impatience. Hers hinted at expectation, excitement at his arrival, and a cool sense of assurance he found oddly disquieting.

"You honor us with your presence, Counselor Noble Treappyn."

"I know." Peering past his hosts, he found himself eyeing a line of Dwarra who were slowly and intermittently filing into a nearby barn. Periodically, the line would advance as an individual or family group entered. Wholly stoic up to now, his bodyguards likewise found themselves straining to see what might lie beyond the single enigmatic, open door. Much to his surprise, Treappyn discovered that he was suddenly unaccountably nervous.

This won't do, he told himself firmly. He could not appear anything less than completely confident in front of these country folk. "I am told you are housing a creature from another world here. I demand to be taken before it immediately."

His hosts exchanged a look, touched Sensitives, then turned back to him. The female's voice was apologetic, but firm. "I am sorry, Noble Treappyn, but we can't do that."

He did not try to hide his shock. "Do you realize to whom you are speaking?"

"Without question, Noble." Ebbanai hurriedly picked up the refrain. "But it cannot be done like that." Twisting around slightly at the waist, he used a pair of forearms to indicate the large barn. "The alien Flinx will not allow it."

"Really?" Treappyn hardly knew how to respond. "It will not allow it. And it has a name, too. *Flinx.* The sounding smacks of barbarism."

"I assure you, Noble," replied Storra, "he is very sensitive, and cultured. I am sure he will see you—in his own good time."

"*His* own good time? What about *my* own good time? I am on leave from the government. *Your* government." He gestured sharply behind him. "Do you expect me to camp out here like the rest of this mind-addled rabble?" He indicated his bodyguards. "What if I and my escort decide to walk straight into that miserable building and confront this—whatever it is you're hiding in there." His voice tightened. "If this is some kind of clever fraud you have concocted to extort money from naïve fellow citizens, I promise you here and now that you will not survive the consequences!"

He did not know whether to be pleased or disappointed when neither of them reacted fearfully. "It is no fraud, Noble," the female assured him. "The alien is tense and uncertain at times. We do not know how he is armed, or to what degree, but have heard him say that he is; thus, we consider it sensible not to provoke him." She hesitated meaningfully. "Though he prefers to see supplicants in the order in which they arrive, it might be possible, given your eminence, to bring you before him sooner."

Under the curse he uttered silently, Treappyn could not help but admire the audaciousness of the couple confronting him. He no longer had any compunction against paying them their requested bribe. If this was all a skillful swindle, he would get his money back along with pieces of their limbs. If it was something more than that . . .

If it was something more than that, then the packet he now handed to the grateful net-caster would be money well spent.

Having finally been persuaded to make a contribution, he expected to be led into the "presence" immediately. But there was one more formality to conclude.

"Apologies, Noble," Ebbanai told him, "but your raiment is far too elaborate. Such flamboyance seems to upset the alien. Perhaps you have simpler garb you could don for the audience?"

This was really too much, Treappyn huffed. Well, he would force himself to play along. Reckoning would come soon enough. At any moment he expected the couple to disappear, along with his money.

They did not. Leading him quietly toward the barn, clad now only in his plain cloth undergarments, they passed beside the line that stretched outward from the building. Surprisingly, none in the queue objected to their advance. Equally surprisingly, his hosts allowed the Noble's bodyguards to accompany him—also in their undergarments, but in possession of their weapons. More than anything else, Treappyn was thankful none of his counterparts from court was present to witness the droll procession.

And yet, not a suggestion of humor arose from those standing silently in line. More than anything else about the situation, he found unsettling the graven solemnity of the queued commoners.

Then he and his guards were inside the barn, advancing deeper into the simple country structure. He thought he was prepared for anything he might see.

He was wrong.

CHAPTER

8

The young female had been carried in on a pallet of woven seashan stiffened with the oversized spines of some unknown plant, the sharp tips of which had been trimmed down so that the makeshift stretcher would not harm its bearers. As she was gently placed before him, Flinx could see she was in considerable pain. Days of working with ill and injured Dwarra had attuned him to the meanings of their expressions. Although their faces were not as flexible as those of a human, they were quite capable of communicating a wide range of emotions.

He did not need to see the pain in her angular, somewhat stiff face, of course. She was outputting her feelings without any attempt at moderation, her Sensitives weaving hypnotically and out of control, as if searching for someone, anyone, with whom to make emotional contact. The expressions of those who had carried her in and laboriously lifted her up to the platform inside the barn where he was working were equally eloquent. As for their feelings, they were a roiling jumble of hope and hopelessness. It was a combination he had come to know well since he had started helping the natives.

Holding the Dwarra-attuned, portable medical scanner he had brought back from his last visit to the *Teacher,* he prepared to pass it over the part of her body that was heavily bandaged. Both she and those who had brought her in looked alarmed. To allay their fears, he projected feelings of assurance onto each of them. That was another of his abilities he'd had ample opportunity to practice lately. They looked surprised, feeling relaxed when they felt they should not. What mattered was that no one moved to interfere with his work.

It took only moments to diagnose the young female's problem: a shattered pelvis. What frightful accident had caused the damage, he did not know. It didn't matter. What was important was stimulating the healing process. No one objected when he removed her bandages. After days of dispensing medical aid, the peculiarities of Dwarran anatomy no longer held any surprises for him. Using his recalibrated healer, he worked on the badly injured female for nearly half an hour. From her resting place nearby, Pip occasionally lifted her iridescent, emerald-green head to spare a glance for her master's activities.

His efforts concluded, Flinx sat back and regarded the young female's handlers. From experience, he knew they might be relatives, close friends, hired helpers, or a mix of all three.

"She's healing now. Reapply the bandages and try to keep her as still as possible for as long as possible." He checked the readings on his healer. "If everything goes well and there are no setbacks, she should be well enough to walk by herself in an eight-day or two."

"Master Visitant!" The senior of the four males who had carried the patient in started to press his Sensitives to Flinx's forehead, looked surprised as he remembered that the alien had none, and settled instead for bending to push them against the human's free hand. "My life is yours. You have restored my only female offspring to me."

"Not yet." Gently, Flinx reached down and raised the elder's angular, bony face. "Let's see how her healing goes before you promise me anything."

Gesturing with gripping flanges and Sensitives, the weathered native indicated understanding. But the gratitude that flowed out of him filled Flinx with the warmth he had come to know well over the preceding days. It was nourishment of a kind even the *Teacher*'s advanced food synthesizer could not provide.

It had been a particularly complex procedure. "That's enough for now." Peering down the line of disappointed hopefuls, his gaze found his hosts and the three males who were accompanying them. Unusually, two were armed. Sensing a change in her master's emotional state, Pip raised her head from its resting place once more. This time she half unfurled her pleated pink-and-blue wings.

"Ebbanai, Storra," he called down to them. "You've brought along some people who don't appear to be ill."

Below the simple platform, Treappyn started. The mere sight of the broad-bodied, limb-deprived alien had been shocking enough, and more than sufficient to instantly confirm the basis for the multitude of rumors that were spreading through the countryside. Watching it work on the crippled young female, without making contact and by simply passing several cryptic instruments repeatedly across her broken body, had been less conclusive. It wasn't as if she had suddenly stood up and danced, miraculously cured. To the chary counselor, the painless, bloodless procedure smacked of outright fraud.

But how had the astonishing creature known that his new visitors were different from those who had preceded them? How could it tell he and his bodyguards were not seekers after healing like all who had gone before? Plainly, it had no Sensitives, nor any other visible means for perceiving what those around it were feeling. Yet the rumors insisted it was capable of doing so.

It should be easy enough to determine the truth. In his position as a counselor to the Highborn, he had long ago learned it was better to ask an awkward question than squat on comfortable ignorance.

"How do you know that there is nothing wrong with any of us? With myself, for example?"

The alien peered down at him. "Your present emotional state is not that of a sick person." It was wonderful, Flinx felt, to be able for the first time in his life to be so open and honest about his Talent. Liberating, even. "The same is true for those who accompany you. You project wariness and curiosity. Those with you project wariness and tension."

Remarkable, Treappyn decided. Though his whole world was spinning around him, he did not lose his balance. Drawing himself up, stretching all four forelegs to their limit, he announced, "I am Noble Treappyn, counselor to His August Highborn Pyrrpallinda, ruler of Wullsakaa. I have been sent by my government to ascertain the truth of your existence as a visitor among us."

"Well?" Flinx flashed the slightly sardonic smile that many he had encountered, human and otherwise, had come to identify closely with his personality.

"I intend to say in my official report that I consider it verified—and then some." Tentatively, he started toward the wide stairs that led up to the platform on which the alien squatted. No, he corrected himself. It was not squatting, as was normal and natural. Instead, it had somehow folded its body in the middle and was resting most of it on a wooden storage container. It was a feat of protean flexibility not even the most adroit Dwarra could duplicate.

"As representative of my government, I request an official audience."

"I don't give official audiences," Flinx replied.

Treappyn thought fast. It was his best attribute. "Well then, can we have an informal chat?"

No hostility radiated from his new visitor, no overtones of deception. Flinx grinned. This individual was as different from his hosts as he was from the suffering he had helped. The Dwarra was not the only individual in the barn whose curiosity needed to be sated.

"Come up and have a seat," he told the counselor. His fluency had increased to the point where he only occasionally needed the assistance of the translator hanging from his neck. Although the counselor could not take a seat, the idiom Flinx employed conveyed the same sentiment, if not the same biological requirements. "Just you," he added when the counselor's bodyguards moved to accompany him.

The two muscular soldiers looked uneasy, and Treappyn was less than thrilled with the stipulation himself. He was not by nature a bold individual. But curiosity overcame his caution.

"Remain here," he told them. "Arms at the ready, but physically and mentally at ease." He did not look up at the waiting alien as he spoke. "Though it has no Sensitives and makes no contact, it is already clear to me that the Visitant can tell what we are feeling."

One of the bodyguards muttered a curse. "A creature of the Dark Pools."

"We don't know that yet," Treappyn admonished him. "Myself, I tend to think not. Those who dwell in the Dark Pools do not bestir themselves to heal on behalf of the sick. Be alert, and wait for me."

Turning, he started up the stairway, his stout form forcing him to labor. Climbing was not at the top of the list of his favorite activities. Approaching the last couple of steps, he was surprised when the Visitant, seeing—or perhaps feeling—the trouble Treappyn was having, extended a single right hand to help him ascend the rest of the way. The hand itself was conspicuously alien. Instead of splitting into a pair of flexible gripping flanges, it terminated in five short, bony digits, like miniature forearms. Wrapping themselves around the counselor's wrist, they pulled gently but firmly.

Despite their small size, the strength in them was astonishing. Treappyn felt himself practically lifted up onto the crude wooden work platform. Nearby, he saw another fantastic creature resting on a pile of gathered seashan fibers. Brightly colored, winged, and limbless, it resembled nothing he had ever encountered outside of a dream. Or a nightmare.

Below, Storra and Ebbanai looked on with concern, though they tried not to show it. Or rather, to feel it, lest their unease be perceived by the alien. They had not been invited up onto the platform to join in, or to monitor, the conversation.

"It's not a problem," Ebbanai whispered to his mate as he touched Sensitives with her. "They will talk, the counselor from Metrel will leave, and things will go on as before."

"Yes," she agreed shrewdly, "but for how long?"

Ebbanai was unconcerned. "For as long as can be hoped." His joy communicated itself to her through their entwined Sensitives. "We have already made more money than ever we dreamed of."

"You never had much ambition, mate-mine," she chided him—but gently. "Don't be so quick to concede to the government that which is our discovery. Depending on how events develop, we may yet turn this encounter to our advantage." Her eyes, contracting, studied the interaction taking place on the platform above. "For example, all may not go well between Flinx and this counselor. In that case, our services as intermediaries will be more necessary than ever."

Contrary to Storra's hope, however, the conversation between Flinx and his new visitor was going very well indeed.

Experienced in the ways of political intrigue, if not interspecies interlocution, Treappyn had settled himself into a comfortable squat near the edge of the platform. From there, he could leap to safety should something untoward suddenly occur, and it also provided his uneasy bodyguards with an unobstructed view of the important personage who was their responsibility. But the longer he conversed with the alien, whose mastery of the Dwarrani language was crude but serviceable, the more relaxed he became.

"So you really do come from the sky? From a world like this one?"

Relaxing between supplicants, Flinx nodded. "A world that circles a sun not unlike your own." Though his guest could not perceive the difference, Flinx waxed wistful. "It's a beautiful place, with dense forests and sculpted deserts." Smiling, he raised a clenched fist and with an upraised finger drew a circle partway around. "It has partial rings, that gleam in the night sky."

"It sounds fascinating," Treappyn confessed, without entirely understanding. "And there are other worlds inhabited by your kind?"

"Many," Flinx told him. "And even more inhabited by intelligent beings as unlike myself as I am unlike you."

Treappyn could hardly believe what he was hearing. The answers to mysteries Dwarran scholars had debated for thousands of years were his for the asking. "Are all your kind as strong and knowledgeable as you?"

Flinx's smile widened. "I am not so knowledgeable. I just seem to pick up bits and pieces of information in my travels. Which are, I admit, extensive. When I look back on my life—where I've been, everything that's happened to me . . ." His voice trailed away and he suddenly stared at Treappyn so hard that the counselor wondered if he had said or done something wrong. "What about you, Noble Treappyn? Do you ever look back on your life? Do you ever wonder what you might have done differently?"

The counselor met the alien's inflexible gaze without flinching. "We are not so very different, I think."

Flinx leaned back against a thick piling. "As for my strength, that's an accident of physics. The gravity on my homeworld, and the worlds where I tend to spend most of my time, is stronger than it is here." He tapped one foot against the platform. "The pull of a planet goes a long ways toward determining the musculature with which species evolve. Though you look to be healthy enough, on my world, for example, you would have trouble just walking."

Not so similar, then, Treappyn mused, wondering as he reflexively waggled his Sensitives if he understood what the alien was telling him. "So there are others of your kind who are physically more powerful than you?"

"Yes. And other species who are stronger still, or faster. And some who are weaker. Although, especially in the past few years, I've grown taller than most of my kind." His voice fell to a contemplative murmur. "I hope *that* kind of growth, at least, has stopped."

"And your companion." Treappyn indicated the dozing flying snake. "Not intelligent?"

"Not in the way of you or I, no," Flinx informed his guest. "But like the Dwarra and myself, she's extremely sensitive to emotions. Even in the absence of Sensitives. Her name is Pip."

Treappyn shifted his stance slightly. Below, his bodyguards tensed, then relaxed. "Then all other species where you come from are able to perceive the emotions of others?"

"No," Flinx told him. "As far as I know, there's just the Alaspinian minidrags—and me. Though," he added as an afterthought, "there may be others. It's something I've tried to learn more about all my life." He gestured broadly. "I never expected, in all my journeying, in all my travels to distant places, to find a place like Arrawd where every member of an entire species can read the emotions of their friends and neighbors, just by making contact with special organs. It's strange—in some ways, I feel more at home here than anyplace else I've ever been."

"I am glad you are comfortable among us." Treappyn's thoughts were racing ahead of his words.

Flinx shifted his seat to more directly face his visitor. Treappyn found the movement astounding in its flexibility. "That's one reason why I've gone against the regulations of my own government and spent so much time helping your people. Aside from the fact that it's just the right thing to do, the sense of gratefulness I can perceive from each and every one is deeper and more meaningful than almost any such emotions I've been able to receive elsewhere." He hesitated. "It's almost as if in your species and their ability to read emotions I've found the nearest thing to kindred spirits that I've ever encountered."

"On behalf of my people, I am flattered," Treappyn replied simply. "I myself have often looked up at the stars at night, and wondered about them."

Below, near the entrance to the barn and away from the platform and the counselor's bodyguards, Ebbanai and Storra worked to calm and reassure the waiting line of supplicants. As they did so, they glanced repeatedly up at the raised area and fretted.

"This isn't going well," Storra muttered. "By which I mean to say," and she gestured toward the platform, "it is going all too well."

Conscious of the line of hopefuls stirring impatiently outside the door, Ebbanai was, as usual, less unsettled than his mate. "Thanks to our fortunate relationship with the alien we have already gained more income than you could make weaving and I fishing in ten years. We should not be greedy." He touched Sensitives with her to be certain she understood how he was feeling.

"Besides, there is nothing we can do," he added as he drew back. "The Noble Treappyn is counselor to the Highborn himself. If Flinx chooses to return with him to Metrel, we'll only be putting ourselves in a bad light if we try to object."

Storra considered thoughtfully. "You are a wise male, Ebbanai. Simple and uncomplicated, but wise. I agree: all we can do is wait, and hope. Why should Flinx go with the counselor, anyway? His sky ship is here—something I would still very much like to see for myself. Maybe they will just talk, and then the counselor will leave, and things will go on as they have—for a while longer, at least."

"Sometimes, when waiting for a big catch to swim into the net, the best thing to do is just that: stand quietly, and do nothing."

She gestured understanding. "Especially," she added, "when one has no choice in the matter. Unless, of course, this counselor tries to force Flinx to return to Metrel with him."

Ebbanai gazed up at the platform where the counselor and Flinx continued to engage in animated conversation. "If I was Noble Treappyn, I don't think I would do that. Flinx mentioned to us that he could defend himself. If his means of doing so is as advanced as his medicine, I think it would go badly for the counselor and his bodyguards to try and make him do anything against his will."

"The last thing we want is trouble with the government." Her expression conveyed dry humor. "They might find out about how we've 'assisted' the alien in helping others, and want to tax the results of what we've done out of the goodness of our hearts."

"And for the goodness of our purses," Ebbanai added, eyeing the platform afresh.

Feeling more and more comfortable in the alien's presence,

Treappyn straightened and moved closer to the biped. Below, his bodyguards stirred restively as they lost clear sight of the counselor. Under strict orders not to interfere, they could only fidget nervously.

"This government you speak of, whose regulations you have defied to help poor and suffering Dwarra: what is it like?" Aside from his boundless personal curiosity, Treappyn had professional reasons for inquiring. He was, after all, here on government business. "Is it ruled by a Highborn, as is Wullsakaa? Or," he added tentatively, "by a Kewwyd, as is Pakktrine Unified?"

"The government that rules the region I come from is called the Commonwealth. Many different kinds of intelligences are part of it. They all work together for a common goal, more or less, and to defend its constituents against challenges from outside."

Ah, Treappyn thought. So the alien did not hail from some mystic, idealistic utopia. Conflict and dispute existed beyond Arrawd, among species other than Dwarra. The revelation both pleased and disappointed him.

Allies. Always, the Highborns of Wullsakaa had sought allies against those who would seek to absorb them. Here, undoubtedly, was the chance to secure the most powerful ally in the history of the realm.

"Do you think your government would entertain the notion of an alliance between it and my government?"

Flinx tried not to smile. "Only world governments are considered for membership in the Commonwealth, not individual tribe—nation-states." He indicated his surroundings. "From what little I've seen, and from what little is known about you and your world, you would qualify for a certain limited status, yes. But that would be for your whole world, not just Wullsakaa. I'm sorry, but membership in the Commonwealth requires a certain degree of racial and social maturity that I'm afraid your kind has yet to achieve." He tried to sound encouraging. "Perhaps in the near future. Technologically, you appear to be moving in the right direction."

"I understand. To meet the requirements to join this Commonwealth, all Dwarra must, essentially, apply as one." And what if that *one* was under the direction and domain of great Wullsakaa? he mused. If, according to this alien, one dream was not easily achievable, might there not be a way to work another and, in so doing, accomplish both? By now he had a good idea how intelligent this alien was. What was yet to be determined was how smart it was.

He stayed as long as he dared, openly enjoying the conversation while acquiring as much useful information as he could. When the alien indicated that it wished to return to helping the sick and injured, Treappyn did not try to force the issue and prolong the visit.

"I hope we can meet like this again," he told the biped. The emotions he was projecting were genuine, but not entirely for the reasons his host thought.

Flinx shrugged. "Time determines all such things." He didn't add that he was likely to be long gone, the *Teacher*'s repairs completed, before the counselor returned again from the city. On the other hand, if Treappyn made haste, he would be perfectly happy to sit and chat again with the government representative. He was highly educated and interested in everything Flinx had to say. But he had no intention of lingering to fulfill the longings of the counselor or any other Dwarra. More important matters required his attention, futile as his efforts on their behalf might be. As comfortable as he was on this world, with its all-pervasive emotional projections that he could sift through or block out at will depending on his mood, he could not face Tse-Mallory or Truzenzuzex again knowing he had made less than a halfhearted effort to locate the wandering Tar-Aiym weapons platform.

So he would continue with his time-killing but very fulfilling work, healing the sick among the local poor, until the *Teacher* informed him they could depart. He would then take his leave. Regretfully, to be sure, but driven by more than one greater necessity. Try to save a few individual nonhumans today, try to save the galaxy tomorrow. And all the while, hope that some day, some how, some where, he might encounter someone or something capable of saving him.

He felt that Ebbanai, for one, would gladly do so, if only the gentle, unsophisticated net-caster possessed the necessary means.

Later that evening, when the last supplicant for the day had been treated and Flinx was enjoying the simple but filling meal Storra had prepared, his host could not refrain from commenting on the meeting that had taken place earlier that afternoon.

"Beware of government representatives, friend Flinx." Ebbanai's Sensitives swayed gently forward and back, as if through the constant motion their owner could somehow duplicate his guest's ability to read emotions in the absence of such appendages and without physical contact. "They are not interested in you. They are interested only in their own interests."

"Interesting," Flinx replied around his food, without cracking a smile. "Don't they represent you as well?"

"Only outside Wullsakaa." Storra spoke from her position near the cooking pot. "Within its borders, they best represent themselves. When the interests of individuals collide with those of the state, I would not want to find myself in the position of having to side with the first against the second."

"How is it among your people and your government, Flinx?" Ebbanai asked, genuinely curious.

Flinx sipped at his soup. By now he had become familiar with and used to the oddly shaped utensils. Pip had no such concerns, accustomed as she was to sticking her head into whatever food happened to be available, or sticking it into her.

"It depends on the people. It depends on the government. No species is entirely altruistic. There are always those for whom greed supersedes selflessness. For example, the society of one species that's not part of the Commonwealth, the AAnn, is founded on the idea of individual advancement above all else. It seems to work for them." He took a long swallow. "It doesn't work for me. If it did, I think I might be a happier person. But I'm afraid I'm just not cut out for selfishness."

"You have already abundantly shown that, Flinx." Storra stirred her dinner. "You have helped so many Dwarra, and without asking for anything in return."

"Happy I could do so," he told her sincerely. "I wish I could stay longer and help everyone who needs it, but when the time is right, I'll have to go. There are others I have to assist."

"How many others?" Ebbanai wondered as he sucked off the tip of a grain stick.

"I'd rather not discuss it. Too many," their guest murmured. "Too much responsibility for one being. I didn't ask for it, and I don't want it."

"Then why not just pretend the problem doesn't exist?" Storra could be startlingly direct. "Wouldn't that make you feel better?"

He eyed her evenly. "I wish I could. I wish it would. But I'm not made that way."

Made, he mused. What a lousy choice of words.

"Well then," wheezed Ebbanai, "we are pleased to have you among us for as long as you see fit." Storra glared at him, but at times the net-caster could be as stubborn as his mate. "But while you remain, I warn you again to think carefully on anything a representative of the government says to you. Especially suggestions."

Flinx chuckled softly, and the two Dwarra marveled at the interesting sound. "I'll be careful, Ebbanai. Don't worry. I've had, and handled, problems with governments and government agencies before. Government agencies and representatives somewhat more sophisticated than the counselor Noble Treappyn."

"Don't underestimate him," Storra warned. "Despite his youth he has a reputation as big as his belly. He's very clever."

Flinx bit down on one of the grain sticks, using teeth to accomplish the cutting where the Dwarra utilized their powerful, muscular round mouths. "If he intends me ill, I'll sense it."

That was true, Ebbanai reminded himself, focusing on his food so his emotions would not betray what he was really thinking.

Unheard by Flinx, the stories swapped by those who now crowded the homestead in hopes of seeing him continued to escalate in both stature and outlandishness. And unheard by him, they metastasized unchallenged. Tales of the Visitant and his abilities had ballooned from rumor, to wary fact, to phenomenon. In these stories, medicine gave way to miracle. Supplicants had become pilgrims.

None of this was known to Flinx. While doing nothing to dissuade such supposition, his kindly, caring hosts ensured that such thoughts were not voiced in his presence, explaining to those who trekked to the homestead for an audience with the virtuous Visitant that his natural modesty forbade the bestowing of such pious accolades. All arrivals were assured that in the presence of the alien, humbleness worked best, and all mention of veneration was banished. That did not prevent the pilgrims from gossiping among themselves. Indeed, while waiting in the winding, steady line to see him, there was little else to do.

"I hear the Visitant is twice the height of a Dwarra," announced one hopeful as he struggled to keep his crippled, aged male parent upright.

"No, three times," insisted a young metalworker from the northern Wullsakaan city of Pevvet. "And that it can leap over castle walls without straining."

"It doesn't have to leap," declared an elderly female from behind both of them. "It is never seen without a flying creature that lives in a hole on its back. When the Visitant wishes to travel, it just abides the small alien, who carries it wherever it wants to go."

The metalworker, whose missing half face had been destroyed in a smelting accident and was concealed by a makeshift mask, nodded somberly. "It is said that while the Visitant cannot fix every injury, it has been observed to perform miracles that are beyond the skills of our greatest physicians." A pair of left hands reached up, the tips of the four gripping flanges lightly stroking the curving mask. "I came all the way from Pevvet hoping it can restore some of my face."

"I don't see why not." With a wheeze, the first speaker re-assessed his grip on his silent sire, struggling to ensure he remained upright. "I heard that one of the instruments it uses can cause lost bone to come back. That's what we need. Maybe it can also give you a new eye to replace your missing one."

"I'm not greedy. I can do without the eye." The younger male shuffled forward a couple of steps as the slow-moving line grudgingly made another of its small, deliberate advances. "But I would like to be able to be rid of this face covering. With it, I am not considered a suitable candidate for mating."

The elderly female sympathized. "I hope the Visitant will do right by you. My hopes are more modest." With one right forehand she gestured in the direction of the barn; so close, yet so unapproachable. "The blessed couple who serve the Visitant say that the required donation is enough to gain access to it, but I myself am taking no chances. I have been praying ever since I started for this place." She seemed well-satisfied with her decision. "The proof that it worked is that I am now here, not far from the Visitant itself, while others in need of its aid remain back in my village, bickering among themselves." All eight gripping flanges were wrapped tightly around the tall walking stick she used to support herself.

The metalworker and the male supporting his master looked at one another. "Perhaps we should pray to the Visitant, too," the metalworker declared. "It might make this line move more quickly."

Releasing one set of flanges from the walking stick, the insightful elder wagged a knowing limb at him. "What matters is not the speed with which the line is moving, but what the Visitant decides when at last you stand before it in all its glory. It is then that it will know of your honest prayers—or lack of them."

Both males found this line of reasoning more than sensible. "Perhaps you could instruct us, offer some suggestions?" the one holding up his male parent inquired politely.

"I am happy to do so. The more mollified is the Visitant when we four reach its presence, the more likely it is to grant our requests."

This suggestion traveled swiftly up and down the line, accompanied by much muted discussion and entwining of Sensitives. By the time it reached the barn at one end and the beginning of the line on the other side of the homestead, the steady susurration of softly voiced prayers formed a polyphonic counterpoint to the subtle shuffling of hundreds of foot flanges. Taking note of this new development, Ebbanai and Storra did nothing to discourage it. If the supplicants now chose to regard their guest as not merely gifted, but divine, it could only enhance their prospects. Who would question the payment of tribute to a god?

Knowing Flinx as they did, not simply as a sophisticated alien but as an earnest individual, they understood that if he became aware of this new development he would probably try to discourage it.

Aware that he already had a great deal on his mind, in addition to being swamped with desperate supplicants, they thoughtfully decided not to tell him about it.

CHAPTER

9

"He is not a god."

Counselor Noble Treappyn sat in the bath beneath one of several stone spouts carved in the shape of a vomiting cyklaria, letting the warm, mildly acidic liquid that spilled from its gray-blue mouth cascade over him. The smelly solution exfoliated his skin and enhanced the flexibility of his gripping flanges. One just had to be careful to keep the eyes closed when submerged, or when enjoying a shower as he was now. A little of the sparkling fluid would clear the eyes. Too much would start to dissolve them.

Across from him, the Highborn Pyrrpallinda lay half in and half out of the elaborate bath, the four forelimbs of his August body sprawled in all directions. It was not a dignified posture, but other than Treappyn and counselor Srinballa there were none present to see it. Given the especially sensitive nature of Treappyn's report, even the usual attendants had been banned from the royal bath.

Unusually for him, Srinballa looked satisfied. "Then it can be killed."

"In theory, yes." Treappyn had no hesitation in agreeing with the senior counselor's assessment. "In practice . . ." He let the implication trail off.

Srinballa was persistent. "What is to prevent such a course of action, should someone wish to take it?"

Raising one pair of forearms, Treappyn used them to stroke clean first one Sensitive, then another, dipping the appendages forward down toward his eyes to make them easier to reach. He did not need a mirror to see what he was doing. It was an instinctive, and ancient, Dwarran behavior.

"It is difficult to see how an assassination might be successfully carried out on a being who can sense the emotions of anyone in his vicinity merely by perceiving their intent, and without having to make physical contact via Sensitives. Also, the alien, who calls himself Flinx, is never far from the company of a small winged animal that he claims can do the same and, furthermore, has the ability to spit a deadly toxin." Sliding out from beneath the gushing spout, Treappyn steadfastly regarded the other counselor who was his senior in age if not authority.

"That is what I have learned from having observed and spoken with the creature. Of perhaps more significance is what I was not able to observe. This being possesses many wonderful instruments for healing. It would be foolish in the extreme to assume he does not also possess similarly advanced means for defending his own person."

"Why would we want to kill it, anyway?" Shifting from a slanted to a squatting position in the deep rectangular basement pool, Pyrrpallinda allowed one of the tiny chouult that lived in the acidic hot-water spring to scour and scrub his lower body for parasites. "It hasn't threatened us and it heals, without asking for payment, the ill and injured of Wullsakaa."

"Well, not entirely without payment, Highborn." Treappyn proceeded to detail the means by which the alien's hosts went about extracting money from arriving supplicants.

Pyrrpallinda wheezed a combination of indifference and mild

admiration. "Good for them. I am always appreciative of those among our citizenry who prove enterprising. You say the alien receives none of this income?"

"Based on interviews with others, I don't think he's even aware of it." Treappyn moved nearer to the Highborn and leaned back slightly against the tiled wall of the pool. "In fact, from my conversation with him, I am of the opinion that if he knew, he would disapprove."

Pyrrpallinda's eyes contracted as he pondered the unprecedented state of affairs that had been thrust upon him. "So. What are we to do with this alien altruist who has dropped uninvited into our midst?"

"We could kill it," Srinballa suggested, apparently unable to put aside that morbid line of thought, "and appropriate its wonderful devices for our own."

"And do what with them?" Pyrrpallinda appreciated the elder counselor's guidance, but in this matter the Highborn felt his senior advisor was out of his depth. "Do you know how to operate them? Or repair them if they fail? And what do we know of this being's provisions for its own welfare? Suppose, despite what it said to Treappyn, it is required to regularly report its status to others of its kind. What happens when they don't hear from it, and possibly come looking for it?"

"He says he travels alone, out of a desire to be alone," Treappyn put in.

Pyrrpallinda made a sound of distaste. "Have you learned so little of the way things work? Or having met and been enchanted by this creature, do you think it incapable of lying?"

Abashed, Treappyn let his Sensitives fall flat against his forehead. To show that he was an evenhanded admonisher, Pyrrpallinda also turned his ire on the second counselor.

"We're not killing anybody. At least, not without good reason. Besides," he murmured introspectively, "a live god is potentially far more useful than a dead one."

Both young and old counselor perked up. "Your Augustness has something in mind," Treappyn observed sagely.

"A small something, perhaps." The Highborn was nothing if not modest. "You say this Flinx is not a god. Yet hundreds, perhaps thousands, of common folk have come to regard it as such. Gods can be useful to have around, if only for reasons of public relations." He eyed each of them meaningfully. "Especially if it's *your* god. Most especially if it's not someone else's god."

"You speak possessively," Srinballa commented.

"With eloquence, I hope." The Highborn waited for his counselors to digest the implications behind his comments, and to counsel.

As expected, in this matter Treappyn's mind was racing ahead of that of his senior. "I think I see where you are leading this, Highborn. However, such a course of action will not be of much use to us if, as the alien insists, he intends to leave soon."

Pyrrpallinda had anticipated the objection. "Then a means must be found to induce it to remain among us. And by *us* I mean, of course, not the Dwarra as a species, but specifically the citizens of Wullsakaa."

By now Srinballa was wheezing to himself. "To claim a god for our own . . ." He peered across the softly steaming water at the half-submerged Highborn. "This is a dangerous game. Attempting to gain advantage through bluffing is always dangerous."

Pyrrpallinda was not put off. "What if it's not a bluff? What if we really can claim this creature as our own?" He turned expectantly to Treappyn.

Put on the spot, the younger counselor was unable to stall. "I don't see how we can do that. He's already told me that he regards all Dwarra as one people. I don't think he'd side with Wullsakaa, or any other territory, against another. He has already expressed remorse that he's interacted with us to the limited degree that he has."

Beneath the water, the Highborn adjusted his stance to allow the busy chouult better access to his nether regions. "Even aliens may react to circumstance. As wise Srinballa points out, if we put the pieces of this proposed game in motion, the consequences could be dangerous." His voice was strong and devoid of indecision. "The rewards could be proportionate to the stakes. We could lose everything—or gain everything."

"August Highborn, I am not sure that I—" Treappyn began.

Pyrrpallinda cut him off impatiently. "I will lay it out so that even an immature offspring could understand. If word reaches the abominations of Pakktrine Unified, or the vile scions of Jebilisk, or any of the other neighboring and nearby territories that covet the lush fields and bountiful fisheries and industrious lands of Wullsakaa, that a god from the sky not only dwells among us, but dispenses miracles in our favor, it will not only give pause to their traditional belligerent intentions toward us, but also enormously strengthen our flanges in any future dealings with these meretricious governments. This hugely beneficial intangible would be, of course, in addition to any material assistance we might persuade the alien to render."

Treappyn's response was muted, but specific. "As you state, August Highborn, it is a proposition fraught with great potential." He employed a forearm to gesture to his left. "It is also, as counselor Srinballa points out, one that floats atop an ocean of risk. If the Kewwyd of Pakktrine, for example, were to discover the ruse, their outrage at any resultant circumstances would be exceeded only by their fury at having been so thoroughly duped. I have to believe that in such an instance they would initiate a response more significant than coarse language."

Using legs and arms, Pyrrpallinda boosted himself up onto the smooth tiled edge of the pool. Disappointed chouult, their work not entirely finished, fell away in droves from beneath his skin flaps in their rush to return to the acidic water of the bath. From a distance, it looked as if the flanks of the Highborn's body were weeping silver.

"That is the beauty of it. If those who yearn to attain mastery of Wullsakaa decide to attack us, for reason of perceived insult or anything else, we can then call upon our own 'god' to respond."

The counselor was taken aback by the audaciousness of the

Highborn's plan. He chanced risking everything on the reaction of an alien about whom little was known. Treappyn felt he would be shirking in his duty as advisor if he did not hurry to point out the potential flaws in his respected ruler's reasoning.

"August Highborn, such a stratagem greatly multiplies the risk of simply letting loose the rumor that a god dwells among us. To employ such a commoner's tale to our diplomatic advantage is one thing. But to rely on the alien to actually come to our aid in a moment of dire need perhaps presupposes too much."

Pyrrpallinda was not dissuaded. "That's where you come in, counselor Treappyn."

As decorously as he could manage, a horrified Srinballa scuttled as far away from his younger colleague as the tiled boundaries of the steaming pool would allow.

Treappyn swallowed, his round mouth contracting so tightly it barely allowed a squeak of a response to emerge. Further reflecting his distress, his Sensitives alternated as they bobbed back and forth. "I, Highborn?"

Enjoying the effect his announcement had produced, the ruler of Wullsakaa squatted on the side of the pool while the cool circulating air rising from the fortress's lower regions dried his gaunt, angular form.

"You are the only one besides the two country folk who have been its hosts who knows anything about this creature; about its mode of thinking, about its likes and dislikes, about its desires and greater intentions. You must persuade it to remain longer among us and, preferably, to come here to Metrel." Pyrrpallinda gestured expansively with all four pairs of gripping flanges, his skin flaps lifting in unison away from his body.

"Tell it that it can continue its work here. Etrenn knows there is plenty to do. As many are sick in the city as in the countryside. Perhaps it can also instruct, imparting some of its superior knowledge to our own willing but technically wanting physicians."

Desperately, Treappyn tried to think of a way out of, or at least around, Pyrrpallinda's proposal. "The alien will sense the deception, Highborn."

"What deception?" Confidence underlined every word of the ruler of Wullsakaa's response. "Is not the capital infested with the ill? Am I not honestly seeking to help them? Are we not all at risk, every day, from enemies on all sides?"

"I told you, Highborn," Treappyn reminded his liege, "the alien will not side with one group of Dwarra against another."

"No one is asking it to do so. We request only that it continue its work here instead of away out on that forsaken, empty peninsula. If it wishes, as you say, to spend its time among us helping the unfortunate, there is far more opportunity for it to do so here." Mouth and eyes contracted in knowing concert. "And if the minions of Pakktrine Unified, or Great Pevvid, or anyone else should take offense at that good work or, worse, feel threatened by it sufficiently to respond, it might just be that the alien will be compelled to react proportionately in order to ensure its own safety."

"But what if it does not, Highborn?" Though uncharacteristically silent during much of the foregoing conversation, Srinballa had missed nothing. "What if, say, the Kewwyd of Pakktrine does feel threatened, and reacts accordingly—and the alien responds by doing nothing? Or, worse, decides that that is the time for it to leave our world."

Ever the far-seer, Pyrrpallinda had anticipated the elder counselor's objection as well. His rejoinder, however, was less than reassuring. As it had to be.

"I have recognized that this strategy carries risks. The opportunity to gain extreme reward often demands the taking of extreme risk." His skin flaps now lay flat and tight against his body, hugging his flesh. "I have said that by putting this plan in motion we could lose everything. We could also see the last of our old enemies. Not until the next skirmish, not until the next disputation, but permanently. Is that not worth taking some risk?" Prudently, neither Treappyn nor Srinballa responded.

Well content with the reaction he had provoked, a nearly dry

Pyrrpallinda straightened to his full height. "Then it is settled. You, counselor Treappyn, will return to the Pavjadd and utilize every iota of your considerable skills to try and convince this alien to shift its good work to the capital, where all might be improved by its efforts." He turned to his right, where Srinballa stood hoping to be spared.

"You, good counselor, will lay the groundwork for the alien's arrival." Pyrrpallinda drifted into contemplation. "It should be properly respectful. Impressive without being garish." He eyed Treappyn. "That would be the right approach, yes, counselor?"

Treappyn found himself gesturing concurrence. "Quite, Highborn. Nothing flashy. It doesn't suit this creature."

"So much the better," Pyrrpallinda murmured. "Ceremony is expensive. Srinballa, I will leave it to you to maintain the ambiguity surrounding our visitor's possible divinity. There is to be no open worship, no raising of body flaps in prayer. Those at court are to be instructed to keep their personal feelings to themselves."

"A fine notion, Highborn," Treappyn readily agreed, "with only one drawback."

Frowning, Pyrrpallinda turned back to the younger counselor. "And what might that be, Treappyn?"

The younger advisor's mouth pulsed slightly as he replied. "In the presence of the alien, it is *impossible* to keep one's feelings to oneself."

The elegant yet functional riverboat carrying the Kewwyd of Pakktrine Unified was reflective of the progressive country through which it was presently cruising. The people of Pakktrine were proud of their steady development, of their advancements in science and technology and modern agriculture. Unlike reactionary regimes such as those that ruled neighboring Jebilisk and Wullsakaa, the Kewwyd of Pakktrine encouraged new ways of thinking. Its government promoted speculation and subsidized experimental ways of doing things. Driven by steam instead of sail, the multiwheeled riverboat was a prime example of such forward thinking, and the pride of the land-bound territory's riverine navy.

At present, all three members of the Kewwyd were lounging on the forward deck, relaxed in squatting postures as they contemplated both the seralune-lined islands through which their craft was loudly motoring and the looming crisis that might be nothing more than energetic rumormongering on the part of their enemies. In addition to the slender trunks of the pink and maroon carnivorous seralune that dipped thousands of barbed fronds into the slow-moving water, the islands and the opposite shores were thick with tall, mauve-colored spreading teraldd, their feeding branches turned into the wind from upstream, and muddy green thickets of puourlakk trees. It was a lush, productive environment, one much envied by the citizens of sere Jebilisk and windswept Wullsakaa. In their turn, the Kewwyd lusted after Wullsakaa's access to the sea, and Jebilisk's desert mines.

Noble Kechralnan twisted her body to the right, her attire ballooning stylishly around her as she gazed moodily down at the turgid green water. "It all sounded like so much talk. Bereft of ideas and philosophy, not to mention intelligence, the Highborn Pyrrpallinda resorts to unimaginative innuendo in a transparent attempt to frighten us into making concessions at the next round of trade and territory talks." She wheezed contemptuously. "How typical."

Across from the youngest member of the Kewwyd, Noble Essmyn Hurrahyrad rested his narrow backbone against the railing that fronted the prow of the shuddering boat. "Yes," he murmured, "except we now know from the latest reports supplied by our agents in that benighted and misruled land that it is not innuendo. The rumors are true. Incredible as it seems, an alien from the sky, from another world, has made its home in Wullsakaa."

"We do not know that is true." Though she often disagreed with them, like each of her colleagues Noble Peryoladam had been equally unsettled to learn that the ridiculous rumors that had ridden rampant throughout the territory for some time now were in fact grounded in reality. "We know only that the alien has set down among the Wullsakaa and is living among them." The skin flaps on her exposed face and arms flexed meaningfully. "That is very different from making its home there."

"We positively must determine the truth or falsity of that. Even more than the reality of its existence, the degree and depth of its involvement with the Highborn and his ilk must be ascertained with accuracy." Hurrahyrad was deeply troubled. "Where this astounding creature is concerned we must also try to separate fact from lie." He eyed his colleagues. "For example, it is said that it can leap all but the tallest fences and outrun even a mounted soldier."

Peryoladam was not too deep in thought to respond. "It seems incredible. If this being's existence had not been confirmed by multiple, trusted sources, I would dismiss it as an invention of the Highborn conceived solely to worry us. Yet the same reports that speak of this creature's physical abilities also say that it is no taller than the average Dwarra."

"No taller, but much broader." As she addressed the urgent matter under discussion, Kechralnan made time to drink in the beauty of the river. "I confess I am curious to see it for myself."

Hurrahyrad wheezed dissent. "If the Wullsakaans have managed to bind the visitor to them as tightly as some would like us to believe, you might not find such a meeting felicitous."

"*Phuzad,*" she snapped. "It is in the Wullsakaans' interest to have everyone believe the stories they spread. I am not intimidated by any alien, no matter how strong or agile it may be. I venture to say it is not fast enough to outrun a barbolt fired by a skilled sharpshooter." Her mouth contracted in a rictus of a smile. "Although if the accounts are true, it would be able to use its abilities and its devices to quickly heal anything short of a mortal wound."

Hurrahyrad was displeased by his colleague's cavalier attitude. "You are not pondering deeply enough, Noble Kechralnan. Think: if this being possesses devices that can heal the sick more rapidly than can our best physicians, and a vehicle capable of carrying it between the worlds around stars, might it follow that it also has at its disposal the means of protecting itself? Even from sharpshooting barbolters?"

She refused to concede. "The reports say that despite wild stories propagated by the Wullsakaan government, the alien's sole claim to defense has thus far taken only the form of cautionary words and a small flying thing that never strays far from its side. If the creature has other means of protecting itself, it has not chosen to demonstrate them."

Though apparently engrossed in watching syl-lynn spin their multiple legs across the surface of the river, relying on surface tension to keep them from sinking, Peryoladam had missed nothing of the conversation between her two colleagues.

"Maybe it doesn't need to," she suggested softly. "Such continued reticence implies appalling stupidity—or supreme confidence." She turned away from the semi-transparent ballet playing out atop the water. "I leave it to each of you to decide which is the more likely."

The elder's analysis did not sit well with her companions. It raised all manner of unpleasant possibilities. Still, unpleasant or not, the escalating crisis had to be dealt with.

"We know nothing of the alien's craft," a grim Hurrahyrad pointed out. "Rumor says that it is bigger than the fortress at Metrel. That is hard to believe—especially since no one except some rustic provincial has claimed to have actually set eyes upon it. If it mounts weapons—something like an oversized barbolt, for example—their number and nature remain unknown." He eyed each of his colleagues in turn. "I think that to be safe we should proceed on the understanding that the creature can possibly call on something for defense that is more effective than an equally alien flying pet. That does *not* mean it is all-powerful. Invincible beings, gods from the sky, do not carry with them elaborate devices for repairing injuries. Therefore I think it is reasonable to assume that it can be killed."

"Before we enter into talk of killing," Kechralnan mused aloud, "we must resolve the problem you posed earlier, Noble Hurrahyrad.

Has the alien bound itself to the needs and aims of Wullsakaa? Personally, I don't understand why it would. Why should a visitor from another world, a representative of another species, wish to involve itself one way or the other in the problems and disagreements of people who are not of its own kind?"

Peryoladam gestured with all four hands, the gripping flanges opening and closing in unison. "My feeling also. Invulnerable or not, superintelligent or not, why should it care about the needs of Wullsakaa? Or for that matter those of Jebilisk, or Pakktrine Unified?"

"I don't know," Hurrahyrad admitted as he moved toward the broad prow of his territory's flagship. Emerging from two pipes in the stern, the smoke from the fires that drove the ship's multiplicity of small paddle wheels was kept clear of the Kewwyd's conversation. "But I do know that we ignore the possibility at our peril. Our country folk, those who chose us to be their Kewwyd, will not soon forgive us if we act ineffectively, or too late." He eyed Peryoladam intently.

"Can we take the chance that this alien intends us no harm, and cannot be swayed to their will by the clever Wullsakaans? Dare we risk ignoring the increasing volume of stories emanating from that benighted place and the increasingly belligerent declarations of the Wullsakaans, on the assumption that whatever they intend, this alien and its manifestly superior technology will not be employed on their behalf?" When neither of his colleagues responded, he continued.

"We cannot sit idly by. We must take steps. It is the proactive who survive catastrophes. The best way to prevent a disaster is to anticipate it and stop it before it can eventuate."

A reflective Kechralnan glanced at her senior. Peryoladam's round eyes said all that the younger representative needed to know. She turned back to the third member of the Kewwyd. "What would you suggest, Noble Hurrahyrad?"

Though he inhaled deeply, his sallow, bony chest expanded only slightly. "We cannot take chances. If we wait for the Highborn to further cement his relationship with this creature, there is no telling what might happen. There is no knowing what it is capable of doing. Thus far, it has restricted its activities to healing the sick. We cannot imagine what it might do if swayed by the lies of the Highborn and his court. By moving now, swiftly and decisively, we may hope to prevent such things from ever taking place."

Kechralnan was not convinced. "By taking action, we might also spur this alien to react accordingly."

Her colleague did not back down. "Would you prefer to wait until the pestilential Highborn Pyrrpallinda has convinced it to act on Wullsakaa's behalf? In moving now we may not only prevent that, but catch this being off its guard." His voice lowered, and all four forearms were gesturing meaningfully. "By all accounts, it is carrying out its healing activities away from the vessel that brought it here. If we move quickly, stealthily, we have the chance to cut it off from its ship. No matter how strong it may be physically, no matter how advanced its technology, it will then be isolated from any support, reliant entirely on what few devices it carries on its person." He straightened to his full height and extended every skin flap to the maximum, acquiring a look that was almost feathery.

"At the same time, we will deal once and for all with the Wullsakaans, and teach them a lesson they will not soon forget."

Peryoladam was gesturing with both Sensitives. "All admirable goals, Noble Hurrahyrad. The alien is, of course, an unknown quantity. Wullsakaa and the strengths and weaknesses of its perverted leadership are more familiar to us. The question is: can it be done?"

"By its very nature, the operation against the alien demands a small force, comprised of the best Pakktrine's military can provide. A parallel assault on Wullsakaa will be expensive and dangerous, but familiar. I believe we have no choice but to try." Advancing, he extended his Sensitives.

The Kewwyd was emotionally locked together when a small boat, with its ranks of oars designed to be worked by four hands instead of two, requested and received permission to draw up alongside. The triumvirate disentangled their Sensitives to greet the singular visitor. His arrival turned out to be as welcome as it was un-expected.

"I, Tywiln of the Red Sands, extend greetings to my brothers and sisters of Pakktrine Unified from the Aceribb of Jebilisk." The coni-cal, traditional attire the visitor wore was embroidered with thread and beads of brilliant hue whose sheen matched the slickness of the envoy's voice.

While the ferocious but well-behaved fighters who had accom-panied Tywiln assumed tense squats and settled themselves restively onto the deck of the boat, equally well-armed sailors stood watch nearby. The necessary additional formalities were exchanged, where-upon Noble Peryoladam inquired as to their visitor's purpose.

The representative of the Aceribb then proceeded to very conve-niently alleviate one of the Kewwyd's greatest qualms regarding Noble Hurrahyrad's proposal.

"We of Jebilisk find ourselves facing an unprecedented problem. Most uncharacteristically, the Aceribb and his council are uncertain how best to deal with it. We know that our government and that of Pakktrine Unified have had their differences in the past, but the situa-tion that brings me here and to this meeting is of such momentous-ness that it brushes aside all other concerns. Old enmities must be forgotten in order that new troubles be effectively dealt with." Letting the upper opening of his garment slip lower around his slim shoul-ders, Tywiln of the Red Sands lowered his voice conspiratorially.

"Believe it or not, we have confirmed stories that an alien god presently walks and works among the Wullsakaans! We are fearful of what this implies for the relationship between our sometimes hostile peoples, and wonder at what steps can be taken to ensure that the present political, military, and social balance is not upset. The Aceribb realizes this is an outlandish assertion to make, and so I have been in-structed to bring with me and to present openly to you as much proof as we have been able to obtain."

The three members of the Kewwyd of Pakktrine Unified looked

at one another and said nothing. Betraying no reaction, Kechralnan leaned slightly toward the envoy and fluttered her Sensitives.

"Perhaps we do not regard your claim as quite so outlandish as you may think. Tell us more of your reason for coming here, Tywiln of the Red Sands. Tell us what you know of this extraordinary phenomenon, and don't spare the details."

CHAPTER
10

"I think we should tell him."

Storra looked over at her mate from where she was supervising the preparation of the evening meal. Two younger females and one male bustled about, hurrying to comply with her commands. For their efforts they received no recompense: only a vague promise by their new masters to try to intercede with the Visitant on their behalf. They would be gone, dispersed among the milling crowds now camped all around the homestead, before Flinx arrived to eat. It would not do, Storra knew, for their guest to see her servants hard at work. His interminable curiosity where matters Dwarra were concerned might inspire him to ask awkward questions of the unpaid help.

So the three hopefuls, each of whom had an ailing relative waiting out in the expanding camp, worked faster. Despite never having aspired to anything so semi-grand, Storra found that she had adapted to power quite easily.

Effortlessly, she entwined Sensitives with her husband. Right away she recognized that he was upset. Coupled with what he had just suggested, it was clear that his resolve was weakening. He was a good mate, was Ebbanai, but too principled for his own good. Not to mention hers.

"Dear mate-mine, what troubles you to feel so strongly?" One set of flanges served to grip his left shoulder reassuringly while the other three continued to gesture emphatically at the workers.

Round eyes of pale violet stared back into hers. "Everything." The net-caster gestured at their surroundings. "How we are exploiting his caring nature. How we are making obscene amounts of money from what he believes to be deeds of pure charity. How the whispers about his true nature are spreading, and being spread, by those who seek to raise him up and portray him as more than what he actually is."

She indicated her understanding, but pulled back from contact with his Sensitives. "First, mine-mate, we are not exploiting his caring nature. No one is forcing him to heal the sick. That more and more seek him out is not our doing. We do not advertise. Should he wish to stop what he is doing, no one could complain. Debate gently, perhaps, but not complain. He would not continue with his efforts if he was not deriving some kind of pleasure from the results. That is not exploitation.

"Second," she added briskly as he showed signs of wanting to be elsewhere, "I see no reason why the terms for 'obscene' and 'money' need appear in the same comment. We feed him, we shelter him and his sloe-eyed pet, and it is not wrong that we should be reimbursed for our efforts."

Ebbanai turned his gaze away from hers and lowered his voice. "We have already been reimbursed to a degree that you could buy a small castle, and I my own ship and crew."

"Just so," she agreed, gesturing boldly with all four forearms, her skin flaps quivering. "As for myself, I happen not to think that a *bad* thing. Lastly, as for those who persist in trying to elevate Flinx into some private pantheon of their own, who are we to challenge their individual beliefs? What right have we?" She indicated their surroundings. "We still live in the same homestead as your ancestors. Yes, we have profited from our fortunate meeting with the alien Flinx. But only monetarily. Others who suffer from truly serious sicknesses have gained far more from their encounters with him than we have. Those are encounters that we have encouraged, and facilitated." She straightened as much as her physique would permit. "Myself, I am proud of what we have done; yes, proud!"

His partner had such a way with words, Ebbanai thought to himself. More than once, he had thought she'd mated below herself. She could have been a village organizer, or maybe even a tertiary counselor to the Highborn's court. Still, his feelings toward her were so often mixed.

As they were toward the alien, who arrived unexpectedly in the cooking area. The three servants eyed him with a mixture of awe and terror.

Flinx sensed those feelings immediately, of course. They only confirmed what he had recently learned. Expression grim, he indicated the trio as he spoke to his host. The flying creature riding in its familiar position on his shoulder appeared unusually agitated.

"Ebbanai, Storra—we need to have a talk."

"Of course." Moving to one side, Ebbanai indicated the storage locker that had been modified with the addition of a wooden back to serve as a "seating" platform for the unnaturally flexible alien. As Flinx moved to take a seat, Storra swiftly and quietly dismissed the three kitchen helpers.

"Is there a problem, friend Flinx?" Storra took up a stance directly in front of their guest, not coincidentally blocking his view of the retreating servants.

It didn't matter. As it developed, Ebbanai did not have to agonize over whether or not to inform the alien of the procedures that had little by little been put in place behind his back. He already knew of them.

"Ebbanai," Flinx began sternly, "what's this I'm hearing about you charging the sick and the ill admission just to get onto your land, and a further fee to see me?"

Ebbanai swallowed hard, a visual expression of how he was feeling made all the more visible by the nature and design of his thin, stiff neck. "Friend Flinx, many of those who come seeking your help have spent all they possess in order to make the journey. They need feeding, and shelter." A pair of hands gestured in Storra's direction. "You know that my mate and I are poor people. Some way of paying for these needs had to be found."

Flinx was not so easily satisfied—or deceived. "I'm told that your income considerably exceeds what you're putting out on behalf of those who come to see me." As he leaned toward his host, there was a glint in the inflexible alien eyes Ebbanai had never seen there before. On Flinx's shoulder, Pip's head was swaying hypnotically from side to side. Ebbanai decided he liked the look in the flying snake's eyes even less than that in those of her master.

"You and Storra are making a *profit* off what I'm doing here. I'm engaged in what I'm doing to help the sick—not to make money off them."

Storra stepped forward hurriedly. "Surely, friend Flinx, you wouldn't forswear a little money to those who took you in and have devoted all their time ever since to helping you with your good works? Is there no wealth where you come from, in this Commonwealth of yours?"

Flinx turned sharply on her. "Too much. There was a time, when I was very young, when I thought that was all that I wanted. Then all I wanted was to find out the truth about my parents. I still want that, and even though an unwelcome set of circumstances has been forced on me I still want to do what's right and help others in numbers you can't imagine, in ways you can't envision. But I don't do any of it for wealth."

"Perhaps," she replied sagely, "wealth means nothing to you because you already have enough of it."

"No, that's not . . ." He hesitated. From a physical standpoint, did he *not* have everything he wanted? Food, shelter, a surprisingly large line of credit, even a space-going ship of his own? Who was he to criticize if some Class IVb native saw an opportunity to make a little money and was smart enough to take advantage of it?

It struck him suddenly that he had been morally outmaneuvered by a being with more limbs than knowledge.

"I don't think it's right," he snapped, "and I don't like it. Just as I don't like where this seems to be leading. I thought I could help some nativ—some of your fellow Dwarra—and that would be all. Clean, simple, and helpful. Now I find out that some of them are fighting among themselves just to get to your homestead, and to gain access to me." His expression shifted from one of determination and mild anger to that of genuine uncertainty. "And by the way—what's this I'm starting to hear about a 'Cult of the Hallowed Visitant Flinx'?"

Ebbanai exchanged a knowing glance with his mate. "Ah, religion," the net-caster murmured. "Every aspect of Dwarran society has its favorite deity or gods. As a net-caster, I make frequent obeisance to Vadakaa, lord of the seas and all that dwell beneath the waves. A farmer would pray for good rains to Seletarii, god of weather. A forest harvester, perhaps to Lentrikee. I do not believe in either of the latter two, of course. My interest is only in Vadakaa, whose intercession I seek to help me in my work." Perfectly round eyes that were not so innocent met those of the alien. "Those who seek salvation from their pain and sickness, from their ills and injuries, entreat Terebb or Nacickk or Rakshinn. It is not unusual, or unprecedented, for people to change their allegiance to still another divinity, especially if they believe it will do more for them than its predecessor."

His host was not trying to hide anything, Flinx sensed. Ebbanai was only telling the truth.

"But I'm no deity. I'm only another individual, like you, or Storra, or anyone who comes this way."

Ebbanai gestured understanding. "We know that." Observing

that her mate was handling the situation unusually well, Storra kept silent. "So do most of those eights and eights who keep coming, who are even now camped patiently and hopefully on our land. But others do not. Or deep down they know the truth, but want to believe otherwise. It makes them feel better to think that they are seeking help from a god. Isn't that what religion is for? To comfort the insecure?" He straightened a little more. "I know that when I am out alone in the shallows, casting my net in the dark of night while hoping for calm weather and a good catch, I frequently pray to Vadakaa for aid. I do this even though I have never seen him, or a recognizable manifestation of him." He nodded in the alien's direction.

"To many Dwarra you, Flinx, have become far more real than these traditional, far more mysterious and unapproachable gods."

"There is no harm in it." Storra finally spoke up. "What does it matter what those who come seeking help think of you, so long as you help them? Isn't that what's important? Your help, and what results from it?"

"I don't know." For simple country folk, his hosts were proving surprisingly adept at argument. Or maybe, he thought, they just did not want to let go of a good thing. It did not take him long to come to a conclusion. One he probably ought to have implemented some time ago. And would have, he told himself, if his innate compassion for the needy had not kept him from putting it off.

"I'm leaving," he told them abruptly.

His hosts were clearly agitated. While he could perceive their distress, his Talent was not precise enough to let him identify the reasons behind it. It might be the money, or they might genuinely be sorry to see him go. Or it could be a combination of those factors, he told himself, or something else entirely of which he was serenely unaware. It didn't matter. He'd become so involved in helping the genuinely needy natives that he'd let slip the reason for stopping at this world in the first place. His motives for becoming so involved with the locals might be sincere, but it was becoming clear to him now that his rationale was slipshod.

Besides, the *Teacher* had informed him that the necessary repairs were almost completed. Even if he wanted to remain longer, to help more of the needy, it was time to go. Destiny had placed a greater claim on his time.

"But Flinx," Storra protested, gesturing toward the front of the domed dwelling, "what about all the others? All those who have trekked here from towns and provinces distant and difficult to reach? Can you just walk away from them?"

"I have no choice," he told her firmly. "While I might personally like to stay, I have important business elsewhere." A cosmic wild-goose chase, he thought to himself. But one to which he was committed. "Others have placed prior demands on my—help. I have to go."

Was their interest in him so great that they might try to restrain him? He doubted it. Of all the Dwarra he had met and dealt with, his hosts were more familiar with his capabilities than all the others combined. Besides, as he had just learned, they had apparently done very well out of hosting him. They should have nothing to complain about.

"Well then, if your mind is made up . . . ," Storra began. Before she could finish, Ebbanai trundled forward, extending all eight gripping flanges in addition to his Sensitives.

"We were proud to help you when you hurt your leg," the Dwarra net-caster exclaimed, "and proud to have been able to help you help other less fortunate ones of our kind. We wish you well in your future journeying, and may your net always come back to you full."

Following Ebbanai's brave and honest declaration, the contrast in emotional reaction between male and female, Flinx noted silently, was almost comical. Neither wanted to see him go, but for an empath like himself who could read the emotions of others, there was no mistaking which of them was the more perturbed by his announcement.

"Close the grounds to new arrivals," he told them both. "I'll attend to those who are already here. But no more. No new cases, no more supplicants. Then I'll be on my way." Reaching up with one hand to absently stroke the back of Pip's gleaming, triangular head, he smiled. "I've enjoyed my stay here, and I feel like I've done some good. Now it's time I was on my way, if only to put a stop to this ridiculous 'cult' before it has a chance to grow and do real damage. If the Dwarra are going to venerate gods, it's important that they stick to their own."

With that, he turned and left the room, heading back to the part of the barn that had been modified to serve as his quarters. Only after she was sure he was gone did Storra turn to her mate.

"What did you have to go and wish him farewell for? Couldn't you see that he still feels sorry for the sick who have come? With the right words and emotions, we might have been able to persuade him to stay longer among us."

Ebbanai frequently deferred to his mate's judgment, but not this time. "He is determined to go. Didn't you hear? He has other commitments. Better he should leave with our blessings than with us clawing at his ankles, begging him to remain. At least this way, he will depart with good feelings on both sides. Maybe that will induce him to return someday." Turning slightly, he reached toward her with his Sensitives. She remained where she was, but jerked hers back. "Or did you have thoughts of trying to hold him forcibly?" He felt compelled to ask the question even as he feared the possible answer.

"Thoughts, perhaps," she admitted. "But they were never more than thoughts. Even if we could separate him from his devices, we would still have to find a way to deal with that flying creature of his. And we don't even know what it can do, except that Flinx said it was poisonous." Her gaze, like her thoughts, shifted back in the direction of the departed alien. "Perhaps you are right, mate-mine. Let him go freely, in hopes that someday he may come back."

Ebbanai gestured agreeably. "It is the best course to take. The only course to take, I think. I am glad you concur."

But in his hearts, her mate knew that once Flinx was gone, it was most unlikely they would ever see the alien again. Unlike her, unlike the majority of his fellow Dwarra, the net-caster had spent too many long nights standing alone in the shallows of the sea, staring up at the stars. He had sometimes tried to count them, but there were too many for him.

Though probably not for someone like the Visitant Flinx, for whom they were the home he was now in a hurry to return to.

The priest Baugarikk was not pleased. In the Sanctuary in central Wullsakaa, he had squatted and brooded for some time now on what ought to be done. The possibilities were many, but whichever was chosen, it could only lead to one outcome.

Acolyte Kredlehken smoothed his swirling, heavily embroidered robes down over his legs. He had attended the High Priest for more than a year and thought he knew him well. But until now, he had never imagined the intensity with which the elder Dwarra could focus his mental energies. That the gods did not respond directly was unsurprising. As he had learned, they tended to make their needs known in ways that were as subtle and mysterious as their origin.

There was nothing subtle or mysterious about the High Priest's meditations. They stemmed from, and related directly to, the arrival outside Metrel City of an alien being. Though it insisted it was not a god, but only another creature like the Dwarra themselves, more and more simple folk were coming to believe that the creature's own denials were intended to dissuade them from worship, and to conceal its true nature. By Rakshinn, they would call it a god and honor it as such even as it denied such tribute!

The problem was that while they were doing so, they were paying less and less attention to Rakshinn himself and his Holy Eight. The result was that not only was proper veneration down at the Sanctuary, but so were collections. It was on this, and related matters, that the High Priest Baugarikk had been meditating for so many days.

His superior had been so quiet and introspective for so long that Kredlehken was nearly startled out of his ceremonial slippers when Baugarikk suddenly rose and turned on him.

"Acolyte!"

"Yes, Most Holy One. I am here." Kredlehken spread both arms and all four forearms wide, inclining his Sensitives toward his superior in a gesture that was both respectful and reverent.

"I know what has to be done." The High Priest's eyes were not especially wide, but they were ablaze with assurance. "It was conveyed to me by the minions of Rakshinn himself!"

"Most Revered!" Kredlehken hissed softly. Who could doubt the holiness of the High Priest, who communicated directly with the gods? "What are we to do?"

Placing a pair of left flanges on the acolyte's shoulder, Baugarikk turned the younger cleric and led him out of the sanctuary. Together, they mounted the steps that led from the subterranean meditation chamber back up into the somber but well-lit hallways of the main temple.

"This creature that has come among us is clearly an abomination. It turns the faithful from the path of righteousness and beguiles them with tricks and subterfuges. In order for all to be returned to the Right Path, the falsity of the being's reality must be shown to them in a manner that none will be able to deny."

Kredlehken was gesturing enthusiastically. "Of course, Holy One. And how is this to be done?"

"Rakshinn has told me. At hearts, it is really a simple matter. The people must be shown that the Visitant is not divine, but exactly what it claims to be: a mere mortal like themselves, meddling in and muddling the ways of the world. While it may have access to science more advanced than our own, it is not something to be worshipped. It must be restored to the ranks of the ordinary."

"By what method is this to be achieved, Holy One?" the acolyte inquired earnestly.

"By the method most direct and incontrovertible. The Visitant must be killed. Only by its death will the people be convinced of its mortality, and that it is not, and never was, a thing to be worshipped—a thing that dared take them away from the Right Path of Rakshinn and the Holy Eight."

Kredlehken halted beneath a famous mosaic of Toryyin, the Fifth of Eight, and swallowed hard. "Holy One, it is known that the Visitant possesses great powers of healing. It is also whispered that it has at its disposal the means to defend itself from any hostility that might be directed toward its person."

Baugarikk gestured knowingly. "Of course such things will be whispered. And what is the source of these whisperings? Why, the Visitant itself! If it can convince everyone that it is untouchable, it need not trouble itself with the means to protect itself. It is an old and wise ploy; one apparently known to creatures other than ourselves."

"The stratagem does not invalidate the original claim," acolyte Kredlehken was compelled to point out.

"There is one way to find out." Baugarikk was unrelenting. Once again, he placed a pair of flanges on the younger cleric's shoulder. "The honor falls to you, Kredlehken, to ascertain the reality of this troublesome visitor. You will be provided with everything necessary to carry out your task. I have been in touch with those who honor and revere Rakshinn in Pakktrine Unified. They have agreed to provide us with whatever aid we may request. Subsequent to the successful completion of this action, I daresay you will find yourself swiftly promoted from the ranks of the acolytes to that of full priest, with all the responsibilities and honors that implies and entails."

Though nervous, Kredlehken had never been one to shirk his sacred duty—which was just one reason why the High Priest had chosen him for the task. And if the zealous youth was to fail, well, other means could be tried, and what was the loss to the temple of one acolyte, more or less?

"Do not fear," Baugarikk assured him. "Rakshinn will be with you, and the rest of the Eight, and all the resources that the temple can muster. You go forth only to dispatch a dishonest pretender, not a god. Its death will restore the full faith of the people, and return them to the temple that is their true spiritual home. I know you will not fail."

"I will not," Kredlehken exclaimed forcefully. "Rakshinn himself will guide my sword!"

The High Priest looked thoughtful. "Better to use barbolts. Mortal as it is, the truth of the creature's physical abilities is no rumor. There is no need to engage it at close quarters. Like doctrine, extermination is better carried off when conducted from a distance."

CHAPTER

11

Ebbanai wished Storra had come with him. Or better still, Flinx and his winged companion. The net-caster had been unable to sleep the previous night for contemplating what he was expected to do this morning. Only a little could go right, while a great many things could go wrong.

Without volunteering to join him, Storra had done her best to bolster his spirits. "You yourself are the one who kept saying this day was inevitable. Now that it's here, you must have the strength to see it through."

He gestured emphatically. "Why can't you see it through with me? Why can't Flinx?"

Soothing noises bubbled from her mouth. "You know very well why. Flinx must minister to the ills of the last group of supplicants, and one of us must be here to attend to him, and to our home." She eyed him sternly. "You have been the one who has first dealt with the arrival of every group, Ebbanai. You are practiced at it, you are good at it."

"I know, I know." He locked Sensitives with her. As was often the case, her emotions reflected a familiar deep, underlying affection that belied her demanding words. "I will go and do it." He turned for the doorway. "But if I have not returned by sunfall, you might come and have a look for what's left of me."

"Don't be so negative," she chided him. "A few words spoken, perhaps a few questions to be answered, and the thing will be done." She let out a soft whistle of resignation. "All good things must come to an end, I suppose. But you are right, mate-mine. We have done well out of this."

"Very much so." I just hope I live to enjoy some of it, he thought to himself as he exited the house.

Maybe he was overreacting. If all went well, it would transpire as Storra had said: a few words, and done. But as he made his way up the slope and down the much-improved dirt path that led toward the main road, his apprehension grew rather than diminished.

The yard was largely empty now. All that remained were the temporary quarters of the final group of supplicants. Flinx would be done with the last of them by tomorrow. Ebbanai found that he would be sorry to see the alien go, and not just because it would mean an end to the highly profitable enterprise he and Storra had put together based on his presence. The strange but benevolent creature had been a part of their lives for a number of eight-days now, and aside from the fortune he had brought their way, the net-caster had grown used to his company. He had learned much from their visitor, knowledge that was unknown to the most venerable scholars. Quite a step up for a simple net-caster.

He glanced skyward. Beyond lay thousands of stars and, if the visitor was to be believed, dozens of races whose achievements and intelligence frequently exceeded those of the Dwarra. Flinx had described many of the wonderful places he had been. But for all his wisdom, and all his travels, Ebbanai did not envy him.

No matter how hard the Visitant tried to project otherwise, Ebbanai could not escape the feeling that his estimable and friendly guest was not happy.

His thoughts and his leather-shod foot-flanges had carried him close to the tollgate that barred the entrance to the homestead. It was a barrier in import only. Anyone who wished to could simply go around it. No one did, because it was widely known that without permission from the landowners, from Storra and himself, they would never get to see the Visitant. What would happen now, when he delivered his announcement?

He would know shortly.

Though it was quite early, a sizable crowd had already gathered and was waiting impatiently for the gatekeeper's arrival. Bent and twisted elders wrestled for position with anxious young families. Solitary hopefuls whose skin flaps barely had the energy to rise and fall clung to the flanks of the line. Wealthy suppliants fidgeted in their wagons or on their individual mounts, annoyed at having to wait their turn like commoners. Ebbanai had dealt with them all equally. Today would be no different.

Except that it would be for the last time.

The restless buzz and bubbling faded as his appearance was noted and his approach remarked upon. He halted just behind the wooden gate, knowing that any protection it afforded him from the crowd was purely symbolic. There was no point in delaying. When the crowd had quieted enough for those in back to hear, he thrust his Sensitives straight up to indicate he needed their attention.

He'd given considerable thought to just what to say and exactly how to say it. Storra had helped. In the end, both decided it was not the sort of thing one could drag out in hopes of muting the impact. Like butchering a dead and dried-out baryeln, it was a thing best done quick.

"The Visitant cannot see you." The response he and Storra had expected to this pronouncement was loud objecting, and he had prepared for that. Instead, an eerie silence settled over the throng of would-be suppliants. It was not a good sign. Not knowing what else to do, not having anything else to do, he continued as planned.

"He is leaving," the net-caster declared, raising his voice slightly despite the hush. Raising both right forearms, he pointed all four flanges skyward. "To return to his home among the stars. He feels that his work here is done." Improvising, he concluded, "He hopes one day to perhaps return to us to continue the work he has begun." With that, he turned to leave.

It didn't work.

The protests began almost immediately, rising rapidly in frequency and volume.

"How can the Visitant leave now, when my family and I have been waiting here for a two-day?"

"What of my infirm son? Who will help him now . . . ?"

"I paid good money to gain this place in line . . . and for what?"

"See here, net-caster," exclaimed a tall, thick merchant as he stuck his head out from the depths of his ornate travel wagon, "who are you to tell us what the Visitant will and will not do? I demand to speak to him myself."

"Yes, yes!" insisted a female poorer in worldly goods but not in determination as she pushed herself to the forefront. "I have come all the way from Derethell Province to seek a cure for my blind nephew, and I will not be denied by such as you!"

"The Visitant, the Visitant!" As the crowd took up the refrain Ebbanai, even in the absence of physical contact with any of their twisting, coiling Sensitives, could see emotions beginning to boil among them as ferociously as one of Storra's spiced stews.

"Didn't you hear me?" he yelled. "He's going home!" he added, raising his voice as much as he could while continuing to back up. "Don't you think even the Visitant has a right to do that?"

"What does a god need with a home?" someone shouted from the center of the crowd. At any moment, it threatened to turn into an aimless mob. "His home is wherever *he* happens to be."

"Also," an increasingly desperate Ebbanai informed them, "he is out of many of the medicines he dispenses, and needs to replenish them and do maintenance on his instruments."

"Instruments!" The young female was so angry her Sensitives

were quivering as if a current were being passed through them. "What does a sanctified one need with instruments?"

From within the flamboyant coach, a well-dressed oldster with wrinkling skin flaps appeared. "All this talk of science is a cover, a mask, for the miracles the Visitant performs! We all know that such things are a fantasy, to mollify the rabble, and that the holy one's cures are the result of spells and magic."

Rising from his driving squat, the coach's tethet wrangler turned angrily on his employer. "Either way, my money is as good as yours, and the Visitant as likely to heal my bad leg as your inconstant bowels!" Louder argument between master and mastered ensued, which culminated in several in the crowd taking up the driver's side. They started to rock the coach with an eye toward putting it over on its side. On the other side of the vehicle, adults and Nursets with offspring scrambled to get out of the way. Rising shouts of anger were joined by the first screams of panic.

"The Visitant should see to the common folk first!" someone was yelling indignantly.

"I hear he takes those with the most money before any others, no matter how serious their afflictions!" exclaimed another angrily.

Tightly curled flanges formed smooth, fingerless fists. Blows began to fall among disputants, their resentment fueled by the fear that in spite of all their hopes and demands, the net-caster's words might hold true. None in the throng was ready to accept that they might have come all this way, with hopes so high, for nothing. A loud crash came from the center of the developing mob, where the fancy travel wagon had finally been tipped over. Still yoked to the vehicle, the three in-line tethets that drew it began to kick out with their short but powerful legs. Fresh injuries were added to those the supplicants had brought with them.

Momentarily forgotten, Ebbanai wisely took the moment to turn and run.

Would any of them follow? Given the crowd's overwhelming need to entreat Flinx, it seemed almost inevitable. For at least some, their desperate need to seek his aid far exceeded their fear of how an angry Visitant might react to their uninvited attention.

Had he handled it badly? Ebbanai thought wildly as he raced back down the dirt track. What else might he have done, what else could he have said? He and Storra had worked out what he would say to the crowd beforehand, and his words had not proven up to the task. A glance backward showed the first supplicants surging around the simple gate. The weight of the mob pushed others forward. Splintering sounds reached him as the gate crumbled beneath their combined weight. As he increased his stride, he could hear individual voices clearly: an unholy mix of prayer, hope, and anger. He had no idea how to cope with such fury.

He wondered if the Visitant would.

Flinx sensed the mob long before he could hear it. He had finished attending to the injured individual who was not only the last patient of the day, but the final Dwarra set to receive medical attention at his hands. Simple folk, the last of them filed out of the baryeln barn chatting contentedly among themselves. As usual, one of his hosts was waiting to escort him back to the house for something to eat. This afternoon, it was Storra.

He had done well here, he convinced himself. Had done good things for deserving people, and damn the Commonwealth's aged, obscure first-contact policies. With the *Teacher*'s repairs completed, there were only final checks to be run on newly refurbished components. Then he could depart this interesting world and resume his seemingly impossible but committed search for the wandering Tar-Aiym artifact.

Storra was talking to him, murmuring something about having prepared a special meal for his last night among them, when he halted on the open ground halfway between the domed house and the barn. In his mind, all had been peaceful, calm, and at ease—until now. For the first time since he had stepped out onto the surface of Arrawd, the emotional aether accessed by his Talent was genuinely disturbed. For the first time, the general tranquillity he had come to savor every morning when he awoke was unsettled. His Talent sensed anger, resentment, fear, and fury. The serene emotions that usually surrounded him, emanating from Storra and his recent patients and the others who worked at the homestead, were suddenly inundated by a thundercloud of hatred and dread, panic and anxiety.

Most disconcerting of all, he perceived that he was at the center of it all.

Storra's Sensitives dipped toward him. Her expression reflected concern as she looked from his face into the east and back again. "What is it, Flinx—what's wrong?"

He did not reply; just kept staring into the distance. Before long, a single figure appeared, running hard in their direction. It plunged down the slope so fast Flinx feared for the runner's safety. Gasping, Ebbanai pulled up alongside his mate. The glances he cast in Flinx's direction were revealing, though Flinx did not have to meet them. He already knew what was coming.

Yelling, screaming, praying, fighting among themselves, the mob that had shattered the gate and the protocol it represented crested the low rise and came marching down the hillside in an angry wave of the needy. Heading for the house, they swerved to their right the instant several of their number caught sight of the Visitant standing there. Her confidence shorn in the face of the advancing multitude, Storra joined her mate in taking refuge well behind Flinx.

From his shoulders, Pip launched skyward as the seething crowd slowed. Having gained their destination, none of them knew how to achieve their goal. Desperate for and desiring of his help, they realized they did not know how to force him to provide it. They surged back and forth, from side to side, pushing and shoving as they muttered uncertainly among themselves.

Flinx faced them squarely. His head did not hurt, but his stomach was churning. He was the cause of all this. In doing good, he had raised unreasonable expectations. The more Dwarra he had helped, the more had come seeking his help. They would not be denied. Nor would dozens, perhaps hundreds, of others who were presently making the long trek to the lonely peninsula and its fabled homestead.

He saw clearly now. For every native he had helped, for every injured individual he had healed, there would be a dozen or more he would have no choice but to leave behind untouched. Over time, their disappointment would turn to bitterness. He would depart revered by some, but hated by far more. In his desire to lend a hand, he had miscalculated.

Fool, he reproached himself as he confronted the crowd. Experienced but still youthful. He should have seen it coming. Bran Tse-Mallory and Truzenzuzex would never have made such a mistake. This is what comes of trying to help those who don't have the background and maturity to understand the nature and limitations of that help, he thought cynically.

Well, what was done, was done. Come whatever, he was leaving. Leaving to help find a solution to an infinitely greater, more threatening problem. He had done what he could for as many of the locals as he could, only to have misjudged the eventual results.

"Help us," a crippled female in the forefront of the crowd implored him. Her words were fraught with desperation, but her emotions were seething with anger. He had better *not* leave without helping her. A similar mix of need and rage fueled the feelings of the rest of the crowd.

Alien or not, he reflected, it seemed that every individual of every sentient species had a public face and a private one. It was his ability and curse to be able to see both simultaneously.

"I can't help any more of you," he told them, and they quieted so as to be able to hear his words. "I've helped as many as I could. Now it's time for me to go. I have work of my own to do."

A pair of young males stumbled forward and, awkwardly, prostrated themselves. "What hurries a god, who can make and take his own time?" declared the elder who had accompanied them. "Only an evil, uncaring god would refuse aid to the most needy!"

The rush of inimical emotion that flashed through the mob threatened to make Flinx physically ill.

"I am not a god!" he yelled at them, communicating the denial with all the force of the fluency he had acquired during the preceding weeks. "I am only a mortal being like yourselves. A traveler with work to do who stopped here for a short time. While here, I ended up helping a few of you—and then more, and still more." Turning slightly, he glared back at Storra, who under that furious alien gaze tried to shrink out of sight behind her mate.

He looked back at the seething, desperate crowd. "I've helped as many as I could, as many as was feasible. Now *I have to go*. You have to let me go."

Their fury and frustration was an emotional storm in his head. The wonderful, matchless peace he had known since landing on Arrawd was gone. Shattered, blasted away by the desperation of the sick and injured, and by their selfishness and individual need. He had found paradise, and in trying to improve a small portion of it, had forever ruined it for himself.

And to think, he told himself as he kept a careful watch on the crowd, that I once actually thought of settling down here. He had underestimated reality and overestimated his environs. Like a quantum state, his presence had disturbed his surroundings to such a degree that they would never be the same.

"Heal us!" a gravid female yelled from the front of the crowd.

"Please put right my offspring!" howled another as she pushed Nurset and damaged progeny forward.

It was as if they hadn't heard, or comprehended, a word he had said. Those in front began to surge forward, urged on by the press of disheartened bodies behind. Terrified, no longer resolute, Storra clung for protection to her equally alarmed mate.

There were too many, Flinx saw immediately. Too many, too close, to try to influence with his Talent. Fortunately, albeit reluctantly, he had access to resources other than his unpredictable ability.

He pulled his gun.

The beamer had been set to kill. Now he adjusted it and pointed it at the crowd. Those in front hesitated, pushing against those shoving from behind. All eyes focused on the device held in the alien's strange hand. It did not look like something for making magic. It looked solid and functional, like a piece of well-maintained tethet tack.

Muttering to himself, perhaps not even fully aware of what he was doing, the elder who had placed the mantle of evil on the Visitant's head took a couple of steps forward. Swinging the muzzle of the beamer around, Flinx triggered the weapon. The tip glowed softly, briefly.

Suddenly the oldster was jumping and swatting at his simple raiment. As flames began to start from the fabric, he frantically tore at the fasteners and flung the burning pieces onto the ground. A few blisters began to appear on his sensitive, exposed skin where the epidermal flaps had not closed. As the crowd gawked at this exhibition, Flinx adjusted the strength of his handgun's output a second time.

"This weapon heated that person's clothing and skin. I have now set it to kill. I've spent these past many eight-days attending to the sick and carrying out healing among your people. Please don't force me to do the opposite to any of you."

The silence that ensued fell over the homestead like a heavy cloak. Then, in twos and threes, in family groups and as individuals, the mob began to break up, bits and pieces of it flaking off and shuffling back the way they had come, with the majority following in a downcast, disconsolate body. The emotions they generated threatened to eradicate the memory of all the good and grateful feelings that had been projected by those Flinx had helped.

As an agitated Pip settled herself back down on her master's shoulders, Ebbanai and Storra moved up to rejoin the visitor. Though outwardly concerned for her guest, Storra's feelings as she eyed the weapon reflected an unmitigated greed she could not suppress.

I have definitely stayed here too long, Flinx thought wearily. He had not stopped here seeking a refuge and, despite his initial impressions of Arrawd and its people, it was now clear he had not found one. There was no such place for him, anywhere. There was only the need to do what he could to try to save others: the few he could count as his friends, and the billions he could not.

He had nearly forgotten all about his driving youthful desire to try to ascertain the identity and truth of his parentage. Nearly, but not entirely.

"They are ungrateful."

Turning, he saw Ebbanai staring back at him. No hint of falsehood or deception colored the humble net-caster's observation. He was genuinely apologetic for the behavior of his kind.

"You know that I can't stay here, forever healing the sick among you." Flinx's anger faded as he spoke to his host. "Even if I wished to do so, I have a limited supply of certain items that my ship can't continue to perpetually synthesize."

"You have done more than enough for the Dwarra," Storra put in. "They should be grateful for the time you have spent, and the efforts you have made on our behalf. Many have benefited."

Not the least of whom have been you and your partner, Flinx added silently. But if Storra was more overtly acquisitive than her modest mate, she was no less honest in her thanks. He mumbled something about having tried to do his best and turned away, heading for the house.

Ebbanai's confusion was reflected in his words as well as his feelings. "But—you said that you are leaving, friend Flinx?"

"First thing in the morning." It was late, and he didn't feel like walking in the dark all the way back to where the *Teacher* was waiting for him.

He could have called out the skimmer, but that vision, at least, of Commonwealth technology he had managed to keep from the sight of the locals. Also, he was tired from his final day's work of healing and from the unpleasant confrontation with the irate crowd. Nor did he relish leaving Arrawd under cover of night, speeding away inside the skimmer's protective bubble. It smacked of demoralized flight.

No, he would leave as he had arrived: under his own power, crossing the peninsula on his own two feet. Could he at least hope for a last good night's sleep?

Ebbanai gestured with two forearms in the direction of the path that led eastward toward the junction with the main road. "I don't think any of them will be back to bother you, friend Flinx. The demonstration of your powers was instructive, and the threat sufficient to discourage even the most persistent supplicants."

Arrive with questions, stay to help, depart on the murmur of a threat. As he entered the pleasant house, made fragrant with expensive local perfumes paid for with money extorted from hopeful travelers by his ever-helpful hosts, he determined to leave future first contacts to those Commonwealth teams specially trained for the purpose. He did not feel he had done too badly, but he certainly could have done better.

Ebbanai was right. None of those anxious supplicants he had so summarily dismissed dared return to risk the god's wrath, and he slept better than he expected.

CHAPTER

12

Morning saw his spirits improved. Now that the decision to leave had been made, and the memory of those he had been forced to turn away had receded somewhat in his mind, he was able to eat with some enjoyment the last native morning meal Storra—or, rather, Storra's new servants—prepared for him. He did not even object when she pleaded to join her mate in escorting him back to his vessel. She had made her desire to see the *Teacher* plain on more than one occasion. It was a simple enough request, a last request, and he decided to accede. Despite her avaricious nature, she had only done what she believed to be best for herself and her mate. If her motivations had been slightly less than altruistic, she had nonetheless been genuinely solicitous of his welfare.

They started out early, the two Dwarra packing food and drink for their return journey, Flinx doubly eager to be on his way now that the moment to depart had come. So much time had he spent on Arrawd and so focused had he become on healing its ill and injured that it was hard to believe he was actually leaving. None of the new servants his hosts had hired with their semi-ethical gains bothered to see them off. They had work to do.

As the trio crested the first rise Flinx glanced briefly back at the homestead. There the domed house, now much transformed by expensive improvements, there the baryeln barn, beyond it the small garden where Storra grew basic foodstuffs. It was a far more domesticated view than many of the other alien landscapes he had trod: Midworld and Jast, Longtunnel and Terra, Moth and New Riviera.

New Riviera. His thoughts went out to that world, though they could not reach it, that was home now to close friends and to one woman in particular. So very far away. Taking a deep breath, he filed Arrawd with them in his mental catalog of worlds visited and turned away, setting his gaze and his stride toward the center of the peninsula. He had some dedicated spatial wandering ahead of him, and would not see any of those other worlds until it was concluded.

The disappointed ailing masses of Arrawd left him and his unpretentious escort alone, but the wildlife of Dwarra seemed reluctant to let him go.

"Vuuerlia," Ebbanai told him as a flock of the creatures wafted through the waist-high growth around them. The inoffensive flying creatures stayed aloft more by gliding and riding the air currents off the nearby ocean than by flapping their paper-thin, meter-wide wings. Though the pale, ivory-hued appendages were so thin as to be translucent, Ebbanai informed Flinx that the membranous tissue was strong enough to cope with even the occasional gales that blew across the peninsula. The front of each long, slender brown animal was tipped with a single piercing bill that was half the length of the creature itself, while the aft end terminated in a pair of flaring tails. One vertical and the other horizontal, they helped to steer and stabilize the creature in the roughest weather. In their appearance the vuuerlia were elegant and angular—not unlike the Dwarra themselves.

The three trekkers stood and waited while the flock of nearly a hundred passed over and around them. This gave Flinx time to

observe how the creatures would fly as close to the tops of the surrounding vegetation as possible, skimming the crests of the grass-
like growths as they used their long, pointed bills to pick off any
plant-dwellers foolish or unlucky enough to be lingering near the top
of the sward. Once it had its prey pinned, the vuuerlia would flip it
into the air and catch it neatly in the small, surprisingly flexible mouths
at the base of each bill. It was like watching a flock of anorexic
hawks attack in slow motion.

The vuuerlia had exceptionally sharp eyes, or some other means
of perceiving what was in their path. Except for the occasional brief
brush from a feather-light wing tip, Flinx and his companions had
no contact with the flock that glided over and around them. Not that
a direct collision was anything to fear. He doubted the heaviest
vuuerlia weighed more than a kilogram, and flew no faster than he
could run.

As for Pip, she delighted in the opportunity to swoop over,
around, and through the flock, disconcerting the placid creatures
with her slashing, brightly colored presence. Utterly alien to their experience, the vuuerlia did not know what to make of the winged, serpentine shape that darted through and among them, teasing the
uncertain and intercepting the leaders, only to keep just out of reach
as they made futile attempts to stab her with their bills.

"Once again, I marvel at the agility of your pet," Storra commented as she watched the display.

"She is that," Flinx agreed, "when she's not sleeping, which is
most of the time."

Pushing forward as the last of the vuuerlia coasted past, he had
covered another ten meters or so when he suddenly pulled up short.
Ebbanai came up alongside the alien and gazed into his face. During
the past many eight-days, he had learned to recognize certain human
expressions by connecting Flinx's words with the concurrent distor-
tion of his facial muscles. But he did not recognize the one that was
featured on his alien friend's face now. He waited for it to change,
and it did not. This was in itself, the net-caster felt, significant.

"Friend Flinx, is something wrong?" As Ebbanai spoke, he noted that Pip came rocketing back from where she had been playing with the disappearing flock of vuuerlia, showing speed the net-caster and his mate had not seen before. Whatever had brought their visitor to an abrupt halt, it was clearly serious.

Flinx proceeded to confirm this. "There are other Dwarra approaching. Many." He scanned the tops of the surrounding verdure. They had entered into a part of the peninsula where the grass-like growths, though still single-bladed, grew tree-high. "They are intent on," he added without the slightest change in tone, "killing. Whether just me or all of us I don't know."

A froth of bubbles and gargling issued from his companions. Not knowing what else to do, unable to see or hear the potential assassins the alien had somehow perceived, they moved closer to him. Ebbanai drew his longknife. It was all he and Storra had brought with them. What need was there for serious weapons on a stroll through their beloved peninsula, where potential dangers were few, far between, and most often encountered at night?

"Who are they?" Storra strained to see through the surrounding greenery.

"I don't know." Pip remained airborne, hovering a meter or so over Flinx's head. She had sensed the same approaching animosity as her master. "I can't perceive identities. Only emotions. Homicidal ones, in this instance." Reaching down, he drew his pistol, made sure it was still charged. If the feelings he was picking up were anything to go by, when those projecting them finally showed themselves there would be no time for demonstrations or illustrative examples of what his weapon could do. He was likely to need stopping power.

Why bother? a part of him wondered unexpectedly. Why not end it all here, now, today? This was as good a place and time as any. Put an end to all the wandering, internal conflict, and frustration. It was a mark of his depression that he would even entertain such a thought. It did not last. He couldn't let any locals kill him, he reasoned, even if he did welcome such an end. Could not, because if a discontented contingent of them were allowed to kill a beneficent "god," when word of what had happened spread to the wider population at large it could very well incite even more fighting and killing as those he had helped took up arms to take revenge on his killers. Reflecting on the possibilities inherent in such a demise, not for the first time he found himself marveling at the irony that underlay so much of his existence.

I can't even let myself be killed, because it wouldn't be the moral thing to do.

As he stood pondering the incongruity of it all, the emotions he was perceiving reached an intensity that reflected the proximity of their promulgators to his present position. Clad in conical clothing that covered their bodies from head to foot-flange, a dozen or so Dwarra burst from the surrounding vegetation. Like so many maniacal, multicolored pinwheels, they converged from two directions on the alien and his terrified companions. They were armed with long, thin, sharp-edged swords and clumsy but effective-looking hand weapons made of wood and metal.

Storra screamed "barbolts!" and fell over onto her side. Ebbanai replicated her desperate fall a moment later. His own emotions a disturbed fusion of dogged determination and sorrowful regret, Flinx raised his weapon and put a shot into the nearest attacker as that individual raised the device he was carrying.

The burst of energy made a neat hole in the center of the assailant's chest. A few tiny flames flickered from the front of his tapering attire where the blast had entered and from the back where it had exited. Ceremonial raiment smoking, the attacker crumpled to the ground like a collapsing building. At the same time, Pip dove toward another of the attackers and spat directly in his face. The corrosive venom had the same effect on the onrushing Dwarra as it did on any carbon-based tissue. Smoke immediately began to rise from where the toxin hit and began to eat away at the eyes and surrounding flesh. Screaming madly, an uncontrolled stream of bubbles emerging from his mouth, the struck assailant stumbled and staggered backward into the undergrowth from which he had emerged.

Taken together, these two defensive responses were more than sufficient to cause the dead assailants' companions to pause in their attack.

At his feet, collapsed in on themselves as much as their muscles could manage, Ebbanai and Storra were torn between watching their attackers and gazing in awe up at Flinx. Despite what he had casually told them about his ability to look after himself, until now that ability had only been buttressed by words. The disquieting demonstration of alien power, both technological and organic, found them eyeing him with an entirely new mind-set. For the first time since he had arrived at the homestead, they were afraid of him. More afraid than they had been when each of them had initially encountered him.

As a consequence, something had been lost, and even though he was preparing to depart Arrawd forever, Flinx was not happy about it.

Before he could depart, however, he still had a dangerous number of potential assassins to deal with. Overcoming their initial shock at seeing what the alien and its pet could do, they began to advance anew, urged on by their leader.

"For Rakshinn!" Kredlehken swallowed his fear as he strove to rally the other acolytes and their Pakktrinian allies. Trying to keep one eye on the murderous alien flying thing, he raised his barbolt. Fearsome or not, there was still only one of the two-legged aliens. It could only shoot one of them at a time. With luck, a barbolt or two might strike him. Once wounded, Kredlehken was certain the creature of flesh and blood could be finished off with ordinary swords.

As he took aim at another of the advancing attackers, Flinx was struggling with the same conundrum. If they all came at him in a rush, and fired together . . . should he dodge left, or right? Shoot the nearest of his assailants first, the biggest, or their apparent leader?

Unexpectedly, a flood of fresh emotions coursed through him. They were not his own, nor those of his two terrified companions, nor even those of his would-be assassins.

"FOR WULLSAKAA AND THE HIGHBORN!"

Whirling, he was just in time to see a host of armed Dwarra explode from among the tallest growths. Unlike his ceremoniously garbed attackers, these newcomers wore strips of metal and leather armor designed to protect their limbs and vital parts. Crested helmets with slits in front allowed their Sensitives to protrude freely. They wielded lances as well as different examples of the complex, pistol-like barbolts. The mounts they rode were like slimmed-down versions of the horned, heavy-bodied tethets whose appearance Flinx had grown accustomed to: similar in origin but an entirely different breed. These new animals were as greyhounds compared to mastiffs.

Ebbanai and Storra cowered at his feet, certain now that death was only moments away. High above the scene of battle Pip hovered uncertainly, reading her master's feelings for clues as to how to proceed. Flinx raised his pistol in the direction of the nearest of the new arrivals—and promptly lowered it. Their emotions were certainly murderous—but they were not directed toward him. Instead, they were channeled unmistakably, and gratefully, elsewhere.

Falling in among the conically clad assassins, the newcomers proceeded to spread havoc and death. Their attention diverted by the armored arrivals, the well-armed attackers managed to bring down two of the newcomers. Then, their number swiftly halved, the survivors scattered into the surrounding undergrowth. With single-minded determination, the majority of the newcomers went after them. The sounds of pursuit, and the grisly end to first one and then another, resounded from different locations within the tall foliage.

Those who had not joined in the pursuit approached Flinx. Recognizing the insignia they wore, and seeing that—so far, anyway—their rescuers meant them no harm, Ebbanai and Storra struggled to their feet. One of the newcomers immediately slipped off his steed, went up to her, and entwined his Sensitives with hers, then carried out the same exchange with her mate. Their sense of relief was immediate.

Dismounting with some difficulty due to his unusual bulk, the leader of the newcomers was panting audibly as he staggered over to

Flinx. As he did so he struggled to straighten his helmet, which had been knocked askew on his head during the battle.

"Your pardon," he wheezed. "Unfamiliar as I am with such martial exertions, I find myself more than a little out of breath." He started to extend his Sensitives before remembering yet again that in that regard the alien was lamentably disadvantaged.

Flinx eyed the speaker for a moment. Recognizing both the face and emotional state of the Dwarra confronting him, he holstered his pistol. Descending in a sharp spiral, Pip settled down on his right shoulder, her tail curling firmly around his neck.

"I know you. Teelin . . . ," Flinx quickly corrected himself. "Treappyn."

The counselor to His August Highborn Pyrrpallinda sucked in a long, deep breath. It helped. "As I said on the occasion of our previous parting, I hoped we should meet again—though I never could have imagined it would be under such shameful circumstances." Turning slightly, he gestured with a pair of flanges in the direction of the thick vegetation that had swallowed Flinx's attackers and the squad of Wullsakaan soldiers who were still pursuing them.

"The fanatics who attacked you are minions of a major deity who is popular throughout Wullsakaa and elsewhere. They dishonor their teachings with this cowardly attempt on your life."

Behind Flinx, Ebbanai and Storra listened to the words of the counselor and found themselves wishing they had chosen to remain behind and bid their otherworldly guest farewell from the reassuring confines of their own home. Now it was too late, and they found themselves involved with something that promised to be more awkward than simply seeing off disappointed would-be supplicants.

Flinx was genuinely puzzled. "Why would followers of a local divinity have anything against me?"

Though he of course did not comment on it, Treappyn marveled to himself at the naïveté of this supposed sophisticated visitor. "Why, they perceive you as competition for their Order. If worshippers switch their allegiance—not to mention their contributions—to another god, then their own deity and 'his' income suffer corre-spondingly."

"Income." Turning, Flinx glared at his hosts, mindful of the revenue they had acquired while supervising and "facilitating" ac-cess to his charitable exertions. A new expression had consumed the alien's visage. Ebbanai did not recognize this one, either, but decided right away that he did not like it.

"Fortunately," the counselor continued, "the Highborn has eyes and ears in many places." Once more he gestured in the direction taken by the majority of the stymied assassins. "We learned of this plot almost too late."

Flinx nodded, politely grateful. "I appreciate your help." As he spoke, another plaintive, whistling cry echoed over the foliage, indi-cating that yet one more unlucky servant of Rakshinn had been run to ground and summarily dealt with. "But I could have handled it. I can take care of myself."

"Without question, without question. None who know you would dare dispute that." Having no diplomatic alternative to agree-ment, Treappyn readily concurred with the alien, though he doubted even one as powerful as Flinx could have simultaneously coped with so many dedicated killers. "Still, as an honored and respected guest in our country, your well-being was of considerable concern to all of us."

Despite the well-meaning counselor's assurances, all Flinx could think of was that a number of natives had met untimely deaths be-cause of his presence on this world. That they had fully intended to kill him did not alter that realization. Clearly, his continued presence here was complicating local relationships in ways he had not, and could not, have foreseen, and the sooner he was on board the *Teacher* and on his way, the better it would be for all concerned. He said as much to Treappyn. To his surprise, this declaration was met with less than enthusiastic agreement.

"Actually, friend Flinx," the counselor responded, "I have been instructed to ask that you return with me to Metrel, as the guest of the

Highborn himself. Originally, this invitation was to be extended so that you might continue your good works there, where many might hope to be the beneficiaries of your miraculous ministrations."

"I'm done doing that." Now that his would-be assassins had been seen to, Flinx was growing impatient to be on his way. Reflecting his eagerness, Pip fidgeted on his shoulder, partly unfurling and then collapsing her brightly colored wings. "I've helped as many as I thought I reasonably could and now I have obligations of my own to carry out." To emphasize his determination, he took a step forward.

A visibly anxious Treappyn scuttled quickly to stay in front of him. Interestingly, the soldiers who had remained with him and several of those who had gone in pursuit of assassins and had now returned shifted their positions accordingly.

What now? Flinx wondered as he halted. Over the years, it had become an all-too-common thought.

"Note that in reference to this invitation I said *originally*," the visibly uncomfortable counselor murmured. "Subsequent to that intention, events have occurred that have forced a change not only in the nature of the invitation, but in the reasoning behind it. Urgency and not wishfulness now guide the Highborn's appeal. It is no longer a question of whether you can come back with me. You *must* come back with me."

Hearing this, Ebbanai and Storra tried to edge their way out of the small clearing. If they could just get into the taller vegetation behind them, the net-caster thought worriedly, they could slip away without being noticed. Unfortunately, there were a couple of soldiers standing between them and welcoming obscurity. In the absence of applicable orders, the soldiers blocked the flight of the net-caster and his mate. Like it or not, they were caught up in whatever was to come.

Flinx eyed the counselor, studied the attentive, well-armed soldiers. On his shoulder, Pip shifted as if preparing to take to the sky. Reaching up, he placed a gentling hand on her body between head and wings, indicating that the time for such things was not yet.

"Must?" he repeated. "I'm flattered, I suppose, that your leader wants to see me so badly. Why? Is he, or someone close to him, seriously ill?"

Pleading for the alien's understanding, Treappyn spread his four forearms wide, forming an interesting X-shaped pattern in the air of the clearing. "There is an illness afoot, yes, but one that afflicts all of Wullsakaa. The realm, may I remind you, that has been your home ever since your arrival on our world.

"Wullsakaa is under attack. Even as we speak, Metrel itself is threatened with siege by the armies of not just one but two long-established rivals: Jebilisk, and Pakktrine Unified. We need your help, venerable visitor from the skies."

It was not the explanation Flinx had expected. While he was distressed by the news, as he would have been at the announcement of any warfare, it did not change anything.

"I'm sorry to hear that, Treappyn, and I wish you and your people well in their defense of their land, but it still has nothing to do with me—and I'm still leaving. Your internal disputes have nothing to do with me." He took another step forward.

For a second time, Treappyn and his troops moved to intercept his path. "Your pardon, friend Flinx, but in this instance, they do."

Now he found himself confused as well as angry. "I don't follow you, Treappyn."

Looking thoroughly embarrassed, the counselor forced himself to meet the alien's unblinking eyes. *"Ah-humm*—it seems that the Aceribb of Jebilisk and the Kewwyd of Pakktrine, knowing of your presence and your remarkable work among our people, are fearful of what you might do on behalf of Wullsakaa if you decide to move your base of operations from the country to the capital itself. These fears have motivated them to embark upon a ferocious and unannounced pre-emptive action." Taking a cautious step backward, he added, "So you see, friend Flinx, through no fault of your own, it seems that you are indeed the cause of this current conflict."

As he stood there, quietly stunned, it came home to Flinx more than ever that the minds who had promulgated those early, silly Commonwealth regulations governing contact with less advanced societies and species might after all have had some small idea of what they were doing, and good reasons for it.

"But I'm not going to Metrel, to help Wullsakaa's government or for any other reason!" He pointed eastward. "I'm going back to my ship, and by tonight I'll be so far away from Arrawd that even with their best telescopic instruments your people won't be able to find me."

Treappyn was gesturing with the patience of an experienced diplomat. "That is exactly what the despicable diseased servants of Jebilisk and Pakktrine would expect us to say, in order to put an end to their assault. All sides, you see, employ skillful deceit in the service of their goals."

Then I'll go to Metrel and tell them myself! Flinx mused angrily. No, wait—he couldn't do that. It was exactly what Treappyn and his conniving Highborn wanted. Once he was in the city, they would doubtless try to use him to further their own political ends.

He did not know whether he was more appalled or disgusted.

"I'm sorry about all this," he told the waiting Treappyn firmly. "I can see now that I never should have had any contact with your people. I should have stayed in my ship until it was ready to leave and, failing that, certainly shouldn't have remained among you to minister to as many of your sick and ill as I did. But I wanted to *help*—and I was curious." Not exactly the first time, he reflected, that his curiosity had gotten him into trouble.

"I'm leaving now. I'm more sorry than I can say that in only trying to do good, I seem to have ended up causing so much trouble. You'll just have to sort it all out among yourselves as best you can." Treappyn had told him that Wullsakaa and these other two political entities were traditional enemies. That suggested this was not the first time they had gone to war with one another, and probably would not be the last. His presence or absence among them would not change that. He felt a little better. He started forward.

Yet again, Treappyn and his soldiers moved to block the alien's path. This time, the soldiers seemed to hold their weapons a little more tightly. The business ends of a couple of loaded barbolts were not quite, but almost, aimed in Flinx's direction. What had started out as uncomfortable was rapidly metamorphosizing into ugly. He'd already shot and killed one native, while Pip had dispatched another. Was he going to be forced to do so again?

"All right," he told Treappyn. "If you'd rather I travel in the direction of Metrel, so be it."

The relief on the counselor's face was immense. Flinx did not add that he would be traveling in the direction of Metrel because that was the general direction of departure the *Teacher* was going to take from Arrawd. But before he could supervise his vessel's departure from this world, he had to get to it. Preferably without causing any more deaths among the locals.

"I am more pleased to hear you say that than you can begin to imagine," Treappyn told him honestly. Turning, he gestured to the commander of troops and barked orders. A riding tethet that had belonged to one of the two fallen soldiers was brought forward and made ready for the visitor.

"As soon as the last of our avenging troops returns from his work, we will start for Metrel." The counselor was now relaxed and at ease, feeling that he had successfully accomplished the uncertain.

"Your pardon, counselor, friend Flinx." With Storra following close behind him, Ebbanai approached. "What of us? What are we to do?"

Treappyn glanced at Flinx, who showed no reaction. With a dismissive flick of one left flange, the counselor gestured in the direction of the distant homestead.

"You have no part in this and may return to your home. Unless," he added, eyeing Ebbanai appraisingly, "your patriotic nature impels you to accompany us, to fight in defense of the city and your country folk."

The alacrity with which Ebbanai and his mate vanished into the surrounding verdure was something to behold.

Flinx was fiddling with the gear on his survival belt, alternately unfastening and checking one piece of equipment after another. At first Treappyn observed this activity with interest, but when nothing unusual manifested itself as a result, his attention rapidly waned.

"What do you expect me to do when we get to Metrel?" Flinx asked the counselor.

"Your reputation for remarkable deeds is known and feared among our attackers," Treappyn replied conversationally. "It may be that your presence alone will be enough to halt the assault. Failing that, the Highborn and his counselors presume that you have at your disposal the means to repel the invaders, or at least give them pause as to whether or not they should continue their offensive."

"Reasonable assumptions, on their part," Flinx agreed. As Treappyn turned to speak with his troop commander, Flinx turned away slightly, just enough so that the counselor did not notice him whispering ever so softly into the most recent piece of equipment he had removed from his belt. After speaking less than two short sentences into the com unit, he returned it to its resting place on his right hip.

Now there was nothing to do but wait.

"How *would* you go about discouraging the forces of Jebilisk and Pakktrine?" a curious Treappyn inquired, turning away from his commander of troops and back to the alien. "Could you perhaps start a great fire? Or cause large stones to be dropped on advancing soldiers?" His tone indicated that nothing would please him more than to witness exactly such a demonstration.

War, Flinx mused. With him as the cause. If he got away from this world in one piece, he vowed, he would never intrude on the affairs of less advanced species ever again. Stones and fire. That was the ultimate in weaponry the otherwise good-natured Treappyn could envision. Meanwhile, as soon as he departed Arrawd's system, Flinx's obligations required that he resume searching for a single ancient weapon capable of destroying entire worlds. Who rested more comfortably at night? he reflected. "Advanced" species such as his own and the thranx who were aware of the existence of such terrible devices, or species like the Dwarra who dwelled in ignorance of them?

His thoughts were distracted by a soft, distant humming. As he stood listening, it grew at once louder and more familiar. Blinking at the unfamiliar sound, it was clear that Treappyn heard it, too. So did the soldiers.

Responding to his terse, whispered emergency request, the *Teacher* had dispatched the skimmer with haste. The sleek, compact vehicle came in low and fast over the waving crests of the tallest growths. As contemporary surface transport went, it was a comparatively quiet machine. The Wullsakaan soldiers, however, had never heard or seen anything like it. It was not large, but in any case it was not the skimmer's size that impressed them. On a world where the most advanced form of aerial transport consisted of hesitant experiments with gas-filled balloons, the sight of something the size of a large freight wagon humming along with no visible means of support or propulsion several body lengths above the ground smacked more of magic than science, exactly as ancient human philosophers had predicted.

With the attention of his friend-captors momentarily distracted by its arrival, Flinx bolted for the oncoming, descending vehicle, utilizing the lesser gravity to cover the rapidly shrinking space between them in long, graceful, bounds. Pip stayed above him, providing cover where none was needed, as he pulled the small com unit from his belt and began to direct the transport.

Treappyn was torn. He liked the alien. It was clear to him now that Flinx was not going to come back to Metrel City voluntarily. But the counselor had his orders. And much as he would have liked to have traveled among and seen the other worlds the alien insisted populated the night sky, Flinx was not the person to whom Treappyn ultimately had to report. He raised his right forearms.

"Bring him down! But aim for the legs—the Highborn needs him alive!"

Galvanized out of the momentary trance into which the appearance of the skimmer had placed them, soldiers raised their weapons. Lances and swords could not reach the retreating alien, but barbolts could. Mechanisms were cocked, crude ranging devices aligned, and half a dozen short, sharp metal bolts were soon cutting through the air between the sharpshooters and their fleeing target.

At Flinx's command, the skimmer had already commenced a sharp descent surfaceward. The bolts struck its alloy frame and canopy and shattered or fell to the ground. They did not so much as scratch the vehicle's transparent passenger compartment.

Treappyn was already huffing and puffing his way toward his own mount. "Arise, servants of the Highborn! Arise, and give chase!" The admonition sounded futile even to his own ears, but he knew that in the aftermath of this vital, failed mission his actions would be judged, and he had no intention of being found wanting. Besides, there was always the chance some mechanical fault would befall the alien's craft, leading to an opportunity to once again remand him into their safekeeping.

Around him, the other soldiers were swinging themselves up into the saddles of their riding tethets, urging them in the direction of the skimmer. It floated before them, not far away at all, hovering just above the ground as its master and his pet entered the upper, glass-like compartment.

Flinx saw them coming as he settled into the familiar, comforting surrounds of the skimmer's pilot's seat. They were brave, these soldiers of Wullsakaa. He admired Treappyn's hopeless persistence even as he made arrangements to put the counselor's visage behind him forever. Having spent time in the company of a few bureaucrats, both human and otherwise, he was familiar with the pressures under which they functioned. If given the opportunity, could he even explain why he had to go? What would someone like Treappyn, or for that matter his much-exalted Highborn, make of news that some unknown and unidentified force was coming out of their night sky and threatening not just their country, but their whole world, and every star and world they could see in the sky? Such a thing would be beyond their comprehension. They would be convinced he was making it up. Existence would be so much simpler if only he were.

Over open ground, the riding tethets were much faster than he expected. Indifferent to proceedings now that her master's mind was at ease, Pip had settled herself down on the narrow console and gone to sleep. With a sigh, Flinx muttered a command to the skimmer. If the Wullsakaan riders came too close, they might injure themselves on the skimmer, or unknowingly impact on its repulsion field.

The pulsepopper mounted on the front of the skimmer was not large. It did not have to be. The small globe of fiery plasma it discharged in response to Flinx's command caused several of the terrified tethets to halt abruptly enough to dislodge their riders. Despite their multiplicity of limbs, the animals did not rise up in fear. Instead, they slumped down, not unlike a squatting Dwarra, and simply refused to move.

When the plasma ball struck the ground, there was no explosion. Instead, a noise like a deep-throated *whoosh* filled the air. There was a bright flash that caused Treappyn's eyes to contract sharply in their sockets. When he could expand them enough to focus again, he saw that a hole several times deeper than himself and considerably wider had appeared in the earth between his mount and the alien machine. The sides of the cavity were smooth and glassy, like the panes of fine glass that were installed on the better manors and commercial buildings in Metrel. The bottom of the hole was curved. Everything that had once occupied that space—soil, small crawling things, plants—had disappeared. The smell of burning things was strong in his nostril.

He did not have to call a formal halt to the pursuit.

To their credit, several of his troops retained enough of their wits to load their barbolts and fire repeatedly at the rapidly disappearing alien craft. Like their predecessors, those bolts that reached it glanced harmless off its sides. What must it be like, Treappyn thought as he watched the skimmer recede eastward, to have access to that kind of technology? One such machine could sow panic among Wullsakaa's enemies without even having to utilize its magical—no, not magical, he corrected himself—weapon. Such a wish would remain nothing more than that. The alien had declared his intention to leave Arrawd. It was now abundantly clear that nothing on Arrawd was capable of preventing him from doing so.

Even saving the alien's life had not been sufficient to persuade him to stay and render assistance. Although, as he watched the skimmer fade from view, Treappyn was not entirely sure that Flinx's life had ever been really in danger. What he did know was that he had failed in his mission.

Siryst, he thought resolutely to himself as he started to bring his still-trembling mount around. He had done his best. The troops who had accompanied him would be witnesses to the fact, and would back him up on it. What could lances and barbolts do against technology that commanded small pieces of sun? It would be a long, joyless ride back to Metrel district, and then they would have to be careful to avoid outriding patrols of the enemy on their way back to the fortress. Wullsakaa would have to face the combined forces of Jebilisk and Pakktrine Unified alone.

The Highborn's great gamble had failed.

CHAPTER

13

The sea of foliage beneath the skimmer gradually gave way to inter-mittent blotches of green interspersed with the first patches of sand, and then to the lightly vegetated dunes that marked the eastern coast of the Pavjadd Peninsula. Now back in familiar surroundings and completely safe, Flinx allowed himself to relax and examine from above the countryside through which he had previously traveled only on foot.

From the skimmer, he could see the coast approaching. It looked little different from seacoasts he had seen on other Earth-type worlds. Only the lack of real trees prevented the view from being one that might have suggested a landscape on Moth, or New Riviera, or Terra itself. Of Dwarran habitation there was no sign. This low, he could not see any of the inland towns. Looking back the way he had come, he found that he had already traveled too far to the east to lo-cate the rural homestead of his Dwarran hosts, the net-caster Ebbanai and the weaver Storra.

One more interlude in a life that already seemed overfull of them. One more world to add to his catalog of the visited and explored. One more visitation that, inevitably, ended up leaving him with more questions than answers. It didn't matter. He had done the best he could, and now he was going.

There was no one in the vicinity of his ship when the skimmer started down. As it neared a group of high dunes fronting the coast, an opening appeared at the base of one sandy hill. Lights gleamed within. Less than a minute later, the skimmer slipped into its docking receptacle as neatly as Clarity Held's graceful foot into a waiting slipper.

The *Teacher* waited until he had exited the skimmer before announcing itself. "Welcome back, Flinx."

He nodded absently, knowing that the ship's internal pickups would note and interpret the gesture accurately. "Good to be back. Ready for departure."

"Impatient. Always impatient. It's not good for your blood pressure."

He turned down the corridor that led, not to the bridge, but to the relaxation lounge. "Neither were my last days here. Not for the first time, I've lingered too long in a place where I shouldn't have. We have a planet-sized weapons platform to locate. Let's get going."

"Repairs are completed. Unless there is an imminent threat I am presently not detecting, I would prefer to activate the systems relevant to departure gradually, in the event any unexpected fault should make itself known."

"That's right. I'm impatient, and you're overcautious." Slightly miffed, he entered the lounge area. Activated for his return, the waterfall and pool gurgled their own aqueous welcome. Carefully monitored and space-restricted small flying things zipped and darted through the air. Pip opened an eye to track several, then closed it. The lounge held no surprises, and she was not in the mood to exert herself in search of familiar amusements.

Gratefully, he sank into the waiting lounge chair. In its latest manifestation, it had configured itself to resemble a sloping pile of rocks. Preternaturally soft rocks, for all that they perfectly duplicated the look of unyielding basalt. Pip fluttered off to settle herself among some nearby pink plants. Music seeped into the lounge area, and into his consciousness. Something by the Muralian Quartet; soothing and undemanding. The *Teacher* knew him well.

"As soon as you feel comfortable with your condition, go ahead and lift," he mumbled. "I might fall asleep, and there's no need to wake me. Changeover will do that."

"Understood." A pause, then, "You appear discontented."

"A condition you've never previously observed in me," he snapped back sardonically.

"Though your occasional communications were intended primarily to check on the status of my repairs to self, I was given to understand that you had embarked on a mission to heal the sick and injured among the locals. Familiar as I am with the extensive spate of human actions and reactions, I would think this kind of activity would leave you both with a sense of accomplishment and feeling good about yourself and the time you have spent here. Did you fail to heal those who came seeking your aid?"

"Oh, I healed them, all right." Stretching out in the malleable, cushioning quasi-stone, he accepted the cold fruit drink offered up by one rock. "Dozens and dozens of them. And in doing so, I gained the reputation among them of being not a skilled physician or even a traditional shaman, but a god. This utterly unjustified status apparently made a couple of neighboring political entities nervous enough to declare war on the country where I happened to be staying and—helping." He downed half the glass of juice. "All three are presently fighting a war about it."

The *Teacher*'s analysis was immediate. "Then when they learn you have departed, the reason for the war will be removed and the fighting will end."

Staring into the foliage that the ship's automatics so assiduously maintained, Flinx wondered if he should order up a libation stronger than fruit juice. "That was my thought. Then the local politician I befriended, who nonetheless tried to forcibly keep me from leaving, pointed out that the leaders of those attacking this region would think stories of my departure nothing more than a diversionary ploy on the part of those they're fighting." He waved the glass in a small arc. "Based on what this official told me, even if all concerned parties were to see you leave, the attackers still wouldn't be convinced. They might think I stayed behind, or only lifted off to fool them so I could land later and further aid their wicked enemy."

"I see." The *Teacher's* use of metaphor was flawless. "Then all sides need to be convinced beyond a shadow of a doubt."

Blinking, Flinx sat up so sharply that several peculiar-colored vines in his immediate vicinity which had started twisting toward him suddenly drew back, coiling in upon themselves.

"Oh no. No. Didn't you hear anything I just said? I've caused all this trouble by involving myself in local affairs, when I should have stayed on board and done nothing but eat, drink, sleep, and wait for you to finish your repair work. Now you're saying that instead of taking my leave and minimizing the damage I've already done, I should stay and somehow try to persuade these traditional enemies to stop their fighting and go back to the way things have always been?"

"Nothing you can do can make them go back to the way they've always been." The ship-mind's tone was unusually somber. "You have walked among them, and that in itself is enough to change them, and their respective societies, permanently. Once observed and recorded, the reality of Flinx and what he represents cannot be undone. But if you are the cause of this war, and it will not cease simply with our departure, then you must somehow find a way to put an end to it. To not attempt to do so constitutes moral abnegation of the worst kind."

Flinx would have looked away from the admonishing ship-mind, except that in essence he was inside it. No matter which way he glanced, he was still looking at it—and it at him.

"I already have a conscience, thank you very much."

"It would appear not to be in attendance. Did it perhaps get left behind on the surface?"

Thoroughly annoyed, he swung his legs over the side of the

pseudo-stone lounge and sat up, setting his empty glass aside. It immediately vanished into an appropriate receptacle.

"What do you expect me to do? I've already made a mess of things by trying to help these people. I should have adhered to Commonwealth procedure for dealing with Class Four-b civilizations. Any further incursion on my part is only likely to make things worse."

The ship-mind was imperturbable. "Searching my records, which as you know are quite extensive, I am unable to access any record where stopping a war incontrovertibly made things worse for those in imminent danger of dying as a result of it. One who can end such conflict and chooses not to invariably finds himself morally compromised."

Staring hard in the direction of the nearest visual pickup, Flinx narrowed his gaze and announced in the most steadfast voice he could manage, "I've done too much here already. The local Dwarra will just have to work out the matter of whether I'm still on their world or not among themselves. Prepare for departure!" With that, he swung himself back onto the lounge, closed his eyes, and requested that instead of another glass of refreshing juice, the ship's synthesizers provide him with an appropriate soporific.

Having stated its opinion and recorded its owner's reaction, the *Teacher* commenced to do as it was told. Methodically, and at a leisurely pace that reflected prudence as opposed to urgency.

It could not directly disobey an order. But when options were available, there was more than one way in which it could proceed to comply.

The explosive-packed disc was as big as a bale of tethet feed. Landing just short of the rock-and-earthen bulwark that had been hastily thrown up on the west side of the Pedetp River, it detonated with enough force to knock the nearest Wullsakaan defenders off all four of their feet. When the dust and smoke finally cleared, it could be seen that the explosion had left behind a crater deep enough to swallow a good-sized cargo wagon. Dazed but determined, the rattled defenders picked themselves up, dusted themselves off, and prepared once more to defend their piece of sacred ground. But any interested observer could measure the depth of their fear by the width of their oculars. They did not need a seer to tell them what would happen if another such explosive landed in their midst, instead of in front of or behind them.

From his command position atop the highest hill to the west of the river, His August Highborn Pyrrpallinda of Wullsakaa observed the ongoing battle and fretted silently. Always willing to defer to experience and knowledge, he had taken the advice of his general officers and staked the defense of his realm on retaining control of the river.

It was not a difficult decision to take. This time of year, the Pedetp was in full spring flood. Attempts by the enemy to sneak troops across on rafts and boats had been thwarted by the current. Where the Pedetp was narrow, it ran fast, and the would-be invaders could not make the crossing quickly enough to reach the opposite shore before they were discovered and intercepted by Wullsakaan patrols. Where it was wide and ran slow, such attempts were easily spotted in time for defenders to cut the would-be invaders to pieces. After a few such failed attempts, the combined forces of Pakktrine Unified and Jebilisk had focused their energies on the ancient trio of massive stone bridges known as the Dathrorrj Triplets.

Located within shouting distance of one another, the three bridges had been so solidly constructed by the ancients, and so conscientiously maintained by their Wullsakaan descendants, that they were as solid and stable as the riverbed in which their stone supporting columns were deeply grounded. As soon as the disposition and intent of the advancing enemy forces had been perceived, many of Pyrrpallinda's officers had argued for mining and destroying these critical approaches to the capital. Others had deplored the call for destruction of one of the country's most important commercial transit points. By the time it looked as if a consensus might be reached, it was too late: the combined armies of Pakktrine and Jebilisk had reached the bridges. Immediately, enemy barbolt sharpshooters had taken up positions allowing them to cover the bridges' foundations. That rendered the question of mining and blowing up the approaches moot, since any sappers who attempted to get near the structures would find themselves under immediate heavy fire, and would be picked off.

By the same token, repeated attempts by brave but foolhardy Jebiliskai riders to cross and take control of the bridges had been repulsed by clouds of bolts and lances from its Wullsakaan defenders. The Dathrorrj Triplets stood essentially untraveled; a bruised, battered, chipped, and scored no-Dwarra's-land stretching essentially intact across the boiling, surging white water of the snowmelt-fed Pedetp. On its western side, the defenders of Metrel City had rapidly raised defensive barricades and other fortifications. The longer enemy forces failed to gain control of the bridges, the stronger these defenses became.

Until now.

Adjusting the multiscope on its mount, Pyrrpallinda peered through the eyepiece. The series of magnifying lenses was focused on a pair of devices the likes of which had never been seen before. They had been brought up behind the Pakktrinian lines several days ago and had been in action ever since. Pakktrine military engineers had been scurrying busily around both objects ever since they had been detached and rolled into position on their multiwheeled mounts.

The first launch had been a shock; not only to the Highborn, but to everyone on the Wullsakaan-controlled shore of the Pedetp. Shock had given way to response, which had proven notable only for its ineffectiveness, and then to a kind of dull realization. While officers and engineers anxiously tried to think of a way to counter this new means of warfare, the soldiers manning the defensive ramparts could only hunker down and pray to Rakshinn, or whichever deity they favored, that the terrible new weapon would not be aimed in their direction. A disturbingly high and growing number had already seen their prayers ignored, and the death toll continued to grow longer with every discharge of the new Pakktrinian weaponry.

A distant hiss signaled the imminence of the latest launch. Through the scope, the Highborn could see the Pakktrinian operators of the fiendish device scatter for cover. An explosion of vapor obscured his field of vision. Raising his gaze from the eyepiece, his eyes tracked the path of another disc as it described a smooth arc through the cloud-filled sky. The disc grew larger and larger, until it landed well *behind* the multiple defensive lines immediately opposite the approach to the central bridge. There followed another of the horrific explosions that had become all too common during the previous couple of days. He lowered his gaze back to the scope's eyepiece. The Pakktrinian operators were already recharging and reloading one of the two massive steam catapults.

Both weapons had been carefully and strategically positioned well out of range of Wullsakaa's most advanced weapons, and were therefore essentially invulnerable. Taking them out would mean sending a force across the bridge. That, Pyrrpallinda's advisors had assured him, would amount to signing the death warrants of every soldier ordered to participate in such a foredoomed enterprise. So the Wullsakaan defenders could only squat, and watch, and hope, while the increasingly accurate Pakktrinians gradually got the hang of operating their new weapons.

"By tomorrow, Highborn, they'll have the range of all our positions, and should be able to begin targeting them accurately," the senior officer standing nearby told him. The old soldier was forced to hobble about on not one but two prosthetic forelegs, one on each side. There was nothing wrong with his mind, however.

"If they get across the Pedetp," another commented, "we'll have no choice but to fall back to the fortress."

Pyrrpallinda knew that. He also knew that it would leave all the land between the river and Metrel City open to pillage and destruction by the invading forces. He was prepared, to an extent, to accept that loss. Homes could be rebuilt, crops resown, goods replaced.

What troubled him was the obvious fact that these new weapons could stand off at an unreachable distance and slowly but steadily reduce the great fortress of Metrel to a pile of blackened stone and concrete. Not to mention what they could do to a frightened, panicky population crammed inside those walls.

He was torn with indecision, a place he hardly ever visited. If he surrendered, the soldiers of Pakktrine and Jebilisk would take control of the country and keep control until they were satisfied that the alien "god" was truly no longer helping their traditional Wullsakaan foes. An occupation was never a pretty thing. There would be brigandage, assault, and casual murder. But eventually the occupiers would leave, and the realm would survive—albeit at a cost.

Not incidentally, he might also be asked to make a show of goodwill by forfeiting his life, as a gesture of good faith. This might help to shorten the occupation. As Highborn, he was prepared to do this on behalf of his people, though it was a sacrifice he would prefer to avoid.

As he stood wrestling with his thoughts, the horrendous distant hissing of steam being explosively released reached him again. The second steam catapult had fired. The ample package of explosives it flung westward landed not on the bulwark that had been raised up across the approach to the third bridge, but directly in front of it. When the smoke cleared, the aftermath was sobering. A large gap showed in the laboriously raised earthworks where the explosives had blown a hole. The contingent of soldiers who had bravely been standing their ground there had vanished.

Rapidly and in good order, fresh troops were moved forward to defend the gap in the defenses. Laborers worked frantically to move dirt and rock to repair the hole. They would have it repaired soon enough, Pyrrpallinda knew. But it was a losing equation, a fight of attrition whose end was obvious to anyone with the slightest knowledge of tactics. Wullsakaa would run out of soldiers before Pakktrine ran out of explosives.

Silently, he called down a succession of curses on his enemies.

The minions of Jebilisk his army could deal with, and the soldiers of Pakktrine as well, but technologically Pakktrine Unified had always been a double-step ahead of his people. Too few institutes of scientific learning, too many places of unthinking adherence to old ways, had put Wullsakaa behind its long-established rival. He tried not to imagine what other devastating developments the industrious engineers of Pakktrine might have hidden beneath their cowls.

"Highborn?"

Turning away from the scope and its depressing field of view, he found himself confronted by Treappyn, Srinballa, and his two other senior counselors. The quartet of general officers stood behind him. Drawn from the best minds Wullsakaa could produce, these eight were the finest source of advice available to him.

If the battle was lost, they would also be the ones who would have to suffer the orders of the triumphant occupiers, since in that event His August Highborn Pyrrpallinda of Wullsakaa would most likely find his head forcibly separated from his body. He had confidence his advisors would do no less under excruciating circumstances.

Letting out a soft hiss, he faced them squarely, all eight gripping flanges turned upward, his torso raised as high from his lower trunk as his muscles could manage, Sensitives erect, every epidermal flap held open in a gesture of acquiescence. Everyone winced as the latest Pakktrinian bomb landed much too close to the hill on which they were assembled.

"I thought up here we were out of range of these infernal new devices," a senior officer snarled. "We will have to move."

"Yes," agreed Treappyn absently. His concern of the moment was not for his own personal safety, but for the condition of his liege. "Highborn? You wish to say something?"

Thus prompted, Pyrrpallinda put the proximity of the blast out of his mind and addressed his advisors slowly and with care, showing that he had given his words more than casual thought.

In his time as advisor not only to Pyrrpallinda but to his predecessors, Srinballa had seen much. He was not easily shocked. He would have conveyed his feelings to his liege in response to the short, terse speech more directly by entwining Sensitives with him, but Pyrrpallinda kept his distance.

"August Highborn, you cannot mean to turn over the keys to the country with so little attempt to defend it!"

Pyrrpallinda gestured to indicate sympathy with his advisor. "Good Srinballa. Well-meaning Srinballa. What is the use of fighting if one knows the fight is already lost? I would rather see a hundred Wullsakaans murdered by rampaging Jebiliskai in their wild red robes than a thousand brave soldiers brought down by weapons they have no chance of countering." For affirmation, he turned to the quartet of senior officers. Not one of them disputed his depressingly accurate analysis of the present military situation.

The few skin flaps exposed beneath his armor upraising, First Officer Bavvthak was forthright enough to confirm his liege's prognosis aloud. "Our muscle-driven catapults and other heavy weapons cannot match the range of these new Pakktrinian devices. Being as aware of our situation as we are, the enemy will know of our desperation. They will take all measures necessary to protect these weapons. No small team of would-be saboteurs will be able to get near them. A mass thrust across the Pedetp, swarming all three bridges and simultaneously using boats, is the only possible option."

Pyrrpallinda had two flanges clasped in front of him and two behind his back. "And the chances of this option succeeding are?"

Bavvthak exchanged a look with his colleagues before turning back to the Highborn and his civilian advisors. "Personally, I would estimate less than twenty percent chance of success, and that with casualties of at least fifty percent."

Pyrrpallinda gestured accordingly and eyed his counselors. "Such odds I do not like. Better to sacrifice one hundred to save one thousand. Better to abdicate one's position on behalf of the immature offspring of hundreds. Better to open the lands to casual theft and pillaging than to methodical destruction. I will offer myself as first sacrifice to the Aceribb and the hated Kewwyd." Eyes of normal dimension glanced back at his military leaders. "That is, unless one of you can come up with a better alternative."

Bavvthak and his fellow officers looked everywhere but at their liege. Their lack of response indicated they were as bereft of ideas as the Highborn's counselors.

Pyrrpallinda accepted their silence as coolly as he would the enemy's anticipated pronouncement of sentence. "There will be another Highborn to follow me. Eventually, Pakktrine and Jebilisk will grow tired of administering unruly Wullsakaa and its troublesome people and will leave. Or there will be a successful uprising. Or other realms such as Great Pevvid will see an opportunity to attack mutual enemies weakened by their assault on us, thereby distracting the foe's attention from here."

"It will not matter," another of the senior officers glumly pointed out, "if Pakktrine can continue to devise weapons of such magical power as they have employed here."

"Science!" While rendered downcast by the seeming inevitability of events, everyone looked in surprise at counselor Treappyn. Though he was the youngest present, his anger and frustration gave him the will to stare them all down. "This has nothing to do with magic. It is a matter of science, and engineering. The weapons with which our enemies have defeated us are a product of thought and rational thinking, not sacrifices and prayers to indifferent divinities. That is where Wullsakaa has fallen short, and that is what has brought about our downfall."

Although the Dwarra did not smile, the expression on the Highborn's angular face and the tone of his voice communicated something similar. "Worthwhile thoughts to ponder while you all strive to keep your own heads." He turned to his senior counselor. "As the most experienced among us, good Srinballa, I ask you to lead the formal delegation that will present the terms of surrender. The details should not be too onerous. We know what they will want to do with me. I am more concerned about their plans for the people."

Soft-voiced, counselor Meyarrul spoke up. "They'll want to

search every crack and cranny in Wullsakaa for the alien they think still remains to help us."

"Let them search." In his own mind, Pyrrpallinda was already dead. "Let them satisfy themselves as rapidly as they wish. The quicker they are convinced of the creature's absence, the sooner their idle soldiers will cease killing and looting."

With dignity and considerable ceremony, he approached and entwined Sensitives with each of them in turn. More than anything he could have said, this direct and highly personal exchange of emotions convinced them of his determination to proceed with his expressed course of action. The necessary individual interactions concluded, he turned back to stare across the river. Another massive explosion shook the northern branch of the Wullsakaan line. A glance at the graying sky suggested rain. Normally he would have welcomed the precipitation, which fell lightly and regularly across Wullsakaa and made it such a distinguished producer of foodstuffs. At the moment, however, it only mirrored the grimness of his mood.

CHAPTER

14

At first, Nejrekalb had been glad when he learned that his unit had been assigned a position atop one of the highest of the gentle, rolling hills that overlooked the river. That changed with the arrival of the Pakktrinians' powerful new catapults. His prominent position, he felt, only made him and the rest of his squadron more obvious targets. Although, as his close friend Cershaad had pointed out, the enemy appeared to be concentrating its fire on those units immediately opposite the approaches to the Dathrorrj Triplets. He shuddered, his epidermal flaps fluttering weakly, imagining what it must be like to have to huddle helplessly beneath such horrific incoming fire, unable to strike back at your attacker, waiting impotently for orders or death.

Nearby, Cershaad squatted with his back toward the hastily constructed barricade of earth and rock, sharpening his lance. It was well-made. A line of them, properly deployed by trained defenders, would stop even a charge of armored tethet riders. Against the new catapults of Pakktrine Unified, however, it might as well have been made of rotting meat. Which is what he and his friend would become if the Pakktrinians chose to put one of their heavy explosives on top of this ridge.

Pivoting on his forelegs, Nejrekalb watched as yet another bomb landed among the bridges' defenders, and winced as this time he saw bodies as well as soil go flying. The enemy's troops could hang back and relax as their new weapons of war picked off the brave but helpless Wullsakaans squad by squad, line by line. He wondered what thought his superiors had given to dealing with the threat, what unique tactics they might even now be concocting.

A droplet landed lightly on his forehead between his Sensitives, on the small patch of flesh exposed by the necessary hole in his leather helmet. Tilting back his head, he shielded his face with one set of flanges as he contemplated the sky. Rain would be welcome. If nothing else, it might blur the increasingly accurate vision of the Pakktrinian engineers.

His eyes contracted slightly, squeezed by the muscles that surrounded them in their sockets. Puzzled, he called out to Cershaad. Pausing in his sharpening, the other soldier set his weapon aside but within easy reach and moved up to stand alongside his companion.

Raising both left forearms, Nejrekalb pointed skyward. "That big cloud, Cershaad."

Dutifully, the slightly larger soldier scrutinized the indicated portion of graying sky. "A cloud. What about it?"

"It doesn't seem to be acting oddly to you?"

Pivoting his upper body to regard his friend, Cershaad extended his Sensitives forward, but Nejrekalb declined the proffered emotional contact. "Have you been too long without sleep or food? A cloud is a cloud. Clouds do not act 'oddly.'"

His gaze still focused on one particular portion of sky, Nejrekalb was not dissuaded. "This one does."

Expanding his eyes, the other soldier tried to find a source for his companion's absurd claim. "Really? In what way?"

Nejrekalb found it difficult to swallow. "It's coming toward us."

One might have expected a collective gasp, at least from the simpler, lower ranks, when the slowly descending cloud mass that had so attracted one soldier's attention suddenly appeared to shimmer and become something very different indeed. Where the looming cumulonimbus had hovered there now hung what, to Dwarran eyes, appeared to be an enormous elongated mass of metal and materials utterly new to their experience. Lights of different hues and impossible intensity marked its flanks; some winked periodically on and off while others glowed steadily. Despite this, no flames were in evidence. The lights were as smokeless as Arrawd's sun.

At one end of the gigantic structure was a huge, curving disc that emitted a faint purplish radiance. Occasionally, the ethereal glow would expand or contract imperceptibly. When it did so, the vast hovering mass would rise or descend accordingly. From the rear center of the disc a long, solid tube of considerable dimensions extended backward. Sporting a plethora of protrusions whose functions could not be imagined, it eventually terminated in a large oval whose purpose was equally enigmatic.

Those Dwarra on both sides of the river who found themselves located beneath the seemingly solid apparition scattered in panic, fearful that it might abruptly plunge all the way to the ground and crush them beneath its perceptible weight. There was no need for Wullsakaan or Pakktrinian or Jebiliskai soldiers to wait for directions from their officers, because the officers fled alongside their troops. Confusion reigned among defenders and attackers alike.

Normally placid tethets pulled at their reins and wrenched at their yokes. In their haste to flee something as ominous as it was outside their experience, some soldiers threw their weapons down in order to make better speed. Soon both banks of the Pedetp were littered with discarded lances, heavy pikes, barbolts, and other arms. More afraid of being accused of cowardice than of the monstrosity hovering overhead, senior officers and commanders on both sides struggled to maintain some semblance of order among their respective ranks. They succeeded to some extent, though not completely, as terror-driven soldiers broke through reserve lines and fled in panic for nearby Metrel City or distant borders.

Among the thousands present who witnessed the sight, only one was unruffled by the shocking materialization. Mobilized like the majority of his able-bodied country folk for the defense of his land, a certain humble net-caster stood calmly in the midst of his reserve squad while those around him took flight, broke down, closed their eyes, fully retracted their Sensitives, or tried frantically to burrow into the ground beneath their foot-flanges.

"Interesting," Ebbanai murmured to no one in particular as he gazed up at the enormous alien object suspended in the gray sky of morning. "The last time, it was sand dunes."

Transfixed by the sight, His August Highborn Pyrrpallinda and his stunned advisors gaped from their high vantage point. Moving up to stand alongside his liege but unable to pull his own gaze away from the sight, Treappyn offered his own evaluation of the awe-inspiring spectacle.

"The alien told me he was leaving," the counselor observed softly. "It would appear he has decided not to take his leave of us just yet."

"Why now, why here?" Monarch of an extensive and powerful realm, used to commanding all around him, Pyrrpallinda had never felt so powerless. "What does the creature want with us? What does it intend?"

Aware that for a second time that morning everyone's attention was fixed on him, Treappyn did his best to formulate a constructive response—and failed. "If I knew that, Highborn, I would have a better idea myself whether to stand here, run away, or compose the last thoughts of my regrettably brief life."

One of the senior military, an individual known as much for his spiritual bent as for his tactical brilliance, contracted his upper torso down into his trunk and dropped his gaze.

"Perhaps we should pray."

Pyrrpallinda as well as Treappyn turned to regard the officer. "An economical as well as innocuous proposal," the Highborn conceded. His gaze returned to the alien colossus hanging in the sky above the river. His own emotions, isolated by unentwined Sensitives from those of his advisors or anyone else, were in turmoil. How should he react to the unprecedented? Ought he to be afraid, worshipful, respectful, awed, or simply benumbed? Or all of these?

"I would appreciate any advice, however, on precisely who, or what, we should pray *to*."

"The military situation below us," the *Teacher* commented studiously, "is as straightforward as it is primitive. With an eye toward crossing deeply into the native land of Wullsakaa, the invading forces are attempting to gain control of one or more of the bridges that span the fast-moving river directly beneath us. The defenders are attempting to prevent this. The strategic balance appears to be fairly equal, with the one exception I have already noted."

Sitting in the command lounge on the bridge, Flinx studied the several images floating in the air before him. "These steam-powered explosives throwers the attackers have brought into play."

"Yes." The *Teacher* paused and, when its owner failed to reply, prompted, "How do you wish to proceed?"

Flinx sighed unenthusiastically. From her favorite perch atop the forward console, Pip watched from within her brilliantine coils. She felt *for* her master's internal distress much as she felt it within her own mind, but there was nothing she could do for him. So she went to sleep.

"You guilted me into putting an end to this war. But in order to make any peace last, I need to do it in a way that causes as little harm as possible, and leaves the natives who are mounting this invasion convinced once and for all that I'm not aiding their adversaries in Wullsakaa. I'm not good at this sort of thing, ship."

The *Teacher* considered. "At such times you must do that which you always seem to do best."

Flinx's expression twisted into one of mild surprise mixed with uncertainty as he glanced in the direction of the nearest pickup. "There's something I do best? What might that be?"

"Improvise," the ship-mind instructed him.

From their command post, the August Highborn Pyrrpallinda and his advisors looked on as a semblance of order was slowly restored among the remaining ranks of defenders. Officers firmed up lines, sometimes having to utilize threats of violence to force fleeing soldiers back to their positions. Bastions were restaffed. Weapons once more were emplaced to confront potential attackers. Across the river, a similar recovery was under way among the forces of the Aceribb of Jebilisk and the Kewwyd of Pakktrine Unified. Puffs of thick vapor were visible from the hill where the two Pakktrinian steam catapults had been emplaced. Soon, he reflected, it would resume.

What of the alien? What did it intend? To leisurely observe and take notes on the continuing carnage? Only one among his entourage was in a position to even essay a remark on the possibilities. Surprisingly, counselor Treappyn had a comment.

"Look to the alien's vessel," he told the Highborn and his colleagues. "If there is any response, it will surely come from there."

"What kind of response could we anticipate?" As thoroughly intimidated as the rest of his associates, Srinballa was ready to defer to anyone possessing a hint of an idea of what might be forthcoming, even the young upstart Treappyn.

"I have no idea," Treappyn told Pyrrpallinda honestly. Raising a pair of forearms, he pointed toward the ovoid at one end of the hovering machine. "Unless it has something to do with that small part of the craft that is presently in motion."

It did.

Treappyn's eyesight was excellent. Several of the others, including the Highborn, had to expand their oculars to maximum before they, too, could finally locate the source of the young counselor's observation. What appeared to be some kind of tree—except that it couldn't be a tree, Treappyn thought as he stared upward—was in motion, traveling on some kind of track or band that encircled the oval portion of the alien ship at its widest point. It shifted position deliberately and with speed, until the top of the tree-shape was pointing downward.

There was an actinic flash of light. To Treappyn's startled, reflexively contracting eyes, an extremely thin portion of sky momentarily seemed to flare with the brightness of the sun. The slender, perfectly straight line of light that for a split second had been etched across the sky as well as his retinas emerged from the tip of the tree-shape now located on the underside of the alien craft and terminated on the ground below. The tip of it made contact with the center arch of Tynary, the northernmost of the Dathrorrj Triplets. A single stunningly loud, concussive *boom* assaulted his ears and those of his associates. Tynary disappeared.

Or rather, the middle portion of it did so. Where once the immovable stone span had arched gracefully over the Pedetp, there was now a vast empty space in the air above the river. From what remained at either end, accompanied by matching, ascending pillars of dust, bits and pieces of pulverized stone crumbled into the torrent. Everyone around him was staring in disbelief at where the ancient, seemingly indestructible bridge had once stood intact. Not Treappyn.

He was watching the alien ship. While he was as dazed and shocked as everyone else, it did not prevent him from trying to comprehend what he had just witnessed. There was no way he could do so. He simply did not have the minimal necessary scientific background. It was a deficiency of which he need not have been ashamed. In that ignorance, he was no worse off than the finest scientific minds on all of Dwarra. Of one thing he was reasonably certain, however.

What they had just seen and experienced had nothing to do with steam power.

The tree-shape that was now more obviously than ever something much more menacing than a tree shifted slightly on its track. A second eye-shocking line of light struck Bywary, the middle bridge. Its fate mirrored that of Tynary. No one was surprised when Syabry, the third and last bridge, vanished along with its predecessors. Like stone hail, bits and pieces of blasted rock and concrete rained down on the rushing River Pedetp.

A ragged cheer arose from the senior military officers and his other counselors. It was echoed from below as the defenders of Wullsakaa realized what the astounding bit of alien intervention meant. With the bridges destroyed, the armies of Pakktrine Unified and Jebilisk now had no way of crossing the swollen Pedetp except on boats. The invasion had been brought to an abrupt and wholly unexpected halt.

"I won't worship him, but if I ever have the chance," Bavvthak declared with feeling, "I will squat before him and lift my skin in gratitude!"

"He has saved us all." Counselor Goidramm was equally effusive. "By intervening on our behalf he has shown himself to be a true friend and ally of great Wullsakaa!"

Treappyn did not join the celebration. He was still watching the immense alien ship.

Maybe, he found himself thinking. Maybe.

When he spoke again, it was to none of his companions in particular, not even the Highborn. But all paid attention. "Keep in mind that none of us, myself included, knows anything of the alien's true motivations or intentions. As easily as he did away with the Dathrorrj, I imagine he could do so with the fortress at Metrel. Or Metrel City."

"Or Wullsakaa," someone pointed out somberly, picking up the counselor's line of thought.

"Why should it do something like that?" Srinballa was eyeing his colleague uncertainly. "Why would it *want* to do something like that?"

"I have no idea." Treappyn had not taken his eyes off the alien ship. "I am only thinking aloud; only saying that he *could* do it. All I am saying is that before we declare a general celebration of victory and break out the commemorative stimulants, it might be best to consider more thoroughly that which we wish to account an ally. One whose actions may very well be driven by motives other than our own, and are yet to be fully revealed."

Pyrrpallinda gestured approvingly. "When I raised you up to full counselor, Treappyn, I knew you brought intelligence and cunning with you. I had not also expected to find wisdom." Embarrassed, Treappyn did not look in the direction of his liege. Turning to his other advisors, the Highborn continued.

"The counselor is right. Let us withhold our zeal a while longer yet." Lifting his own gaze, he, too, stared at the hovering alien vessel. "At least until this monstrous mechanism has disappeared back into the sky from which it came."

"That should keep both armies separate for now." Using hands and voice to control the images floating in front of him, Flinx studied the smashed bridges and the havoc the *Teacher*'s brief intervention had wrought. "I kind of hoped the demonstration, making the center spans of all three bridges disappear, would be enough to convince both sides to pull back."

"Clearly this is not the case." The ship voice paused. "I could increase power somewhat and make the river disappear."

Flinx's expression twisted. Advanced though it was, it was not beyond the *Teacher*'s ship-mind to miss certain subtleties. "I don't think that's a good idea. Bridges are easier to replace than rivers." There was the slightest sensation of motion; as always, more perceptible when the *Teacher* was within atmosphere than out in open space.

"What was that for? Weather?" On the three-dimensional imagery in front of him, he saw nothing that looked particularly threatening. Only light rain clouds.

"No." The ship managed to inject a thoughtfully calibrated note of surprise into its synthesized voice. "We are under attack."

Even as it issued this amazing announcement, one groundward-positioned image shifted and zoomed in to focus on a specific portion of the Pakktrinian ranks. As Flinx looked on, an explosive-laden disc soared upward, growing larger in the field of view until, at the top of its arc, a hastily rigged internal fuse caused it to explode a good thirty meters below the underside of the hovering *Teacher*. The Pakktrinian engineers had elevated their twin steam catapults to the maximum.

"They're shooting at us," he murmured in astonishment. Give credit where due, he thought to himself. The Pakktrinians were as fearless as they were foolish. He wondered if the operators of the catapults had decided on their own to take the valiant action, or if they had been compelled against their better judgment by orders from higher up. As he looked on, a disc rose from the second catapult. Climbing higher than its predecessor, it detonated a little closer to the ship.

"Response?" There was no concern in the *Teacher*'s voice. "I can continue to ascend and remain out of their range."

"No. Much as I'd prefer to take the easy way out, we can't have them thinking they've forced us to move." A small knot formed in his stomach, as it usually did whenever he thought he might have to hurt someone, even in self-defense. "Remove the source of contention." He peered toward the console-mounted pickup in front of him. "But be as careful as you can, and do your best to minimize injuries."

Fully aware of its owner's outlook on such matters, the ship replied evenly, "I will of course endeavor to do so. Bear in mind that, accurate as it is, my single external weapon is designed to react to and defend us against modern armament mounted on orbiting stations, other starships, and advanced ground-based weapons systems. It was not engineered to carry out excisions of surgical precision."

The shaft of light that parsed matter was no greater in diameter than a human hair. It struck one of the two steam catapults, briefly illuminating a sphere twenty meters in diameter. When those in its vicinity regained their vision and their hearing, they were able to see that where the pride of Pakktrinian military science had previously stood there was now only a smoking hole in the earth. The steam catapult, with its attendant disc-shaped shells, fuel, and raft of elaborate accessories, had vanished. So, unfortunately, had several of its operators.

Observing this, the engineers and soldiers manning the second catapult decided en masse that disobeying orders was preferable to remaining at their posts. They scattered in time to avoid the effects of a second beam that thrust downward from the underside of the immense machine hanging in the sky above them. The second catapult loudly and spectacularly went the way of the first, though this time without any loss of life. As word spread of the destruction, and the effortless accuracy with which it had been carried out, consternation and despair raced through the ranks of Pakktrinian and Jebiliskai fighters.

Not unexpectedly, the response to this judicious yet devastating intervention on the part of the alien was somewhat different on the other side of the Pedetp. Beginning with those troops nearest to the river, a wave of cheering rose and swept back through the ranks of the defenders, accompanied by much fluttering of gripping flanges and skin flaps. Eventually, it reached the hill where the Highborn and his commanders and counselors were encamped.

Just as with the lower ranks, initial shock and astonishment quickly gave way to jubilation. Sensitives were entwined and touched so that the elated emotion of the moment might be fully shared. While senior officers congratulated themselves on this unexpected shift in the strategic balance, the Highborn's counselors were more circumspect. Experience had taught them that no matter how favorable circumstances might appear in any given situation, there were always two sides to happenstance. Forever wary of good fortune as well as bad, they allowed themselves only a moment of elation before beginning to consider its possible downside.

Still, given the display that they had just witnessed, it was difficult not to be optimistic.

Eptpulvv, another of the senior military advisors present, broke away from celebrating with his fellow officers to amble over to the thoughtful Treappyn. As the soldier proffered his Sensitives, the counselor knew it would be ill-mannered to refuse. They shared emotions for a moment, then the officer drew back. His expression reflected his bemusement.

"You are not satisfied? This is a great moment for Wullsakaa!" A pair of flanges gestured across the river, to where the vile weapons that had been tormenting the defenders had been replaced by a pair of smoking craters. "The god Flinx has shown categorically that it stands with the Highborn and his defenders!"

Treappyn was glad that his Sensitives were no longer entwined with those of the oft-honored Eptpulvv, lest the senior officer sense his irritation. "While I am as ready as anyone to applaud such apparent triumphs, I think the cheering premature. The motives and actions of the alien are not so predictable as many seem to believe. And don't call him a god. He's only a person, a creature of flesh and blood and life, little different from any Dwarra." The counselor's gaze shifted away from the staring officer and back to the massif hanging in the gray sky. "The only difference is that he has access to more science, and more history."

Momentarily at a loss for words, the officer recovered quickly. When he spoke again, there was a touch of anger in his voice. "You deep thinkers! Always ready to smother joy and happiness under a pall of gloom." Treappyn felt a pair of gripping flanges pressing strongly on his shoulder. "Can you not be content for once? Can you not trust the evidence of your own eyes?"

The counselor continued to watch the alien's ship. It had not moved. "That is exactly what I am doing. I accept what I have seen—as I will continue to accept, and consider, whatever else may be forthcoming."

Eptpulvv drew back. *"Forthcoming?"*

Now Treappyn did look away from the alien vessel, and back to the senior officer. "Time has not stopped, brave soldier. Not for our enemies, not for us, and not for the alien. Events progress."

As indeed they did.

The shock to the Wullsakaan observers when the alien craft had destroyed the Pakktrinian weapons had been considerable. It was substantially greater when the next narrow, bright beam of energy struck not the routed enemy, but the Wullsakaan side of the river. A sudden, sharp blast, a flash of light that momentarily blinded all who happened to be looking in the wrong direction, and a new crater appeared where an instant before had stood one of Wullsakaa's largest and most formidable catapults. That it was not advanced enough to be powered by steam did not seem to matter to the alien.

This sobering nanosecond of destruction was followed by a second, which obliterated another catapult together with all of its support wagons and equipment. Since the weapons were not staffed at the time, no deaths resulted. There were only injuries; those largely from soldiers who were unlucky enough to find themselves standing or squatting nearby at the moment of impact, and found themselves picked up and thrown through the air by the force of the concussion.

Among the leaders of Wullsakaa, Treappyn was the only one who was neither traumatized nor stunned into momentary immobility by this shocking development. There was no hint of satisfaction in his voice as he pivoted slightly to face Eptpulvv: merely acceptance.

"You see," he told the senior military officer, "the alien has his own agenda. It may or may not have anything to do with the hopes and desires of the people of Wullsakaa—or any other political entity on Arrawd." Turning away, he returned his attention to the alien vessel. Thankfully, the tiny device protruding from its underside did not flare again. "Pakktrine loses two catapults; Wullsakaa loses two catapults. The alien is showing his impartiality."

Used to commanding ranks of obedient soldiers, Eptpulvv found himself at a loss for words. "But—the Pakktrinian offal attacked it, attempted to strike at its ship. We did no such thing." The old soldier's gaze followed Treappyn's. "Why would it hit back at us?"

"I told you." The counselor was patient, knowing that among everyone present, only he had personal knowledge of the alien, his thought processes, and his mind-set. "He is demonstrating his impartiality. You see, commander, where he comes from, political groupings like Wullsakaa and Jebilisk are regarded as no better than primitive tribes. He is not angry with us, I think. Just impatient."

"Impatient?" Unable to grasp the larger import behind the counselor's words, the officer could only gaze back in bemusement. "Impatient at what?"

"I don't know," declared His August Highborn Pyrrpallinda, who while feigning disinterest had been listening intently to the conversation, "but it may be that we are about to find out." Raising a right forearm, he pointed with one flange while every one of his skin flaps opened halfway, signifying uncertainty. "The alien's vessel is moving."

Those who had turned away to argue about the meaning of the alien assault on their own positions now rejoined their companions in tilting back their heads to stare upward at the immense machine. It had been impressive hovering above the Pedetp. It was even more so as it passed directly above them. Below, oblivious to the furious entreaties of their officers, a number of terrified soldiers dove frantically for anyplace that offered concealment from the vast mass passing so close over their heads. Even a few of the senior officers and counselors could not keep from flinching as the alien craft blocked out much of the sky.

Treappyn was not among them. The alien ship, he knew, was not about to fall out of the sky like a rock blasted from the depths of the earth. It was moving slowly, deliberately, and under the complete control of its inscrutable master. That, however, was not what interested him the most.

It was the undeniable realization that the enormous vessel was heading due west, directly toward Metrel City, the capital of Wull-sakaa.

It had not taken long for the August Highborn and his retinue to come to the same realization. Knowing they could not possibly hope to keep pace with the alien's flying machine, they nonetheless raced back to Metrel as fast as their tethets could carry them, leaving First Officers Bavvthak, Eptpulvv, and the rest of the Wullsakaan military command to look to the continued defense of the realm's borders.

Reaching the outskirts of the city, the Highborn's party was thronged by frightened, bewildered citizens pleading to know if the end of the world was at hand. They could hardly be blamed for their alarm given the looming, awe-inspiring presence of the *Teacher*. Flinx's ship had stopped directly above the city and now hovered there, an unfathomable alien mass whose intentions could only be imagined. The unnerved citizens of Metrel had vivid imaginations.

Not all the scenarios they invented postulated imminent catastrophe. Those among them who had been the beneficiaries of Flinx's curative efforts insisted that the alien's intentions could only be of a benign nature. Why heal the sick and injured, they argued, only to later come and rain death and destruction? They were supported in their stance, with much mutual entwining of Sensitives, by those who continued to believe the alien was not a natural being but rather a new god, come to Arrawd to rescue the Dwarra from their own sins and follies. Argument was frequent and occasionally strident, with those of differing opinions sometimes coming to blows.

All of this conflict and controversy the Highborn and his entourage left behind as they sought a semblance of peace within Metrel's inner fortress. The great central octagonal bastion, built on the highest point of land in Metrel, rose multiple stories above the rest of the capital and provided sweeping views over the city and the prosperous lands beyond.

It also allowed those with access to its uppermost levels a slightly closer view of the alien vessel. Rested and refreshed as much as was possible under the circumstances, the August Highborn and his counselors stood in the Great Audience Chamber beneath the roof. The single room extended the entire width and length of the bastion. On the side opposite where they were presently gathered was a reception area, complete with raised dais for the Highborn and his family and a lower one for visiting dignitaries to stand on while paying their official respects.

Of the bastion's eight sides, four were fitted with high, arching portals that opened onto large balconies. From these, the rulers of Wullsakaa could survey any reach of the realm. The one they had currently chosen offered no better view than any of the others. The alien's enormous craft was visible from all four balconies.

Occasionally contracting his oculars against a nomadic raindrop, Pyrrpallinda stared up at the looming machine. Neither he nor any of his best scientific advisors could fathom a reason for the craft's design. What was the purpose of that enormous disc at one end, and why was the bulk of the craft kept separate from it by such a long, narrow, connecting structure? Why did one alien need so large a vehicle? Was the distance between the stars really that great?

And most important of all, what did the alien want, now that it had left the field of battle and come, in all its might and otherworldly magnificence, to Metrel?

His advisors could not tell him. When queried, Treappyn, who knew more than anyone else about the alien, remained maddeningly equivocal. A discerning ruler, Pyrrpallinda knew that the counselor could not be expected to provide answers to questions that had never before been asked—but the resulting ambiguity was vexing nonetheless.

Clarification loomed when one of the other counselors suddenly flailed upward in panic and shouted, "The alien—he's shooting at us again!" before turning and running like a frightened souzhadd for the presumed safety of the bastion's lower levels. Common-sensible if not inherently wise, Pyrrpallinda ignored everyone else's reaction in favor of watching counselor Treappyn. That worthy did not run, but instead stood on the balcony focusing on the glint of light that had sent his more impressionable colleague fleeing.

"I don't think it's a weapon, Highborn. True, it is coming toward us. But at such a moderate velocity that I suspect it to be something else entirely." A moment later he added, reassuringly, "In fact, I recognize it. It is the vehicle the alien utilizes for local, as opposed to far-distant, transport."

Despite the counselor's assurances, several of his associates and other members of the Highborn's staff found themselves backing away as the alien device drew close to the balcony. Below, word of the strange being's approach spread swiftly. Guards struggled to hold back the growing throng of supplicants who, crying and pleading, shouting and praying, tried to storm the main gate leading into the fortress.

As the vehicle drew near, Pyrrpallinda could see the alien, together with its strange flying pet, folded up inside the craft's transparent cover. Treappyn had described how the alien rested by bending its body in half at the middle, but it was one thing to hear a description of such a physical impossibility and quite another to see it in person.

As the alien straightened itself, a portion of the transparent covering slid out of the way. Settling on the Highborn, who had bravely stood his ground, Flinx addressed the ruler of Wullsakaa in heavily accented but otherwise quite understandable speech.

"My name is Flinx." Peering past the thoroughly entranced Highborn, the alien bobbed its head up and down. "Hello, counselor Treappyn."

Treappyn reacted as though he had concourse with alien beings every day. "Good feelings to you, Flinx. His August Highborn Pyrrpallinda and his Council offer their greetings on your arrival at Metrel City."

"Yes." Breaking free of the momentary trance into which he had slipped, Pyrrpallinda stepped forward and formally extended his Sensitives, retracting them as a glance reminded him that the alien had none. "We welcome you to our city. And," he added with a becoming alacrity born of long experience in politics, "we extend to you our heartsfelt thanks for your assistance in helping to forestall the invasion of our land by the perfidious minions of Jebilisk and Pakktrine Unified."

The alien's head bobbed again. It did not appear impressed, either by the great bastion of Metrel's fortress, the elaborate decoration of its interior, the elegance of the Highborn's attendants, or Pyrrpallinda himself. In fact, it seemed rather impatient.

"Thank you for your welcome," it declared amiably enough. "As Treappyn can tell you, I'd enjoy staying and talking. But I have other claims on my time, and I'm kind of in a hurry. So could you please send word to the generals, or leaders, or whoever is in charge of the forces of Jebilisk and Pakktrine that I'd like to meet with them. Here, as soon as possible."

Several members of the Highborn's staff looked aghast. One did not speak to Pyr Pyrrpallinda in this fashion. The ruler of Wullsakaa bristled. Even Treappyn was taken aback. Open to the emotions of everyone present, Flinx found that he did not care. All he wanted now was to settle the local concerns and misconceptions that had led to the present conflict, and be on his way.

"May I at least know the reason for this?" Pyrrpallinda contained himself as best he could, struggling to ignore the obvious fact that he had just been given an order and not a request.

The alien appeared detached, as if preoccupied with other matters. The attenuated flying thing resting on its shoulders was eyeing the Highborn attentively. Finding the intensity of the creature's unblinking gaze unsettling, Pyrrpallinda looked away. The alien was speaking again.

"I understand that the reason for this war is that your rivals are concerned I may be helping you, and might help you further, to their detriment."

"You did nothing to dissuade them of that when you destroyed their most powerful weapons," the Highborn pointed out.

Flinx smiled thinly. "An example I would have preferred to have avoided, and one that I had to balance by taking out two of your own war machines. I intend to assure the leaders of both other countries that I favor no one Dwarran realm over another, and that as soon as I've been given the opportunity to make that point, I will be leaving." He glanced over at the always attentive Treappyn. "Permanently, as I've already informed your counselor."

"What if the odious Aceribb of Jebilisk and Kewwyd of Pakktrine Unified do not believe you?" Srinballa asked sensibly.

Flinx looked at the senior counselor. "If they hear it from me in person, I think they'll believe me. Why shouldn't they? If I was planning to stay, and favor one side against another, there would be no purpose in calling such a meeting." He looked back at the August Highborn. "Well? Can such a conference be arranged?"

Pyrrpallinda was relieved to find that the alien could not read his mind; otherwise, it would already have known the answer to its question.

"I think so. I will send word immediately. If those leading the assault on Wullsakaa are in agreement, it should be possible to guarantee their safe passage here by some time tomorrow." Not knowing if the alien was conversant enough to detect it, he nonetheless took care to keep any hint of sarcasm from his reply. "Will that be soon enough to suit your needs?"

"Tomorrow will be fine." Flinx let his gaze wander past the Highborn and his staff. "Meanwhile, if you want to play host, I don't like to waste time that can be used to gather knowledge. I wouldn't mind seeing some more of your fortress. Alien architecture and culture are always interesting."

Stepping to one side, Pyrrpallinda used two forearms to indicate that the visitor should enter. "I will guide you myself, and attempt to satisfy any curiosity you may have. Counselors Treappyn and Srinballa will accompany us." At this announcement Treappyn looked pleased, while Srinballa remained wary. "I do have a request of my own, if you don't mind."

"What is it?" Flinx asked as he entered the audience room. Pip immediately took off to explore the upper reaches of the high-ceilinged chamber, drawing fascinated stares from the guards stationed around its circumference.

His August Highborn Pyr Pyrrpallinda, ruler of all Wullsakaa, met the gaze of the alien squarely. His restlessness was as clear to Flinx as if it had been neatly scribed on an open scroll and handed to him to read.

"You have talked much to counselor Treappyn. He has related the gist of these conversations to me. But it is not the same thing as hearing them from the source. Tell me if you would, visitor-with-an-agenda-of-his-own, what it is like on other worlds . . ."

CHAPTER

15

"Once and for all time, I've called this meeting here today to tell you that I have no interest whatsoever in helping any one faction of the Dwarra against another, that I do not favor any one realm, religion, or local philosophy above another, and that as soon as all present realize this and accept it, I will be leaving your world—in all likelihood, forever. Nor are any others of my kind likely to come here in the foreseeable future." Flinx's gaze traveled around the Audience Chamber as he tried to meet as many Dwarran eyes and read as many Dwarran emotions as possible. "You will be left alone, to work out your mutual problems and settle your common differences by yourselves. It will be as if I had never been here."

Sensitives entwined and mouthparts worked rapidly as those assembled in the great room of the fortress's central bastion discussed the alien's words among themselves. As a measure of the importance they attached to the conference, the leaders of all three contending forces were present: His August Highborn Pyrrpallinda of Wullsakaa; the Aceribb of Jebilisk, splendid in embroidered, flowing robes; and the more somberly attired Kewwyd of Pakktrine Unified.

Flinx looked on in silence. He had little to add. All they had to do was acknowledge his succinct declaration of intent. With the impetus behind the war removed, fighting would end, everyone would go home, he could depart the interesting world of Arrawd with a more or less clear conscience, and maybe also a little wiser.

"And of course," he concluded, "all hostilities will cease immediately as the forces of Jebilisk and Pakktrine Unified prepare as rapidly as possible to make their way back to their own lands."

The Highborn Pyrrpallinda of Wullsakaa hardly reacted at all to this remark, while the Aceribb of Jebilisk whispered only briefly with his mentor. As was to be expected of a group, the Kewwyd of Pakktrine Unified conferred among themselves. What was not expected was their response.

Turning to face him, the designated spokesperson among them responded with astonishing matter-of-factness. "I am the Noble Hurrahyrad. Though through your intervention we have lost two of our newest weapons, it cannot be argued that we and our allies from Jebilisk remain firmly ensconced on the field of battle and continue to control its destiny. We wonder why we should without objection sacrifice to the whim of a single visitor that which has been gained at some cost and sacrifice."

Fear and defiance mingled in equal measure within the mind of the speaker, Flinx perceived. He should not have been surprised at the query. The more primitive the society, the more obtuse and less rational its reactions tended to be, especially those of its leaders. Also, there was likely a possible secondary motive. By at least posing a challenge to his supremacy, the Kewwyd would be able to return home insisting that they had done their best in the face of overwhelming force. Showing no anger and replying with equivalent calm, he proceeded to elaborate on his reasoning in plain, straightforward, somber language.

"You have seen a brief demonstration of my ship's capabilities. You need to understand that when it destroyed your respective weapons, it was operating at the lowest limit of what it can do." This prompted the expected murmuring among the assembled. Some of them were dubious, but many were willing to accept his claim.

"I've already told you that I'm not an ally of Wullsakaa. I'm also not anyone's enemy. Not of Pakktrine Unified, nor Jebilisk, nor Wullsakaa." He concentrated on the attentive trio of rulers known as the Kewwyd. "Don't make me one. Any side that fails to comply with the demand to cease fighting will find out what my vessel can really do."

It was more or less bluff. Regardless of the response he received, he had no intention of engaging in mass slaughter. If the obstinate Kewwyd refused to withdraw its troops, he would have to find another way of convincing them of the need to do so. Had any of them been able to entwine Sensitives with him, a perceptive individual might have been able to discern the hollowness of his threat. In the absence of such intimate emotional contact, they were left to evaluate the truth of his response based on words alone.

To further drive his point home, he glanced in the direction of the Highborn Pyrrpallinda. "That warning holds for the armies of Wullsakaa as well, should any overeager officer decide to take it upon him- or herself to pursue and harry the retreating forces of the other realms present at this meeting."

A visibly nervous Srinballa spoke up before his liege could reply. "We have already agreed to recall all forces to barracks as soon as it becomes clear that the assault has been called off. I assure you that none of our commanders in the field would dare to initiate the kind of action you cite without direct approval from one of four senior officers, all of whom report directly to His August Highborn."

Regal robes aswirl, the Aceribb of Jebilisk carefully balanced his lengthy, trailing headpiece as he took a step forward. "Jebilisk is ready to comply. Envisaging such a request, I have already taken the liberty of informing my mounted squadrons to start breaking camp with an eye toward beginning the long trek homeward." Executing a quadruple-flanged salute the likes of which Flinx had not seen before that employed all four forearms, the ruler of the Red Sands stepped back among his retinue.

That left only the ever-contentious Kewwyd to agree. As he watched the male and two females muttering among themselves in search of consensus, Flinx found himself growing increasingly impatient with the delay. He was anxious to be on his way. Even their ally the Aceribb appeared ill at ease with their arguing.

What were they so nervous about? Their emotions, as he perceived them, were a confused and roiling mix. Were they going to abide or not? If the latter, then he would be forced to waste more time here, composing some sort of overpowering display that would persuade them once and for all of the futility of squatting on any position other than full compliance. A display, he reminded himself tiredly, that would call for as few casualties among the Pakktrinian host as possible.

He could have summoned up his Talent to mute their emotions, but the temporary pacification would last only as long as he was present to sustain it. Their final decision needed to outlive his presence. They needed to reach the necessary agreement on their own, without any interference on his part.

He wasn't sure why he suddenly looked up. Maybe it was the furtive, hasty glance roofward of the one called Noble Kechralnan. Maybe a slight, unnatural movement of air. Or it might have been the speed with which Pip unexpectedly exploded skyward from her resting place across his shoulders. Whatever the reason, he tilted his head back just in time to see the Dwarra who had jumped through the open skylight in the lavishly frescoed ceiling come plunging straight toward him.

Several items worthy of note impressed themselves on him virtually simultaneously. While everyone else in the great room reacted to this unexpected and violent intrusion with shock and surprise, the triumvirate of individuals who comprised the Kewwyd of Pakktrine Unified did not. As guards reacted and started forward seconds too late and other dignitaries present stood and gaped, the members of the Kewwyd and their entourage turned away and covered their faces and Sensitives with whatever fabric was at hand for the purpose. Most interesting of all, the Pakktrinian who was plummeting toward him was emotionally empty; as dead inside and devoid of feeling as a stone. No wonder neither he nor Pip had sensed his approach, much less his presence or intentions.

The latter were defined by the object the falling native was holding tightly in both hands. As big around as a melon, it smoked slightly and smelled of something burning.

The last thing Flinx remembered seeing before utter blackness overtook him was a clear, unobstructed view of the suicidal bomber's head. It was devoid of Sensitives.

They had been amputated.

Awareness. Intimations of consciousness. Nerves communicating confusion, and pain. His head was killing him. Uncharacteristically, that was a good thing, he realized. If his head was killing him, then he couldn't already be dead.

He was conscious of a weight on his chest. It was not oppressive, and it was familiar. Looking up, he saw a bright green head staring back at him out of lazy coils of pink and blue. Relieved to once again meet her master's gaze and perceive his feelings, Pip slightly unfurled her wings and slithered off to one side, resting close to but not on him.

Sitting up nearly caused him to black out again. The pain in his head, the razor-sharp agony behind his eyes, was as bad as any he could remember. Squeezing his eyes shut again, he rubbed methodically at his temples, his forehead, the back of his neck beneath his hair. Slowly the sting ebbed, though it did not go away entirely.

The next time he opened his eyes it was to see Treappyn staring down at him. Concern flowed from the counselor; honest, genuine concern. Flinx saw that he was sitting close to one wall of the Audience Chamber great room in the bastion of fortress Metrel. That was interesting, because the last he remembered, he had been standing in the middle of that octagonal chamber, starting suddenly at the intrusion of . . .

He looked up sharply. The skylight through which the would-be assassin had plunged was still there, open now to a clear afternoon sky. The conference had taken place during the morning. That meant he had been unconscious for—he checked his chronometer. Six hours, more or less.

"You are alive." Treappyn let his upper body extend to its normal length and height.

"More or less." Still flinching occasionally from the pain, Flinx climbed to his feet. It was a careful, gradual process, designed to ensure he did not black out or fall down. The lighter gravity helped.

He saw that he and the counselor were not alone in the room. Of the Highborn Pyrrpallinda and the other counselors to the ruler of Wullsakaa there was no sign. The assembled representatives of Jebilisk and Pakktrine Unified were also gone. In addition to himself, Pip, and Treappyn, there were only guards. Their general emotional state, as he perceived them, was instructive. Stalwart and alert on the outside, they were fearful within. Furthermore, the source of their current concern was clear.

Him.

"We tried to help you—after," Treappyn told him. "But your pet wouldn't let anyone near you, and not even the boldest among us was willing to chance her disfavor."

"Probably a wise decision." Suddenly shaky, Flinx leaned back and felt against the solid stone wall for support. "That's typically how she'd react in such a situation, not knowing what was wrong with me."

A breeze distracted him. He found himself looking across the chamber, to the far side of the great room. Directly opposite from where he was standing was a hole in the thick stone-and-masonry wall. It was approximately three meters wide and extended from the floor halfway to the ceiling. Through the breach, blue sky could be seen above distant green and brown terrain. As he stared at it, he was aware that Treappyn was speaking again.

"Somehow the assassin succeeded in scaling the outside of the bastion. We think he may have had help." The counselor made a disgusted noise, his epidermal flaps snapping shut against his flesh. "Even the most loyal retainers can be tempted by bribery. When he fell, several among us saw that he was holding some kind of explosive device in his hands. You looked up . . ." Treappyn's voice trailed away as he remembered, forcing Flinx to prompt him.

"Yes. I looked up."

"Your pet flew from your shoulders. I suppose *launched* would be a more accurate description." His gaze flicked to the resting minidrag. "I never in my life saw anything with wings move so fast. Then everything went black."

Just like with me, Flinx thought. Only not like with me.

"When we started to recover consciousness, we discovered that we had all been thrown across the room. Like yourself just now, guards, counselors, advisors, even the Highborn, found themselves lying individually or in heaps piled up against one wall or another. It was the same with the Aceribb of Jebilisk and his retinue. Also many of the representatives of Pakktrine Unified." His tone changed meaningfully. "But not all of them.

"The assassin was gone. He had disappeared. So had the Kewwyd of Pakktrine and a number of those next to them. Only those who had not been standing close to the Kewwyd remained—inside."

"Inside?" Flinx's bewildered gaze shifted reflexively to the gaping hole in the bastion wall.

"The bodies of the Kewwyd and their closest retainers were discovered lying in the courtyard far below, dead and broken where they had fallen. Following his own return to consciousness, the Highborn has busied himself dealing with the resultant diplomatic niceties, as well as reassuring the populace that he himself is alive and well. I was instructed to stay and look after you, in hopes that you would also recover. I am pleased to see that you have."

"So am I," Flinx admitted candidly. He continued to stare at the hole in the sturdy rock wall. The sides of the rift looked as if they had been ripped apart by a giant's hands.

"At first," Treappyn went on, "everyone assumed that the bomb in the assassin's hands had gone off, or that another, unseen device had exploded prematurely, thus creating the breach in the wall. Upon ensuing reflection, none could explain how this would result in the majority of the Pakktrinian contingent being blown *out* through the resultant opening, instead of being torn apart." Turning slightly, he gestured with a pair of forearms. "There are black skid marks on the floor, seared into the wood. They commence where the Kewwyd and those close to them were standing. They end next to the opening. Of the would-be assassin, there is no sign whatsoever. No body in the courtyard below—nothing." He looked back at Flinx, his emotions a shifting mix of uncertainty and wonderment—and not a little fear.

"Are you sure," the counselor asked him evenly, "that you are not a god?"

As the pain in his head continued to recede without disappearing entirely, Flinx tried to recall what had happened at the instant of attack; to reassess the last second or two before he had lost consciousness. For the life of him, he could not. It wasn't the first time his volatile, unpredictable Talent had saved him. Confronted with the possibility of imminent death, the human body experienced a surge of adrenaline and other endorphins. Not him. His body, and most particularly his Meliorare-messed-with, modified, altered mind, underwent—something else.

Nor was it for the first time.

"No, I'm not a god," he muttered, remembering the counselor. "I don't know exactly what happened, Treappyn. I never do, at such times."

"Such times?" Uncomprehending, the Dwarra stared at him. "This has happened to you before?"

"At least once," he confessed. "Only, I didn't have as much control over the consequences then as I seem to now. I expect that parts of me are—maturing. Changing. In ways I can't predict. Funny," he mused, thinking back, way back, "how similar the other situation was." He indicated the flying snake now relaxing at his feet. "Then, as now, Pip was in immediate danger. When I came to—afterward, I was lying on the ground, just like this time, with her resting on my chest. I remember that it was raining. Those who had been threatening her, and me, had been in a building that ended up like this one—damaged." He shook his head sharply, as if the action would loosen an explanation.

"I don't know what happened then, or now. Only that something within me reacted reflexively to protect both of us. The bond between us is strong and very special. She's an empathic lens," he added, overlooking the fact that the counselor would have no idea what he was talking about.

His voice grew wistful as he gazed past the attentive Treappyn, who struggled to comprehend what the alien was telling him. "That was ten years ago, in a city called Drallar, on a world called Moth." He blinked, nodded in the direction of the gaping tear in the wall opposite. "Now it's happened again."

Suddenly he bent double and clutched at his head as the pain he felt had been diminishing struck at him once again from the depths of his modified nervous system. It was bad, but not as bad as before. Pip looked up, alarmed, while concern once again flooded Treappyn's mind.

"It's—all right," Flinx struggled to reassure the counselor. "These pains aren't new, either. They're at their worst whenever my, uh, abilities manifest themselves."

"This Talent of yours is not necessarily always a blessing, then," Treappyn commented perceptively.

Flinx met the counselor's curious, sympathetic gaze. "That, my good friend, is an understatement. Every time it saves me, I think it's going to kill me. It may yet."

"You should seek treatment," the Dwarra recommended solicitously.

Yes, Flinx thought. The next time I have the opportunity to see a doctor, human or mechanical, in addition to a standard checkup I'll just ask him, or her, or it, to please undo the insidious prenatal manipulations of the wicked Meliorares and re-gengineer me to normal.

What he said was, "I'll keep your advice in mind. Before I can act on it, though, I have other more pressing business to attend to."

"So you told me. I am glad you will be able to continue with your work, whatever that might be." As always, there was no guile in the counselor's response, no veiled design hiding among other emotions. "I said to you before, when we talked at that net-caster's homestead, that I would give much to see other worlds, other intelligent beings, other life-forms. But now, after this . . ." He gestured in the direction of the inexplicable but ominous breach in the far wall, with its intimation of incalculable forces unknown. "I don't think I'm ready."

That's all right, Flinx thought to himself. Neither am I, and I have to live with that knowledge every waking moment of my life.

And some of the nonwaking moments, too.

It was not surprising that after receiving reports of the incident from the few survivors among their delegation to the conference and perusing the skin-flap-raising details therein, the senior officers who had been left in charge of the glorious combined invasion forces of Jebilisk and Pakktrine Unified quickly agreed to every one of the alien's demands. Within the day they had begun breaking camp. Well before the end of the next eight-day their long lines of troops and supply vehicles could be seen traveling away from the borders of Wullsakaa, making the maximum speed of which they were capable; those of Pakktrine Unified wending their way southeastward, the riders of Jebilisk heading due north.

They had a good deal to think about and much to occupy their minds as they retraced their steps homeward. The ranking elders of Pakktrine, for instance, were already engaged in active political infighting as to who should be chosen to fill the sudden unexpected triple vacancies at the top of their government. Faced with no such conundrum, the Aceribb of Jebilisk had only to deal with recurrent nightmares in which he found himself standing at the critical moment just a little closer to the now demised former members of the Kewwyd.

While the joyous and much-relieved citizens of Metrel City celebrated, Flinx brooded. He had set down on this world intending only to permit the *Teacher* to conduct some necessary maintenance and repair. Curiosity and boredom had driven him to take a quick, informal look around. He had ended up giving of his time, knowledge, and skills to help hundreds of sick and crippled natives. His good intentions had resulted in war between three local realms and an untold number of deaths, the most recent of which he was directly responsible for.

Why, he thought to himself and not for the first time, can't I learn to mind my own business?

Squatting nearby, Treappyn studied the silent alien. He was cognizant of the cause of the alien's moodiness, having been privy to it for several days now. That did not mean he understood. Having grown comfortable, if still cautious, in the creature's presence, he had learned that it responded most favorably of all to honest opinion straightforwardly rendered. No doubt because, thanks to its remarkable perceptiveness, it could invariably tell when someone was lying to it. Better to court the creature's displeasure and disagreement, the counselor subsequently advised his colleagues and the Highborn, than to engage in mendacity that was doomed to failure from the start.

"I don't understand, Flinx," he told the alien. As always, the counselor tried to divide his attention between the visitor and the flying creature that was currently resting on the projecting shelf behind him. "The Kewwyd of Pakktrine deserved what happened to them.

They sanctioned an attempt on your life." Eyes respectfully wide, Treappyn thrust both Sensitives in the alien's direction. "One that would have succeeded, if not for your invocation of magic."

Sounding tired, Flinx glanced up from where he was sitting on the narrow stone hearth. "I keep telling you: it wasn't magic, Treappyn."

"Then what was it, friend Flinx?" The counselor's curiosity was genuine. "I want to understand. If not magic, then what made the hole in the bastion's inner wall? What blew the Kewwyd and those guarding them out through that hole, to fall to their deaths in the courtyard below? Tell me."

Lowering its gaze, the alien entwined together the ten strange little bony digits it used for gripping things. "I can't, Treappyn. I don't know myself. Like I told you earlier, it's happened to me before, under similar circumstances. I don't know what happened that time, either."

The counselor had to believe what the alien was telling him. For one thing, if he did not, the creature would sense his uncertainty and query him on the reason behind it. "It must be terrible," he remarked thoughtfully, "to possess such powers, yet to be ignorant of how they work, or unable to control them."

Startled, Flinx looked up at the counselor. He knew Treappyn was shrewd, but until this moment he had not realized the depth of the young, lumbering counselor's insightfulness. "Yes, that's exactly right, Treappyn."

Gratified at this, the counselor continued to speak his mind. "If it was me, I would worry that such lack of knowledge and control might one day result in my hurting myself as well as others."

Now there's a promising thought, Flinx mused mockingly. Someday I'll get angry at something and, without ever knowing how or why, blow myself through a wall. Or, worse, someone entirely innocent who's just unlucky enough to be in the vicinity. He had been right in leaving Clarity Held behind on New Riviera. How could he ask someone to live with him when, in a bad moment or fit of pique or even during a dream, he might cause them unimaginable harm? He could not have a life, the ordinary life he so desperately wanted, until he learned how to master not just emotional perception and projection, but every aspect of his mutated abilities.

A rising susurration outside distracted him. Straightening and moving away from the hearth, he headed toward the nearest window. Like all Wullsakaan windowpanes it was tall and narrow, though fashioned of better-quality glass than most.

"Now what?" he inquired of his host with unbecoming irritability.

"It is the people of Metrel City," Treappyn informed him. "And others who have come from distant reaches of the realm. I believe there are also contingents from Jebilisk and Pakktrine Unified."

Flinx frowned. From her resting place on the shelf, Pip looked up curiously. "Contingents? Contingents of what?"

Familiar as he was by this time with the alien's mind-set on certain matters, Treappyn looked distinctly uncomfortable. "Worshippers." Flinx just stared at the counselor. "They have heard of what you did."

Recovering, Flinx replied sharply, "How could they have *heard of what I did*? I don't know myself what I did."

"Perhaps not." As the alien was obviously agitated, Treappyn did his best to employ a soothing tone. "But the *consequences* of whatever it was that you did are well known. The Pakktrinian assassin was there, and then he was not. The Kewwyd of Pakktrine Unified and their entourage were there, and then most of them were not." Raising a pair of forearms and flanges, he gestured in the direction of the gaping rift in the bastion wall, where repairs had not yet begun. "There stood a solid wall of stone, and then it was not. All these things have been attributed to your intervention." Four arms moved in a manner to suggest acceptance. "The 'how' of it has been subject to much speculation; some of it grounded on the eyewitness reports of those who were there, much of the remainder wild and imaginative." He eyed the alien directly, in the fashion both preferred. "You cannot prevent people from speculating on such things."

"Worshippers." Flinx shook his head, a gesture Treappyn had come to recognize. "A stop has *got* to be put to this nonsense—now."

At the alien's insistence, Treappyn escorted him and his pet down a wide, winding stone staircase until they had descended almost to courtyard level. Entering a room that was impressive and lavishly decorated but far smaller than the Audience Chamber they had just left, the counselor indicated a double glass-and-wood door that opened onto a walkway that ran just above and parallel to the noise-filled courtyard. At this lower level, the shouts and yells of the surging crowd outside were much louder.

"Try what you will, friend Flinx. But having listened to and observed some of the talk, I have doubts as to whether even you yourself can succeed in putting an end to the conjecture. Myth begins to layer you like fine cloth."

Disregarding the counselor's pessimism, Flinx moved to the portal and pushed both narrow doors aside. Immediately, the roar of the crowd grew louder: both because he was outside, and because those in the forefront of the eddying, indecisive crowd caught sight of him and immediately raised the volume of their chanting. Echoing eerie and odd from the throats of dozens, perhaps hundreds of assembled Dwarra, cries of "Flinx, Flinx!" began to resound across the courtyard. Hitherto uninterested citizens turned from their tasks to search for the source of the rejuvenated commotion, and not a few interrupted their intended routine to join the multitude for a better look— and perhaps to see what might happen.

Gazing out at the sea of alien faces and bodies, noting the scattering of Pakktrinians and Jebiliskai among them, a despairing Flinx raised both arms. It had the intended affect of quieting, if not completely silencing, the crowd. From within the fortress chamber where he had been conversing with Treappyn, Pip flew out to settle herself on his shoulders and assure herself that the flood of emotion presently engulfing her master presaged no enmity.

"Listen to me!" he shouted in his best Dwarrani. "I am only a person, like you. A visitor, who will soon be leaving your world. You need to forget me and go on with your lives as before!"

"NO—NO—NO!" The massed shouts were deafening. Instead of being dampened by his demurral, they grew louder.

"I am no god!" he bellowed back heatedly.

It didn't make any difference to the half-hysterical crowd. They jostled and shoved to get a better look at their new deity. To get closer to him. Wild eyes were expanded to the maximum. Gripping flanges tugged and grabbed. The weak and immature found themselves roughly pushed aside by eager worshippers locked in paroxysms of ecstasy. Frustrated at his inability to make them understand, much less get them to listen, he even tried to utilize his Talent to project feelings of discord and uncertainty onto the throng. But there were too many of them for him to achieve any kind of focus. The force of his conviction was dissipated by the numbers confronting him, and failed to persuade.

What a mess he had made of the present state of affairs, he told himself. It seemed that the longer he remained and the harder he struggled to clear things up, the worse they became. True, he had stopped a war. Equally true, he had been the cause of it in the first place. Action, reaction, no matter how aloof he tried to be. As the crowd roared and implored, he turned to look back at Treappyn. With a wisdom that belied his years, the hefty, well-meaning counselor gazed squarely back at him.

I can't help you with this, the Dwarra's slightly flexing eyes seemed to say, and the emotions Flinx sensed pouring forth from within the alien advisor only served to confirm his helplessness.

No one could help him, Flinx realized. Like it or not, the well-intentioned visitor had become the all-powerful Visitant.

Unresolved or not, it was time to go before he made the situation any worse. All it took was a terse command whispered into the pickup on his wrist.

Moments later heads tilted backward and flanges pointed skyward as the *Teacher*'s skimmer appeared and commenced a gradual descent toward the courtyard. Conscious of the effect it would have but unable—and too tired—to think of a better way to manage his departure, he boarded the waiting vehicle as it hovered next to the walkway. Thanks to the light gravity, it was easy for him to jump up and in. The leap would have been impossible for the average Dwarra.

Seeing that he truly was leaving their presence and without knowing for how long, the frenzied, chanting crowd surged forward. Flanges flailed at the balcony railing, desperately seeking purchase. Overcome with religious fervor, a few of the more active and athletic worshippers succeeded in reaching high enough to touch the bottom of the skimmer before it rose skyward.

The chanting continued for as long as the small craft was visible and began to die down only when it disappeared into the underside of the hovering mass of the *Teacher*. This was followed soon thereafter by the rise of a muted thrumming. Deep and penetrating, it set skin and bone, earth and stone, to vibrating with its intensity. An audible gasp of collective awe rose from the assembled and still-growing crowd as the alien vessel began its climb through the clouds. As those on the ground watched, the *Teacher* grew smaller and smaller, shrinking until it was the size of a freight wagon, then a writing stylus. And then it was gone.

If not an indisputably god-like ascension, it had certainly been an impressive one.

Alternately confused and bemused, the crowd began to break up. Though daunted by what they had just witnessed, some citizens returned to the work and routine that the alien's appearance and departure had temporarily interrupted. Others joined in groups to discuss its ramifications. A few squatted as deeply into themselves as was physically possible and fell to uttering sorrowful lamentations.

Standing in the balcony portal framed by the open doors, Treappyn eventually turned away from the now vacant sky only to see the silent figure of His August Highborn Pyr Pyrrpallinda standing there facing him. The counselor hurried to stammer his apologies.

"Highborn, I did not know—you should have announced—"

Raising a pair of flanges, Pyrrpallinda forestalled any further apologia. "Calm yourself, Treappyn. I watched as spellbound as any citizen. And as powerless to affect events." Advancing on all four forelegs, he halted just behind the counselor. From there he could see more of the increasingly cloud-mottled sky outside, but was still invisible to the disintegrating throng of would-be worshippers.

"What do you think, counselor?" He gestured heavenward. "Will this new Church of the Alien Flinx endure, or will it eventually go the way of so many cults?"

Treappyn considered carefully. "It is difficult to say, Highborn. He was not long among us, and his immediate influence, while profound, was limited to those few who saw him or were directly helped by him." He turned back to the outside. "Of course, if he, or others like him, were to return to Arrawd . . ."

Pyrrpallinda eyed the younger male intently. "Do you think that will happen?"

"Again, who am I to speculate on matters of the unknowable? But if I were pressed, I would say no. Only because that is what the alien himself told me, and I have no reason to doubt his word. Also, I sense that the longer he remained among us, the greater became his discontent." The counselor gestured in a way that indicated inner confusion. "I don't know why this should be, since we of Wullsakaa, at least, did our best to make him feel welcome among us. But I believe it to be so. I believe it in my bones. I do not think he will be back."

His August Highborn Pyrrpallinda was silent for a while. When he next spoke again, it was as if he was talking to himself as much as to the counselor standing attentively nearby.

"Just as well. No way to predict the actions of the un-Dwarra. A whim might have seen him side later with the Jebilisk, or another of our enemies." Uttering a noise unbecoming a Highborn, he added cynically, "This peace will last as long as most of them do." Remembering that he was not alone, he looked back at Treappyn.

"I intend to convene a full meeting of all senior and junior advisors for tomorrow morning. We have a realm to run." Turning, he started back into the depths of the room. "I'll need cost estimates for the repair of at least one and possibly three bridges. And a bastion wall."

"Yes," Treappyn agreed, trailing respectfully behind his liege. "It should be cheaper if the Treasury can afford to contract for simultaneous repairs. Economies of scale dictate that . . ."

Visiting alien gods all but forgotten, their conversation grew more animated as they made their way deeper into the fortress. Whatever Flinx was, had been, or meant was soon lost in the very real need to manage reality instead of conjecture.

In the courtyard outside, those milling true believers who still remained occasionally pointed but more rarely gazed skyward as they began to compile the beginnings of what would eventually become the Liturgy of the Alien Flinx. Whether this would become canon or whimsy, whether it would remain a provincial curiosity of Wullsakaa or spread throughout the length and breadth of all Arrawd, only time and the perseverance of its tentative but energetic devotees would tell.

"Everything, I take it, is functioning properly, and the repairs we came here to make are holding appropriately?"

"One would have to have access to, or be, a precision instrument in order to tell that any change had been effected," the *Teacher* assured him confidently.

"Ready to leave?"

"I am preparing to implement departure along the new vector you have suggested."

"Good." Slumping down in the welcoming embrace of the

lounge chair, the moist air surrounding him filled with small, colorful, harmless flying things, listening to water cascade into the artificial pond while the striking fragrances of exotic vegetation gathered from several worlds pungently scented the air around him, Flinx stroked Pip's back as she lay contentedly on his stomach. "Then maybe you have a suggestion or two about how to repair me."

The ship-mind's reply was devoid of mockery. "I was not aware that you were broken, Flinx."

"You know what I mean. You're perceptive enough to understand."

The *Teacher* also knew enough to know how to pause for effect before replying. "If you are lamenting the fact that your attempt to sow good among the native population did not eventuate as effectively as you intended, you must not blame yourself. Analysis of cause—you—and effect—one localized war, now terminated, and one incipient religion, future undetermined—suggests that the Dwarra are heavily prone to both, and that your presence only temporarily exacerbated a set of endemic cultural conditions."

Flinx stirred on the lounge, forcing an annoyed Pip to shift her coils to avoid slipping off his restless torso. "Could you put that another way?"

The ship-mind responded efficiently. "The Dwarra would fight among themselves and run through many different beliefs whether you had appeared among them or not."

"Well, maybe . . . ," he muttered, slightly reassured. The *Teacher* had the ability to comfort him without being overly specific. "You try to do good—" he began.

"Perhaps you shouldn't try so hard," ship-mind interrupted him. "It is a historical characteristic of humans that when they try to do 'good' among others, including themselves, their efforts all too often have the opposite effect. You have a strenuous course set before you. Given such conditions, future diffident attempts at ancillary altruism might best be avoided."

Lying back on the lounge and letting it more fully adapt to his weight and frame, he gazed ceilingward. It was not necessary to look for a lens. The ship's visual and audio pickups were everywhere.

"That's not my nature. If I see someone needing help, I feel compelled to extend it. It's because of who I am. What I am," he added thoughtfully. "Maybe it's because I feel I need so much help myself that I feel the need to help others when and where I can." He paused a moment. "Otherwise I'd be setting you on a course straight back to New Riviera, I'd pick up Clarity, and we'd go somewhere pleasant and quiet and live out our lives as normally as my internal modifications would permit."

He could almost imagine the ship-mind nodding tolerantly. "But you're not going to do that, Flinx. You're going to do as Bran Tse-Mallory and the Eint Truzenzuzex suggested, and try to save a galaxy whose inhabitants might not ever know your name or the extent of your efforts on their behalf. Because that's also who, and what, you are."

Folding his arms over his chest above where Pip was resting contently, he growled at no one in particular. "Yeah, I know, I know." He took a deep breath. It didn't help. "And I'm not getting any of anything done lying here swapping inanities with you. Get us moving."

"Right away, master," the *Teacher* replied, in a subtle, suavely modified tone that might or might not have contained just a soupçon of sarcasm.

CHAPTER

16

Bugs everywhere. No, not bugs, Clarity hastily corrected herself. Old cognomens were slow to fade from collective memory. The thranx themselves didn't mind. They found human attempts to avoid comparing their chitinous friends with primitive Terran insects amusing. The thranx sense of humor was dry, but not wanting.

They had landed on Hivehom at Chitteranx and hurriedly boarded an atmospheric shuttle that had transported them down to Yalwez, far to the south on Hivehom's largest continent. There, well inland from the shores of vast Maldrett Bay and not far from the site of ancient thranx civilization known as the Valley of the Dead, Bran Tse-Mallory and Truzenzuzex had introduced her to members of a stealth research branch of Commonwealth Science Central of which the Eint was a prominent member.

She had encountered thranx before, of course. As humanity's closest friends and allies among the known intelligent species and as cofounders of the Commonwealth, the mastiff-sized, eight-limbed insectoids were present in varying numbers on every one of its developed worlds. Their large colonies in the Amazon and Congo on

Earth found their counterparts in the substantial human outposts on Hivehom's Mediterranea Plateau and industrial-commercial interests on Humus.

But Yalwez and the ancient Valley of the Dead were quite distant from such cool highlands, she was very far from her comfortable home on New Riviera, and save for the amiable but sometimes inscrutable Tse-Mallory, she had not seen another human since they had left behind the main shuttleport at now far-off Chitteranx.

She could have stayed on New Riviera. Tse-Mallory had assured her that through their contacts, he and Truzenzuzex could guarantee her privacy from the attentions of inquisitive Commonwealth officials and disreputable groups such as the Order of Null. Besides, it was Flinx such organizations, legal and not, were after—not her. Or, they offered, she could come with them. Having recovered from the injuries she had sustained when Flinx had taken flight from her world, she did not have to consider long. As was proving to be more and more frequently the case, she elected to follow her heart instead of her brain.

Tse-Mallory and Truzenzuzex had sent Flinx on a mission. When he returned from it, whether successful or not, he would obviously report first to them. Therefore, she was most likely to see him soonest if she remained in the company of the unusual pairing of elderly scientist-adventurers who were his closest friends. So she had tidied up her affairs, taken a leave of absence from her job, security-sealed her home, and agreed to follow them. Now she found herself in a new place, somewhere she had never expected to visit: the venerable thranx homeworld and Commonwealth co-capital of Hivehom.

Where she presently found herself, along with Tse-Mallory, towering over Truzenzuzex and the senior thranx researcher who had greeted them. Like those of her female colleagues, Kesedbarmek's ovipositors had stiffened in suspicion at the sight of the unknown human female, until Truzenzuzex had assured her that Clarity had more than earned the same access to restricted information as himself and Tse-Mallory.

"Her status in the ongoing investigation of the singular phe-

nomena that forms the basis of our mutual interest is unique," the
Eint had assured his chary, aquamarine-hued colleague.

Once that declaration had worked its way throughout the surrep-
titious facility, Clarity no longer found herself the subject of recurring stares on the part of its wholly thranx staff. Though, she told
herself, given the nature of their compound eyes, it was difficult to
tell when a thranx was staring at you and when it was not. Already,
she had learned to identify the subject of their attention by looking
not at their large, golden eyes, but at the direction in which their
graceful, feathery antennae happened to be pointed.

Presently, the four of them were walking down a corridor that
was not nearly as high as it was wide. Like the majority of thranx
construction, it was situated beneath the hot, humid planetary surface. Coved corners and reduced but adequate indirect lighting soft-
ened the otherwise utilitarian design that was at once ultramodern
and thoughtfully reflective of ancient tastes. The top of her head just
did clear the low ceiling, allowing the minidrag Scrap to cling to her
neck and left shoulder without having to constantly shift his position.
In contrast, the taller Tse-Mallory had to bend frequently to avoid
bumping into the occasional protruding conduit or other overhead
fixture. The grizzled scientist did not seem to mind the physical limitations imposed by their present surroundings. It was as if he had
spent as much time on thranx-dominated worlds as on those populated principally by his own kind.

Thankfully, she had never been subject to claustrophobia. For
anyone who had been forced to spend day after anxious day wandering in total darkness on the primitive world of Longtunnel, the con-
strictions of thranx construction barely qualified as inconvenient.
Several of the passageways she and her companions had been obliged
to traverse in order to access the current larger one had been sufficiently narrow that if she had extended both arms out to the side, she
would have been able to touch both walls simultaneously.

In deference to the human members of the party, both Kesedbarmek and Truzenzuzex forbore from speaking in High or Low

Thranx. Instead, they employed the well-established Commonwealth lingua franca known as symbospeech. Like any educated Commonwealth citizen, Clarity was reasonably fluent in that hybrid patois, though she did not know all the appropriate hand gestures that corresponded to the expressive movements of thranx truhands and foothands. So while she could make herself understood without any problems, her efforts at interspecies communication lacked polish. Neither of the two thranx seemed to mind, and no one made fun of her occasionally clumsy attempts at visible punctuation.

For several minutes now they had not encountered anyone else. Turning a sharp corner, the quartet of humans and thranx entered a short, slightly narrower corridor at the end of which was a large door deeply embossed with a ribbed design she did not recognize. This was not surprising, since the insignia of certain special branches of Commonwealth Science Central were not widely disseminated. More disconcerting was the presence, this deep into a typical subterranean complex on the highly civilized and largely pacific thranx homeworld, of an armed guard. The single eight-limbed figure stood as tall as he was able, though the valentine-shaped head did not reach as high as her own and did not even come up to Tse-Mallory's shoulders. Truhands and foothands worked together to handle a rifle-like weapon that for all its svelte design looked more than passably intimidating. The lethal device would have been useless in human hands, Homo sapiens being two limbs short of the complement necessary to manage it.

Sticking her head into the metallic, reflective half sphere that protruded from the wall to the right of the portal, Kesedbarmek waited briefly while the security device read the unique pattern of her compound eyes and matched it to the distinctive pattern of her brain waves. As she drew back, the single door rose upward into an accommodating ceiling recess and the guard stepped aside to let them pass. The armed male did not glance in Clarity's direction, nor at Tse-Mallory, suggesting that the two of them were not the first humans to pass this way. As she strode past, Scrap flicked his pointed tongue in the guard's direction and let out a sharp hiss.

"Why all the security?" she murmured to Tse-Mallory as they entered a chamber larger than any they had encountered since leaving the arrival lounge at Yalwez shuttleport.

"There are some things better kept from the general public," he explained, leaning down to whisper to her. Eyes of obsidian black gazed into her own. "Unfortunately, panic is a condition that seems to be common to all sentient species. Certain bits of knowledge are best held in trust by those mentally and emotionally trained to cope with them on a rational basis. I think you know of what I speak."

Though neither of her guardians had spoken directly of the reason for the journey to Hivehom, she was very much afraid that she did.

The far side of the room was marked by a number of study stations: banks of refractive electronics fronting the kind of longitudinal resting platforms that served thranx as both chairs and beds. Two were occupied. Taking note of the newcomers, their operators looked up only briefly before returning to the work at hand.

Halting in the center of the chamber, which for a change was high-ceilinged enough to allow even Tse-Mallory to stand erect without bending, Kesedbarmek moved to a single tapering post that protruded from the floor and addressed it in High Thranx. Clarity caught the meaning of a few phrases, but for the most part the elaborate, if sharply defined, mix of whistles, words, and clicks was beyond her limited store of linguistic knowledge. Flinx was fluent in both thranx dialects, she knew. But Flinx wasn't here. There were only the two thranx and the always affable but sometimes distant Tse-Mallory. The chamber darkened in response to their host's commands. Despite the heat and high humidity favored by the thranx, she found herself shivering.

The chamber transformed into a cartographic habitat. She'd stood in similar rooms before, but this time many of the clouds of stars and nebulae that filled the domed open space to surround her and her companions were unfamiliar to her. It took her a moment to realize why. Instead of the usual map of the Commonwealth or even a greater galographic, she realized that she was standing in the midst of a number of whole galaxies. At Kesedbarmek's command, the view contracted somewhat. One large spiral galaxy was highlighted, tinted a distinguishing green. It was the color the thranx always utilized whenever they wished to indicate the presence of life, whereas humans were as likely to employ blue. Nearby, Tse-Mallory shifted his stance slightly and leaned toward her.

"You are here," he murmured softly.

"Yes, that is our home," Kesedbarmek confirmed. "We are there. And *it* has now advanced to here." Making her way through the three-dimensional representation, the thranx scientist reached out to push one of the four opposing digits on her left truhand into the edge of another galaxy. It immediately glowed red. That, however, was not what drew Clarity's interest. Lacking though her education might be in the finer nuances of higher astronomics, she knew enough to tell that there was something seriously wrong with the cluster that had been singled out.

It was another spiral galaxy, like the Milky Way, but with at least one significant visible difference: at least a third of it was missing. The globular core seemed unusually dim, and the surviving spiral arms were ragged and irregular, as if they had been pulled and distorted by inconceivable forces. Behind it, on the side that appeared to have gone missing, was a vast dark area that extended all the way to the far boundaries of the room. At first she assumed the distorted galaxy was simply located at the edge of the dimensional map, but, looking around, she saw that multiple galaxies extended much farther into the distance off to either side of the partial cluster that had been highlighted. The emptiness behind it took the shape of an enormous extended cone, with its apex penetrating the distorted galaxy like the stinger of some unimaginable predatory insect.

She sensed immediately what it must represent. Monitoring her emotions, Scrap stirred uneasily on her shoulder. She had been present when Tse-Mallory and Truzenzuzex had discussed the phenomenon with Flinx on New Riviera.

The Great Emptiness. The Great Void, as the thranx referred to it. According to Flinx, there was something dreadful behind or within it that was blocked from direct observation by a huge gravitational lens of dark matter. Something horrific that howled and writhed and roared through empty space within an area that was three hundred million light-years across and one hundred million megaparsecs in volume.

Something that was coming this way.

"It's gotten worse." Staring at the image that hovered between himself and the two thranx, Tse-Mallory was not whispering now. "And in measurable time."

Using truhands only, Kesedbarmek gestured to indicate agreement. "Though velocities in the region remain, as previously noted, inconsistent, the process is certainly measurable within the time-compensation limits of our available instrumentation, and is clearly continuing to accelerate." After a glance at Truzenzuzex, their host continued. "You must swear not to reveal anything that is told to you here, Clarity Held."

She felt offended. "It seems like my life is turning into one long litany of things I'm not supposed to talk about."

Truzenzuzex reassured his colleague. "As we have indicated, she knows what we know, and in certain ways and certain aspects may know more of what is happening than do we."

Satisfied by this, Kesedbarmek continued. As she spoke, she used a truhand and foothand to trace shapes and directions in the air. Like ethereal ink, faint lines of lambent bright blue trailed the tips of her shiny, green-blue, multijointed fingers.

"We have been able to keep the singularity in question under study for a while now. As you know, that its true significance was noted at all is due to a combination of diligence on the part of certain of our people"—she glanced in the direction of Tse-Mallory and Truzenzuzex—"and to a report stemming from an informal meeting that took place between a padre of the United Church and the human with whom you exist in close emotional, if presently not physical, contact." This time Clarity had no doubt where those golden, multi-lensed eyes were focused.

"Philip Lynx," she confirmed unnecessarily.

"*Crr!lk.*" Thranx digits wove evocative patterns in the star-spotted darkness as their hostess turned her attention back to the pair of visiting scientists. "The reason for asking you here is that for the first time, extensive and detailed examination of the area of concern has yielded visible evidence of actual destructive activity. Dissemination of this discovery is necessarily limited to an extremely small number of the aware, while ongoing security demands dictate that it not even be trusted to supposedly secure space-minus communications." Within the depths of the map, a quartet of digits moved once more, to half cup the distorted cluster of far-distant stars in their chitinous fingers.

"This galaxy is known to us as Poltebet and to human astronomers as MH-four-three-eight-A. It is smaller than our own, or the one you call Andromeda, but still of considerable size. Note this area." Polysaccharide digits traced the space where missing spirals should have extended outward into darkness. "Offsetting arms should be swirling here. They are not. Furthermore, the center of Poltebet shows signs of a distinctive, unusual, and inexplicable energy deficiency. This deficit continues to increase even as the situation is monitored. Given the time scale on which events of galactic magnitude normally proceed, the rate at which this loss is occurring exceeds anything in our, or your, scientific experience." When she continued, her delicate truhands moved apart to encompass a much larger area.

"Galaxy Poltebet—MH-four-three-eight-A is disappearing, at quantifiable speed and in astronomical terms literally before our eyes." Moving beyond the stellar cluster under discussion, her digits traced blue lines in the blackness beyond. "Something is consuming it. This is not an instance of one galaxy colliding with another and absorbing it, or of a supermassive black hole or other identifiable astronomical phenomenon siphoning off stellar mass. It is unprecedented.

"Beyond, and in the direction of absorption, is the expanse that has been known to human astronomers for hundreds of years as the Great Emptiness and to us as the Great Void. We believe that whatever is consuming Poltebet—MH-four-three-eight-A is the first measurable manifestation of whatever is emerging from that hitherto unviewable region, perhaps a tendril of the actual malevolent phenomenon perceived by the human Philip Lynx."

Along with his companions, Tse-Mallory stared intently at the hovering visual. "A significant and, needless to say, unsettling development. At least we finally have a chance to get a look at the thing, or a portion of it."

Kesedbarmek gestured disarmingly. "So one would think. Unfortunately even our best instruments, compensating for the relevant chronological delay so that measurements are recorded in actual time, detect nothing. The phenomenon continues to reveal nothing of its true nature. We are made aware of its presence only through its catastrophic activity, in the same way that an unseen carnivore reveals itself only through the carcass it leaves behind."

Clarity stared at the glowing representation. It was one thing to listen to Flinx describe what he felt, what he sensed, when he had visions of the indescribable malevolence that lay within the Great Emptiness; quite another to see it rendered in front of her as a visible, almost tangible image, and an unimaginably destructive one at that.

The breathing spicules on Truzenzuzex's thorax expanded as he inhaled deeply. "One would expect some sort of measurable consequent activity: bursts of gamma- or X-rays, something strikingly visible at one end of the electromagnetic spectrum or the other."

Kesedbarmek gestured negativity. "There is nothing. No detectable infall of charged particles, no streams of visible light or heat or energy—nothing. Poltebet—MH-four-three-eight-A is simply vanishing." Compound eyes and antennae turned once more in Clarity's direction. "Unlike the unique human upon whose singular perception we are all dependent, we have no sense of the thing beyond what it leaves behind—which is nothing." She returned her attention to her fellow thranx.

"What of this essential individual? When last we communicated you spoke, with obligatory obliqueness, of an attempt on his part to ascertain the location of a still-functioning Tar-Aiym device of significant potential, with an eye toward attempting to employ it to impact the advance of the approaching cataclysmic phenomenon." Once again, she indicated the ghostly image of the rapidly vanishing galaxy. "Though given the scope of the catastrophe that will eventually confront us I and my colleagues continue to doubt any potential efficacy."

Truzenzuzex exchanged a look with Tse-Mallory, his glance passing over Clarity as it returned to their host. "One seeks hope where one can find it. To the best of our knowledge the individual in question is in the process of doing exactly that. Unfortunately, *srr!lk,* we can not project a credible time frame for possible success."

"You have no way of communicating with him while he is engaged in this search?" she asked.

"He is presently probing sundry portions of the Blight," Tse-Mallory informed the fretful scientist. "For reasons of security—personal as well as otherwise—it was decided that he not engage in communication with anyone, including ourselves, until and unless he has something of significance to report. As you know there are others, including branches of government, whose attentions would only complicate our efforts should they learn of his location and attempt to detain him."

Kesedbarmek indicated understanding. "As time passes, it becomes increasingly difficult to keep knowledge of the phenomenon in question a secret. That hundreds of years might pass before it begins to impact on our civilization would mitigate but by no means eliminate the danger to the moral, mental, and spiritual development of the Commonwealth."

Hundreds of years, Clarity thought. They had told her the same thing on New Riviera. That it might be centuries of years before this advancing horror threatened their own galaxy. She didn't need millennia. She didn't even need hundreds of years. A few decades of happiness with the man she loved was all she wanted. Was that too much to wish for? Was that being selfish, when the future lives of billions of intelligent beings were at stake? All she wanted was for Flinx to come back to her, for them to have *some* time together. Some time to be happy in each other's company. She felt she knew that strange, solitary young man well enough to know that if she asked him to make that choice, if she pressed him hard enough, he just might opt to agree. But if she did, and he responded favorably, would he still be the man she had fallen in love with?

Can't marry. Have to save the galaxy first. Uncomplicated ordinary domesticity later. She stood quietly in the semi-darkness, illuminated by the glow of dozens of precisely imaged, hovering galaxies, watching and listening as the two most intelligent beings she had ever met in her life conversed in a steady hum of words, whistles, and clicks with an oversized insectoid who gleamed like an ambulatory topaz and smelled of orchids and vanilla.

Other couples saw their nuptials blocked by bickering relatives, or protesting friends, or financial difficulties, or medical problems.

She could only fantasize, and yearn hopelessly for, such simplicity.

The first indication that something was amiss came from certain uniquely sensitive plants growing in the *Teacher*'s lounge area. They began to sway and twitch as if in the presence of an electric current. As for Pip, she was lying coiled on the padded bed close to the lounge when she suddenly jerked and twisted. Insufficiently intelligent to interpret the meaning of what she was mentally magnifying, she nonetheless reacted powerfully to the intrusion. After the initial shock, her body relaxed. Quivering on the folds of fabric, she trembled only slightly as the incursion continued full force. For all its strength, it was not harmful. She remained thus, a bioconduit amplifying and facilitating access to the intrusion's final destination.

That individual twitched slightly as he lay on the lounge, ostensibly asleep but far from unperceptive. Tired but recovering from the frustrations engendered by his time on Arrawd, Flinx had taken a mild soporific and fallen into a deep sleep, knowing that the ship would wake him when it was time to depart orbit. As was all too often the case, however, not all of him was wholly asleep.

That distinctive segment of his mind had just been contacted.

THERE IS A DANGER.

I know, a part of him replied.

NO. NOT THAT. ANOTHER. NEARER. DIFFERENT. MORE IMPENDING. IT MUST BE DEALT WITH FIRST.

Confused, exhausted, neither unconscious nor entirely aware, he struggled to comprehend while on the floor by his side Pip quivered like a cable through which a powerful current was being passed.

I don't understand. I don't see. What other? What nearer? What different?

The contact proceeded to show him.

It was everything that was claimed, and more. It was utterly different from anything he had ever encountered before, or imagined. And unlike the immense unknown that lurked within the Great Emptiness, it was not on the borders of the Commonwealth, threatening it from a far-distant place and time.

It was already inside.

Recoiling from what he perceived, he cried out in his quasi-consciousness. *How can I deal with something like that? I am only one.*

YOU HAVE A CLASS-A MIND. I AM NOT THAT EQUAL . . . BUT I AM NEAR. TOGETHER WE WILL DEAL WITH IT. IT IS MY LOT TO DO SO. IT MUST BE DONE CAREFULLY, SUBTLY, CAUTIOUSLY. IN MOMENTS MEASURED. BUT TOGETHER, IT CAN BE DONE.

Perception clarified, ever so slightly. *You are asleep.*

NOT SLEEP. SOMETHING ELSE. LIKE YOU.

Body twisting on the lounge, Flinx fought to comprehend. *One danger, another danger. I'm tired—so tired. If I agree to help . . .*

YOU MUST HELP.

. . . then what happens after?

There was a brief pause, then,

YOU MOVE ON. I GET TO DIE. AND . . . I WILL SHOW YOU THINGS BEFORE THIS IS DONE.

THIS WAY . . .

The contact snapped. Breathing hard, Flinx sat up sharply. Nearby, Pip's eyes flashed open, her pleated wings unfurled, and in a couple of quick beats she had coiled herself so tightly around his left arm and shoulder that he had to coax her to relax lest she cut off the flow of blood to his hand.

Around him, all was peaceful and normal. Decorative flying things flitted through the moist, perfumed air of the relaxation chamber. Exotic flora thrust strange tendrils and leaves toward the artificial light. Bubbles of light water rose toward the upper siphon as water danced and ran down the artificial waterfall that was the centerpiece of the chamber.

It had been no dream. Having experienced dreams and—other things—Flinx knew the difference all too well. But who—or what—had been in his head? Remarkably, with one notable exception it was more like himself than any other mind with which he had ever been in contact. More akin to his own than Truzenzuzex, or Bran Tse-Mallory, or Clarity, or anyone, human or otherwise. Vaguely, it reminded him not of someone, but of something, else. He shook his head, trying to clear it.

The urgency had been profound, the need overwhelming. He felt that he had no choice but to comply. The contact had spoken of its lot. Mine, Flinx thought, apparently is to deal with the needs of others to the exclusion of my own.

Another danger. Impending, the contact had declaimed. Always another danger. Always another threat. Actually, he knew he did not have to accede. He could continue on his way, searching for the wandering Tar-Aiym weapons platform, fulfilling the request made by Tse-Mallory and Truzenzuzex. Until, successful or otherwise, he returned to live out the balance of his abnormal, tormented life with the one person, the one woman, with whom he had grown comfortable.

But—there was something else. Something that smacked of weight and importance. Something nonspecific yet holding out matchless promise.

I will show you things before this is done.

He could not resist. The import of that vow spread throughout his being, saturated his self with suggestion. His damnable curiosity, getting in the way of common sense again. He sighed heavily. Another pause. Another shift. Another detour.

Until this point, the *Teacher* had been silent. Watching, recording, striving to interpret without interposing itself or its own opinions. It had been well-made, and meticulously programmed. Now, as its master sat on the side of the lounge and pondered, it finally spoke.

"All preparations for departure from this system are completed. Shall I resume the vector along which we were traveling when our journey was interrupted?"

"No." Having made up his mind, Flinx did not hesitate. "Change in course, change in plans. We're going back to the Commonwealth."

"Back?" The ship-mind sounded uncertain, a condition with which it was not overly familiar. "But the last known projected track of the object that we are seeking indicates that—"

"New course," Flinx interrupted concisely. "Back to the Commonwealth. We need to pay a visit to another colony world. One we haven't visited before. Which means you will likely have to change your appearance yet again."

The *Teacher* had expressed its uncertainty. Having had it noted, it now proceeded to straightforward compliance. That, too, was part of its noble programming.

"Destination?"

Lying back on the lounge, Flinx stretched out and placed his folded hands behind his head. A few flying things fluttered past between his gaze and the ceiling. Quivering, a curling, animate vine worked its way into his line of sight and hung there, a bright green question mark. A mirror of his whole life, he reflected. He remembered the ship's request.

"Small place," he responded. "Of no particular significance. Out near the border. Repler."

The soft hum of certain physical states of matter being manipulated by energy and higher mathematics penetrated the sanctum. Out, far out at the forefront of the ship, a deep purple refulgence appeared in front of the center of the great Caplis generator. It grew rapidly in dimensions and strength. The *Teacher* began to move. In a short while it had passed beyond the boundaries of the outermost world of the Arrawd system and back out into the emptiness that was the Blight. Changeover occurred and the ship slipped into that otherness of reality that was space-plus, allowing it not to ignore or defy the speed of light but to avoid it.

On a minor colony world within the far reaches of the Commonwealth, something was stirring. Something soul-less and inimical. It had to be stopped, and soon. Not unlike the evil that threatened from within the astronomical masque that was the Great Emptiness.

The difference was that in this instance, instead of seeking help for himself, Flinx had been called upon to provide it for someone else.

About the Author

ALAN DEAN FOSTER has written in a variety of genres, including hard science fiction, fantasy, horror, detective, western, historical, and contemporary fiction. He is the author of the *New York Times* bestseller *Star Wars: The Approaching Storm,* as well as novelizations of several films, including *Star Wars,* the first three *Alien* films, and *Alien Nation.* His novel *Cyber Way* won the Southwest Book Award for Fiction in 1990, the first science fiction work ever to do so. Foster and his wife, JoAnn Oxley, live in Prescott, Arizona, in a house built of brick that was salvaged from an early-twentieth-century miners' brothel. He is currently at work on several new novels and media projects.

About the Type

This book was set in Times Roman, designed by Stanley Morrison specifically for *The Times* of London. The typeface was introduced in the newspaper in 1932. Times Roman had its greatest success in the United States as a book and commercial typeface, rather than one used in newspapers.